NEW YORK REVIEW BOOKS
CLASSICS

A MEANINGFUL LIFE

L. J. DAVIS (1940–2011) was the author of four novels and two works of nonfiction. Over the course of his career he contributed articles to *The New York Times*, *Mother Jones*, and *Harper's*, among other publications. In 1975 he received a Guggenheim fellowship, and his 1987 article "The Next Panic: Fear and Trembling on Wall Street" won him a National Magazine Award. He lived in Brooklyn from 1965 until his death in 2011.

JONATHAN LETHEM is the author of seven novels, including *Motherless Brooklyn* and *The Fortress of Solitude*. He lives in Brooklyn and in Maine.

A MEANINGFUL LIFE

L.J. DAVIS

Introduction by
JONATHAN LETHEM

NEW YORK REVIEW BOOKS

New York

THIS IS A NEW YORK REVIEW BOOK
PUBLISHED BY THE NEW YORK REVIEW OF BOOKS
435 Hudson Street, New York, NY 10014
www.nyrb.com

Library of Congress Cataloging-in-Publication Data
Davis, L. J. (Lawrence J.)
  A meaningful life / by L. J. Davis ; introduction by Jonathan Lethem.
      p. cm.
  ISBN 978-1-59017-300-8 (alk. paper)
  1. Housing rehabilitation—Fiction. 2. Brooklyn (New York, N.Y.)—Fiction.
I. Title.
  PS3554.A935M43 2009
  813'.54—dc22

                          2008041187

ISBN 978-1-59017-300-8

Printed in the United States of America on acid-free paper.
10 9 8 7 6 5 4 3

INTRODUCTION

This can only be entirely personal for me, I have no way around it. Not least because in considering the matter of "the Brownstoners"— those straggling individuals and families, nearly all of them white, who, by laying claim in the 1960s to a few of the aging and tattered row houses in the neighborhoods on the periphery of downtown Brooklyn, set the groundwork for the disaster and triumph of Brooklyn's slow-motion gentrification, so full of social implications and ethical paradoxes, and trailing any number of morbid and comic life situations not unlike those depicted in L. J. Davis's three novels of Brooklyn—I am considering the matters of my own life. My parents were Brownstoners, and the complexly uncomfortable facts in the case, discernible behind Davis's Brooklyn novels and also behind Paula Fox's *Desperate Characters* and Thomas Glynn's *The Building*, are the facts of my childhood. These were the facts I eventually excavated in a long novel called *The Fortress of Solitude*, yet which no matter how deeply I dig, I will never completely demystify.

Not least, but not only. Writing about Davis's book is personal for me because L. J. Davis was my first writer, and by that I mean not in the sense of Lewis Carroll or L. Frank Baum, who were among the first writers I read, but that he was my first captive specimen. L.J. and his family lived on the next block (he still lives in the neighborhood, and so do I), and I was best friends with his son Jeremy. When I first conceived the wish to be a writer, the thought was pretty easily completed by the phrase: "like Jeremy's dad." I liked what I saw. L.J. sat at the back end of an open, high-ceilinged parlor floor devoted to bookshelves. (That I alphabetize my books now is probably attributable to the fact that his were alphabetized.) His desk was massive—I think it had to be, to support the weight of his manual typewriter, which I recall as a piece of epic ironwork wreckage, something you'd seen driven around on the back of a flatbed truck in search of a vacant lot where it might be safely abandoned. In that office, when Jeremy and I weren't shooed away, I was introduced to the existence of the books of Thomas Berger, Charles Webb, Leonard Michaels, and Kingsley Amis ("I was happy to be called Brooklyn's Kingsley Amis," L.J. once told me, "until I had the misfortune of being introduced to Kingsley Amis"), and to Leonard Cohen's *New Skin for the Old Ceremony* LP. These are all tastes I've retained, and the flavor of which seem relevant now to the pleasure I take in L.J.'s novels—rightly relevant, it seems to me, though I could never defy the associative force of childhood memory.

So, Davis's *A Meaningful Life*, along with the true literary thrill it offers on rereading, provides for me a shudder of recognition, or a whole series of shudders. In three of L.J. Davis's four novels, young men who can only be described as sick, chronically ill with self-knowledge of their prejudices and reservations, find their ambivalent fates manifest in scenes of brownstone renovation in downtown Brooklyn, where the joists and pillars of the grand and tempting old houses are too often rotten to the core. More than that of Fox's great novel, close to the bone though it cuts, this is the world I dawned into when my parents moved to Dean Street. The dystopian reality of late 60s and early 70s outerborough New York City can be difficult to grant at this distance; these streets, though rich with human lives, were collectively damned by the city as subhuman, crossed off the list. Firehouses and police stations refused to answer calls, whether out of fear, or indifference, or both. As L.J. told me once, most simply: "Anyone who chose to move to the neighborhood was in some way crazy. I know I was." How precarious this existence was—morally, sociologically, financially—was never exactly permissible to name outside of L.J.'s books, or at least not with such nihilistic glee.

L.J., by refusing to blur the paradoxes of racial and class misunderstanding in idealist sentiment, was "un-PC" before there was such a thing. By being so, he turned some of his neighbors against him, exemplifying a loneliness he, from evidence of his books, already felt as a innate life condition. That he also chose with his wife to adopt two black daughters to raise in his brownstone alongside their two white sons is a fact that still stirs me in its strangeness and beauty. I remember thinking even as a teenager that L.J. had made his home a kind of allegory of the neighborhood as a whole, perhaps partly in order that he might refuse to stand above or apart from it. Then again, with characteristic dryness (unforgivable in the eyes of some local parents), L.J. once awarded a friend of mine and Jeremy's the Dickensian nickname "Muggable Tim," and recommended we avoid walking the streets with him. When after thirty-odd years of personal shame at such stuff I finally managed to open my mouth in *The Fortress of Solitude*, I had L.J. to thank.

L.J.'s novels, like those of Berger and Webb—as well as those of Bruce Jay Friedman and a few other contemporaries—could be fitted into the uncomfortable category of the Black Humorists, an unaffiliated clan of writers who strained European existentialist angst through residual American optimism, arriving at a mordant hilarity just shy of doom. I call the category uncomfortable because nearly any writer ever associated with the label disavowed it, and while most were critical darlings (Davis was), too many bumped to the lower rungs of the mid-list (certainly Davis did). If a concocted literary "movement" doesn't sell books, what good is it? In any event, most of these writers could be called sons of Nathanael West, but unlike

West, giddily free of the formal pressure of modernist aesthetics. In L.J.'s case, he appears to have tempered his West with a jigger of West's brother-in-law, S.J. Perelman, or even of P.G. Wodehouse. "I *like* slapstick," L.J. recently told me, as if guiltlessly confessing a murder.

L.J.'s family home also gave evidence of a fanatical interest in world history, which had been Davis's major at Stanford. He and Jeremy shared a fondness for antique lead toy soldiers, John Huston's adaptation of Kipling's *The Man Who Would Be King*, scrupulously realistic board-game re-creations of European wars, and the Flashman novels of George MacDonald Fraser. Born in Seattle but raised in Idaho, L.J. explained in a typically caustic autobiographical statement (written for the jacket of his first novel, *Whence All But He Had Fled*):

> There is something about Boise, its isolation and its inbreeding and its density, that fosters a specialized kind of hatred of parent for child and child for parent. I think the West, the concept of the heroic West, has a great deal to do with it. The pioneers are closer than they are in other places... It has something to do with the great good place found. The second generation agrees almost by default with the first, and the third can think of nothing but going away. Going away is not easy. Its goal out there is specific: San Francisco, and San Francisco is 642 miles away.

The context of American history, its grand themes of Manifest Destiny and Manifest Disappointment, are terrifically relevant to *A Meaningful Life*, the most pointed and severe of L.J.'s novels of Brooklyn. It is precisely this undertow of pioneer failure that gives the book its oxygen and reach, and which make it undismissable, more than just a brilliant complaint or comic-existentialist howl in the night. By the description of his hero Lowell Lake's failing attempt to pen a novel of—surprise!—"the founding and settlement of Boise, Idaho," and by various other nearly subliminal keynotes (Lake suffers his premarital jitters at Donner Pass), we come to see Lake's disastrous reverse-pilgrimage into Brooklyn, the easy destruction of his tissue-paper WASP idealizations upon immersion in the racial boiling pot of the inner city, in terms of an American incapacity or unwillingness to meet the true implications of its founding promises, made to itself and to the future. Every arrival aimed at some golden San Francisco of the mind falls leadenly short, landing in a Boise of regret and loathing. In this, Davis's America opens unexpectedly into Kafka's unattainable Castle, and the Zeno's paradox hopes of breaching its doors.

"Do you realize that I'm the first member of my family to cross this thing in a hundred years?" said Lowell as they bridged the Mississippi at Saint Louis. His emotions were strange and sinking, but not precise enough to put a name to.

"Big deal," said his wife.

They came to New York at night, hurtling through a hellish New Jersey landscape the likes of which Lowell had never dreamed existed, a chaos of roadways and exits, none of which made any sense, surrounded by smoke and flashes and dark hulking masses and pillars of real fire a thousand feet high, enveloped in a stench like dog's breath and dead goldfish.

In Davis's helpless vision, West collapses into East, the American future into the bloodstained European colonial past. Plus the contractor you hired just wrenched out and demolished the irreplaceable Carrara marble mantelpiece, without asking.

—JONATHAN LETHEM

A MEANINGFUL LIFE

FOR JUDITH

"This is the place. Drive on."
—BRIGHAM YOUNG

"Brigham, Brigham Young,
It's a miracle he survived,
With his roaring rams,
And pretty little lambs
And his five and forty wives."
—OLD IDAHO FOLK SONG

1

Lowell Lake was a tall man, rather thin, with thin sandy hair and a distant, preoccupied though amiable disposition, as though the world did not reach him as it reaches other men and all the voices around him were pleasant but very faint. His attention was liable to wander off at any time and he was always asking people to repeat things. He gave the impression that people bored him, although not in a bad way: actually, they seemed to lull him. He was frequently discovered half-asleep at his desk, gazing vacantly out the nearest window.

One morning not long after his thirtieth birthday, Lowell woke up with the sudden realization that his job was not temporary. It was as though a fiery angel had visited him in his sleep with a message of doom, and he leaped from bed in a state bordering on panic, staring wildly about him. His job wasn't temporary and things weren't going to get any better—not that they were going to get any worse , barring some unforeseen catastrophe like atomic warfare or mental illness, but they weren't going to get any better. That was the whole point. He'd found his level, and here he was, on it. He was the managing editor of a second-rate plumbing-trade weekly, a job he did adequately if not with much snap. It was, he realized with a dull kind of shock, just the sort of job for a man like him. Someday he might rise to the editorship, either of the plumbing-trade monthly or of something exactly like it. Big deal. But it was all he was good for, and he was stuck with it.

"What did you say?" asked his wife sleepily, rolling over in bed and peering at him from under her hand.

Lowell wasn't aware that he'd said anything.

"I thought you said something," she muttered. She yawned. "Maybe you were dreaming or something. It sounded like a groan."

"It's nothing," said Lowell. "I was just, um, stretching." He stretched and groaned elaborately, demonstrating. "Like that," he said. "That must have been what you heard."

"Mum," she said. "Come back to bed and wait for the alarm."

Normally Lowell stayed in bed for as long as he could, fighting wakefulness and never totally giving up. Sometimes on weekends he stayed in bed until noon and then dragged himself heavily around the apartment until it was time to go to sleep again. This morning he looked at his bed with fear and loathing.

"I'm too awake for that," he said. His wife rolled over and went back to sleep.

Lowell dressed furiously. He wanted to be out of the room before the alarm rang and he had to watch his wife hoist on her girdle and buckle on her bra. Usually he was half-asleep when this happened, and he didn't think he could stand it, somehow, awake. Tucking in his shirt with desperate haste, he raced down the hall to the bathroom, first making an inaccurate feint in the direction of the kitchen. The apartment was constructed around a narrow, wormlike central hall, and although he'd lived there for three years, Lowell had never gotten the hang of it.

Peeing, then shaving with considerable speed and indifferent accuracy, he trotted down the hall to the kitchen (having first taken a step toward the living room) just as the alarm clock went off. It was a hateful sound. In a moment it stopped, and he heard his wife beating the pillow where his head should have been.

"Lowell?" she called, not too confidently. "Dear?"

"In the kitchen," Lowell said. "Making coffee."

"Oh," she said. There was a pause. "Oh, yes, I remember. You got up."

"That's right," said Lowell. "I got up." He held his hand in front of his face and watched the fingers tremble. He giggled nervously, then stopped himself.

"Something's the matter with you this morning," said his wife as they sat down to their instant coffee and frozen coffee cake. They were not great breakfast people. "You look kind of funny. Was it something in the news?"

"Thirty," said Lowell before he thought. "I mean," he corrected himself, "no, there's nothing the matter. What makes you think something's the matter? I just woke up early, that's all. Is there something wrong with waking up early?"

"Forget I said anything," said his wife. They put on their coats and went down to the subway together. At 42nd Street his wife got off the train and transferred to the shuttle, which took her to the place where she punched computer keys, or whatever she did over there. Lowell continued downtown, wearing a tweed cap. He stared bleakly at his dim, jostled reflection in the window. It was a silly tweed cap.

"What in God's name is the matter with you this morning?" demanded his boss, a man named Crawford. As a youth, Crawford had developed a fixation about Perry White, editor of the *Daily Planet*, which had molded his character and determined the course his life was to take. He looked back on those days with nostalgia and regret, but he would have cut out his tongue before admitting that his life had been shaped by a minor character in a child's radio serial, the comic-book counterpart not having affected him in the least, but there was no getting around it. Most of the time he managed not to think about it, but every once in a while awareness would suddenly strike him and he would feel like a supreme ass. "Pay attention, Lake!" he barked. "I said, what's the matter with you?"

"I heard you," said Lowell, who had been doing random violence to the papers on his desk, picking up one and throwing it away, scribbling a note on the margin of another, driven by a fierce but aimless need. "Keep your shirt on," he snapped.

Crawford gave a startled little hop and looked at Lowell with a face on which fear was close to the surface. A modest man, not much older than Lowell, Crawford lived in constant terror that one day his job would be snatched from him by a smart subordinate. He firmly believed that an office boy with pluck and stamina could rise to be editor, and he was accordingly careful to select his office personnel for cowardice and lethargy. In fact, he'd never had a spot of trouble with office boys, but he'd once been forced to make life so miserable for a junior copy editor that the man had finally quit, a little hysterically. The somnolent Lowell Lake was just his sort of man, and Crawford had seen to it that he rose swiftly through the ranks to a position where he served as a buffer against any threat from below. The road to the editorship lay through the managing editorship, and even if they got Lowell, it would still be possible for Crawford to pick them off before they were able to gather for another spring. Under these circumstances, Lowell's sudden display of unprecedented energy was alarming indeed, and Crawford scarcely knew how to deal with it. It contradicted nature and defied experience and confirmed his darkest and most secret fears that someday they would contrive to get him no matter what he did to stop them.

"Any idiot could do this kind of work," Lowell snarled, regarding a piece of paper as though some outrageous insult were written upon it. He initialed it viciously, put it in his Out basket, and picked up another. "Any idiot," he repeated.

"Now, see here, Lake," began Crawford hesitantly.

"Do you realize that I've never fixed a pipe in my life?" Lowell raged. "What do I know about plumbing? I'll tell you what I know about plumbing. I don't know shit about plumbing."

"Has everybody around here gone stark staring mad?" bellowed Crawford in desperate mimicry of his hero. He stuck the cold stump of a cigar in his mouth and stormed into his office, braying the name of the senior copy editor, who promptly appeared, only to be told to go soak his head.

"I've got it figured out," Lowell told his wife that night as they prepared supper together. Lowell was cutting up the vegetables and his wife was cutting up the meat. "I know what my problem is. I'm not having a meaningful life. There you have it in a nutshell."

"I knew there was something the matter with you this morning," said his wife.

"There was nothing the matter with me this morning," said Lowell, taking a big swallow of his gin and tonic. He'd been drinking gin and tonic since he came home, and by now he was pretty drunk. "I mean, that wasn't it. It was something else. Do you realize that something has been the matter with me for years? Years?"

His wife looked at him over her shoulder with an expression of perplexity tinged with alarm, as though she considered it possible that he was on the verge of confessing a secret passion for Arlo Povachik, their middle-aged, half-witted doorman who was seldom on duty when he was supposed to be. "I don't understand what you're talking about," she said. "You're not being very clear. Maybe you can explain it better." For a computer expert, she did not grasp concepts very easily, if at all, but she was tenacious and seldom gave up. Her mind was capable of worrying an unclear concept for hours on end, shaking it like a rag doll until she had found out whether it was good for her, bad for her, significant in any way, or utterly meaningless. In recent years, Lowell had grown wary of this apparently incurable tendency, and he was usually able to nip it in the bud with a swift, simplistic lie. He lied now, drunk as he was.

"I don' know what was the matter with me this morning," he said, unsteadily pouring himself a fresh drink with more gin in it than tonic. He returned to the table and began to slice up the carrots every which way. "I must have been having a dream."

"Let me do that," said his wife, confiscating the carrots with a loving expression.

Later, seated alone in the dimly lighted, curiously shaped living room of his apartment, full of dinner, sexually sated, and still pretty drunk, Lowell sipped ice water and brooded about his life. His parents owned a motel on Highway 30, just outside of Boise, Idaho. They were absentminded, pale, thin people who seemed completely unaware that they were running a love nest for downtown merchants, students from the junior college, and state politicians, among whom they were treasured for their permissiveness, probity, and discretion. (Actually, it was mostly just absentmindedness.) Lowell had a pleasant, undemanding childhood, free from influences either stimulating or depressing. He did well in school, largely because he had an excellent memory and an undemanding personality. It was some years before he realized that his parents ran a kind of self-service whorehouse, and even then it didn't bother him much. Nobody else seemed to think anything of it; a couple of the regular girls had been his mother's coffee friends for as long as he could remember, and it neither impressed nor upset him to think that some of the most respected and powerful men in the state took off their pants in rooms he cleaned every morning. He graduated fifth in his high-school class, behind three home-economics majors and a strange-looking veterinarian's son who had bad skin and never talked to anybody, and who committed suicide the following September, the day after Labor Day.

On the strength of his grades (and somewhat to his surprise), Lowell was accepted at Stanford, but his family had never made any money out of their motel despite the fact that it never had a slack season, and they didn't have the money to send him. Lowell wanted to go to Stanford pretty badly now that it had accepted him, and after much thought he screwed up his courage and wrote a letter to the most powerful politician he knew, Judge Lionel B. Crosby. Judge Crosby stopped by the place every once in a while, and he was fond of saying that if there was anything he could do for you, just call. He had often expressed an admiration for Lowell's intelligence, putting his hand on Lowell's head and sort of kneading it as though trying to feel his brain through the skull. Lowell didn't like him very much.

Dear Judge Crosby [he wrote],

I would not bother a man of your importance with a matter that cannot be very important to you, although it is very important to me, except that you have often suggested that if I ever encountered some problem, you would like to talk it over with me. I have decided to take you up on your offer. My problem is as follows: I have been accepted at Stanford University in California but they didn't give me a scholarship and my family can't afford it, so I was wondering if there is any fund or source of funds that the state, county, or other municipal body provides for any of the expenses of (prospective) college students in my position. If you know of any, I would certainly appreciate word of them. If you are too busy to do this, I will understand because I know what an imposition it is and I would not have written if you had not so kindly encouraged me to do so in the past, and I will just have to think of something else.

> Sincerely yours,
> Lowell P. Lake

Lowell read it over and decided it was a pretty terrible letter. It didn't look a bit like the kind of courtly, terse letter people were always writing to Sherlock Holmes when they implored his assistance, and Lowell put it aside. He made three more attempts.

He was unable to finish two of them, and the syntax of the third was so tangled that it made no sense whatever. He scarcely knew what to do, and with a kind of sick despair he mailed the first letter after all. He immediately thought better of it, but it was in the box, and there was nothing he could do about it but sit and wait for someone to come and scold him about it.

The letter frightened Judge Crosby out of his wits.

At three-month intervals for five years, Judge Crosby had met a middle-aged traveling bandleader at Lowell's parents' motel and spent the night with him. The judge thought it was a very dirty, sinful thing to do, but he had yielded to his passions long ago and could no longer help himself. He lived with his aged mother in a big old house in the heart of town, where he had a book-lined study with a bust of Homer and a handsome marble fireplace. In this fireplace he burned certain letters he received on the second Monday of every month and also the various publications that came to him from New Jersey in manila envelopes marked "Educational Materials." In the summer he scattered the ashes in the garden under the shrubs, where they would do the most good. In the winter he put them on the sidewalk with the clinkers, and nobody was the wiser.

For years the judge had lived in constant terror of blackmail and exposure. His mind had dwelt for two decades with the turgid subtleties and intricate sharp practice of the law, until, like a doctor who sees symptoms wherever he looks, he could think no other way, and whenever he tried to imagine what a blackmail letter would look like, it always looked very much like the letter Lowell had sent him. It was the kind of letter the judge would have written if he'd been trying to blackmail someone; the threat was there, but it was nothing you could put your finger on in court. He didn't doubt for a minute that the little son-of-a-bitch had gotten the goods on him; it was plain as a pikestaff, and the chickens had come home to roost. He always knew it would happen someday. The judge's opponent in the next election was an unscrupulous nincompoop who would love to know his guilty secret and who would love telling people about it even more. He supposed that Lowell planned to place the information in his hands if the judge failed to meet his terms. If the judge had been in Lowell's place, that was exactly what he would have done. In fact, he'd already done something pretty much like it, not once but a couple of times.

The judge spent all afternoon locked in his study with Lowell's letter and a bottle of heart pills. He was so utterly certain that he was being blackmailed that it never occurred to him for a moment that he might not be; Judge Crosby had waited so long to be blackmailed that if he hadn't been, it was altogether possible that he would have gone to his grave a disappointed man, kind of relieved to get it all over with but feeling strangely unfulfilled. At the end of the day he put Lowell's letter in the fireplace and burned it, crumbling the ash with the tip of a poker. Then he sat down at his desk and began a hearty, avuncular letter of reply, concerning a confidential private fund, the existence of which was not widely known.

So it was that Lowell went to Stanford. He had a good time at the university and never gave another thought to how he came to be there; things had always had a way of working out for him, one way or another. (Two years after Lowell graduated, Judge Crosby was surprised by his political enemies with his hand in the till and arrested, whereupon he immediately—and profusely—confessed to being a homosexual too, which pretty generally amazed everyone and ended up causing quite a little rumpus.)

At Stanford, Lowell majored in English. It had always been his best subject and it didn't commit him to do anything specific in later life, which was just fine with Lowell. He had no idea of what he was going to do in later life and the very words lacked meaning when he tried to apply them to himself. He thought he might go ahead and get a Ph.D., but he couldn't see much farther than that, and even it was dim. Sometimes it seemed to him that all the grown-ups he'd ever known had been old and calm, the sort of people who made up their lives the same way they made up their beds, neat and clean and tight at the corners and no nonsense about the spread, and although Lowell supposed it must have been very nice for them, it didn't seem to have a whole lot to do with him. Whenever he thought about the future, he vaguely supposed that things would go on much the same as they always had, and that when he left college (provided he ever left college) it would be to take up an existence much the same as the one he'd always known, where people gave him tasks to perform and praised him when he did them well. He did them well consistently, if not with much originality, and he was more conspicuous for his highly developed sense of responsibility than for any keenness of intellect; in his eating club, he was the chairman of the committee that cleaned up after parties.

He met his future wife at the beginning of his sophomore year and immediately nicknamed her Tex for reasons that were obscure even to himself, but the joke, whatever it was, soon wore off and eventually he came to call her by no name at all, or at least none he could use in public. When he wanted to attract her attention in a crowded room he usually called her "dear," which admittedly was a pretty lame expedient and one that always embarrassed him. Her real name was Betty and she came from Flatbush. Lowell couldn't bring himself to believe that there really was such a place as Flatbush, any more than he believed in Allen's Alley and Wistful Vista, and he could no more picture himself marrying a girl named Betty from there than he could imagine himself marrying a horse from Kentucky. As far as Lowell was concerned, her life began the day he met her and it took place exclusively in places that he knew. When vacation came and she went back to Flatbush and became Betty again, it was almost as though she had ceased to exist for a while, like a well-loved character in a favorite book that he'd momentarily put aside. For some reason, he began to feel the same way about himself whenever he went back home to his parents' motel, and after the Christmas of his sophomore year he no longer did so. He told his parents that he couldn't afford it; they believed him and didn't offer to help out. His mother kept in touch with one letter every month, in which she gave exhaustive descriptions of the weather and the state of his father's health, and advised Lowell to wear a tie whenever he thought he should. Lowell liked his parents and was always glad to hear from them. He never failed to write back promptly.

Two days after graduation, Lowell and his wife were married with nonsectarian pomp amid the gold-leafed, erotic splendors of Memorial Chapel. The place looked like a cross between a Byzantine whorehouse and a Victorian ladies' parlor, and Lowell was somewhat at a loss when he tried to comprehend the vision of heaven that had inspired it. He'd always wondered what it would feel like to be married there, and when his future wife suggested it, he figured that it was as good a time as any to find out.

"I'm not sure I like this," said his future mother-in-law grimly as he took her on a tour of the premises the day before the ceremony. In the course of a very few hours she had managed to convince him that there really might have been somebody named Betty from Flatbush. Betty from Flatbush was the daughter of this woman; she was also nobody Lowell had ever known. He was still getting used to being a Bachelor of Arts, he was presently about to become the husband of the girl he loved, and naturally he was a little confused about things, but when it came to contemplating becoming this unpleasant woman's son-in-law, his mind went completely blank. It wasn't anything he knew about, and he simply couldn't imagine it at all. "I don't know if I like this," she repeated, staring unblinkingly into some middle distance where nothing seemed to be. It was a habit she employed whenever she spoke to either Lowell or her husband, and in a very short time it had come close to driving Lowell mad. It made him feel ridiculous and hard-put for a reply, and it worked every time she did it. They continued down the aisle toward the altar, with great gleaming butterscotch columns rising all around them. "I don't know," she said. "What do you think, Leo? Let me just say that, for myself, I definitely don't know."

"It's hard to say," said Leo, Lowell's future father-in-law. He was a little, bald, chickenlike man, and Lowell didn't know what to make of him, either. At the airport, shaking Lowell's hand, he'd said furtively, "Hi. I'm Leo. I guess I'm going to be your father-in-law. That was sure some plane ride, let me tell you. Up and down all the way. Ha, ha, some of the passengers really looked worried about that. You can call me Leo."

At intervals throughout the day he continued to remind Lowell to call him Leo, like a little kid trying to get someone to address him with a nickname he'd just thought up for himself. "I don't know whether I told you, but you can call me Leo even if I am your future father-in-law," he would say, right out of the blue. "You can call me Leo when I'm your father-in-law too. I mean, you can call me Leo anytime. Everyone does, you don't have to be shy. I don't remember if I told you before."

"Right, Leo," Lowell would say. "Sure thing." And they would march on, with Lowell's future mother-in-law (who never asked him to call her anything) beating near-perfect time with her voice, like a drum that yakked instead of boomed. She talked all sorts of aggressive nonsense, but for some reason although Lowell disliked her, he did not feel strange about her; he was used to women who did that sort of thing, mostly on television. It was Leo that made him feel strange. Leo was a puzzle; Lowell had never met anyone remotely like him, at least that he could remember. Most of the men Lowell knew strove either to be tough and mean or tough and nice, and even the weak little men that had come his way had cherished a Henry Fonda of the spirit and rode tall in the saddle in their dreams. Leo, on the other hand, actually seemed to be struggling to project a deliberate image of himself that was about as craven as humanly possible. Whenever there was an opportunity to cringe, he cringed. Sometimes he didn't even wait for the opportunity. It was amazing without being pleasant or very interesting, and after a while it began to get on your nerves and make you snappish, which in turn offered Leo wonderful fresh cringing opportunities. Lowell could see how it would be easy to get locked in a cycle with him, a cycle that would last for years and years. Lowell decided right then that he didn't want to do that. Leo didn't even try to bully, hector, or needle people younger, poorer, less articulate, or more polite than himself—any of that bookkeeper's vast constituency of the ego. He didn't seem to think that he was smarter, cleaner, or better bred than anybody, and Negroes openly terrified him. Apparently he was meek and craven through and through, the kind of man who would always strive industriously to remain beneath any situation that might arise or sort of creep up on him, the kind of man who went through life continually ducking his head. Lowell got the disturbing impression that if somebody finally came and told him it was time to go to the gas chamber, he would hop right into the truck, asking them to call him Leo.

"I'm not sure," said Lowell's future mother-in-law, planting herself squarely in front of the altar and standing there as though waiting for the crucified Christ to make a move for his gun. "I don't think I like it, but I'm still thinking it over. Tell me what you think, I'm open for suggestions."

"We don't have to have it in church," said Lowell. "We could have it anywhere. We could have it in your church. . . . I mean . . ."

"When I want your opinion, I'll ask for it," she snapped, without taking her eyes off the altar. "You can just keep out of this. I wasn't talking about that, so shut up." Then she burst into tears.

"Excuse me," said Leo. "My wife is crying."

Lowell wasn't exactly sure what was going on, but his future mother-in-law was carrying on pretty loudly, and he looked helplessly about the church, alternately hoping that no one would see him and that someone would come and help him.

"It's okay," said Leo to his wife, standing beside her with fumbling, incompetent gestures, patting her like a city boy trying to make friends with a cow. "Look, if it doesn't work out, she can divorce him in a couple of years, it's not like it's forever or anything. Who knows, maybe it will work out. Personally, I think it will work out."

Lowell's future mother-in-law made a kind of strangled noise and struck out at her husband. "All right," she said. "All right. After all, what do I know? Who am I, after all? Only a mother. Who listens to a mother? Just remember, my blood is on your hands."

Lowell couldn't tell whether this incredible threat was directed at himself, Leo, Christ, or some combination of the three of them, but evidently it meant that they were free to go. Moving as though balancing a plate on her head, his future mother-in-law turned and marched up the aisle without so much as a backward glance.

"I don't know if I told you," Leo remarked as they followed her out of the church, "but I'm a cutter."

Lowell wondered if it was an occupation or a pathology. Nothing could surprise him anymore, not even if Leo were suddenly to strip off his shirt in the middle of the quad to show him his collection of self-inflicted wounds. Maybe it had something to do with organized crime, a sort of job title like "torpedo" or "goon." The only kind of cutters Lowell had ever heard about were Coast Guard boats and horse-drawn sleighs, and he was in no condition to think very clearly about anything right now. No matter what it was, if it had anything to do with Leo or his

wife, Lowell didn't want to know a thing about it. He never
wanted to see them again as long as they lived. All he wanted
to do was marry their daughter. These outrageous people
seemed to live in a world entirely different from any he had
ever known, a kind of bizarre parallel universe that had somehow overlapped our own. Once when Lowell was a little kid, he
got the idea if you held your breath and squinted your eyes a
certain way, the sky would turn red and everybody would have
six legs, among other things. Leo and his wife made him feel
like he had finally pulled off the trick, although in a much worse
way.

"You hadn't mentioned it," he said, when it became evident
that Leo would continue to look at him inquisitively until he
made some comment, even if it took hours.

"It's not much," said Leo at once. "It's a living. Don't think
I'm proud of it."

"That's too bad," said Lowell, looking steadfastly in another
direction.

They crossed the quad in a blaze of sunlight, Lowell's future
mother-in-law clumping along ahead of them, looking neither to
the right nor to the left. Behind them rose the immense, hideous
Sunday-school mosaic on the face of the chapel, the Apostles
looking down from it like a dozen Edwardian fags in biblical
drag. Lowell had always thought it was a funny mosaic, but
now he hated it. He hated everything in sight, the palm trees,
the gravel, everything. He began to understand why some people chose to live in sin. It was so they wouldn't have to get married and invite their parents to the wedding. He even began to
wonder a little about his own parents. What did he really know
about them? The last time he saw them, he wasn't even old
enough to drink. Maybe his parents had a whole life he didn't
know about, strange proclivities that would suddenly become
horribly apparent now that their son was about to get married.
He had a sharp, quick vision of his father whipping out a pack

of pornographic photographs and passing them around during the ceremony. He wondered why it didn't seem so implausible as it would have a couple of days ago.

"A lot of Puerto Ricans are coming into it now," Leo was saying. "I've been thinking of getting out. It's the only thing I know. I guess if I got out, I'd just sit around the house and watch television. What do you think, should I get out or not? It's hard to know what to do. All the Puerto Ricans coming in and everything. I think about it a lot. I heard on the radio the other day that Mickey Mantle broke his leg. I wonder if it's true. You never know what to believe these days. I'll bet if Mickey Mantle really broke his leg, you'd never hear about it. They'd hush it up, what do you think?"

Lowell was afraid to open his mouth for fear of screaming in the little man's face. He wasn't even certain he was hearing any of this. He'd never heard anything like it in his life, except once when he was delirious with pneumonia and everybody seemed to be talking about fish.

"Let's elope," he told his future wife that night when they had parked up by the lake in his blue Ford hardtop. They were sitting in the back seat with their clothes off. "Let's run away to Nevada and live in the desert." He was only joking, except that he really wasn't. He really did kind of want to run off to Nevada and try his mettle among all that desolation and vast manly silence.

"You're being silly," said the soft warm girl in his arms. "Yum, that's why I love you. Anyway, my parents will be gone soon, and it'll all be over. If you think you're having a hard time now, just remember that I had to put up with them for years and years. God, years and years. Let's never be parents. Let's have children but not be parents, what do you say?"

"Great," said Lowell, noticing with a sinking feeling that her last sentence had been spoken with her father's inflection and ended with her father's phrase. He'd never noticed a thing like that in her voice before. He began to listen for it, and shortly his fears were confirmed. It was there, all right, coming and going like the odor of burning tires in a rose garden. He listened so hard and heard so much that soon he made himself impotent and unable to think about anything else. He held Betty from Flatbush in his arms, and it scared him.

"It's okay," she said cheerfully as they put their clothes back on, something they had never learned to do either gracefully or well, owing largely to the hump in the middle of the floor. "We've got a lot of time. Pretty soon we'll be married and have a bed."

"How come you're chewing gum?" Lowell asked. "You never chewed gum before."

"What are you talking about? I've always chewed gum. I've chewed gum ever since I was a little girl. What kind of a question is that? Boy, this marriage thing must really be getting on your nerves. Here, fasten this, will you?" She turned her back to him, and he hooked her bra. Try as he would, he couldn't remember ever having seen her chewing gum. Surely he would have smelled it when he kissed her.

"Did you always pop it like that?" he asked.

"Pop what like that? I don't know what you're talking about. You forgot to kiss my back." He always gave her a gentle kiss between the shoulderblades after he hooked or unhooked her bra. It was very important to both of them, and he'd forgotten all about it. He gave her a halfhearted peck, but the whole thing was already spoiled.

"I mean your gum," he said. "I wanted to know if you always popped it like that. I guess it's not important. Let's forget about it."

"You bet your life I'll forget about it, buster," she said, swiftly climbing into her blouse and throwing her skirt around her somehow. "I'm going back to the dorm. I think you'd better take a good long ride and calm down or something. You can call me in the morning."

She slammed the door and strode off down the parking lot. Lowell would have followed her but he hadn't put his pants on yet. He knew he couldn't follow her in his Jockey shorts. The people in the other cars would see him and honk their horns. He imagined himself trying to run back to the car in a half-squat with his shirttail desperately pulled way down. Then he imagined himself actually overtaking her by some fluke and having an argument with her in his Jockey shorts. It was impossible in Jockey shorts; he couldn't argue with anybody. Along with pajamas, Jockey shorts were possibly the dumbest garment ever conceived by the mind of man.

It was far too late to pursue her by the time he got his pants on. Instead, he went back to his dormitory, stole his roommate's tent, and ran away to Nevada.

By the time he reached Sacramento, he began to feel foolish. By the time he reached the Sierra, he began to feel positively terrified. The last of his forward inertia ran out in Truckee. He pulled into a service station, filled the tank, and headed back toward school. It wouldn't work. The life of Thoreau, testing his mettle against a harsh, muscular climate, wresting a living from the barren desert soil—it was not for him. He couldn't do it, any more than a cow could fly, and that was that. In the only plausible vision that assembled itself before his mind's eye, he wasn't struggling titanically with the elements and roaring his defiance like Lear; he was sitting in the middle of an alkali flat waiting for his pocket money to run out or his tent to blow over, whichever happened first. The whole notion was absurd on the face of it. He wasn't cut out for that kind of life. He didn't even know the first thing about it, and he had enough sense to realize that the Nevada desert wasn't the place to find out. He hadn't really wanted to go to Nevada anyway. He really wanted to marry his girl and stay in town. He still didn't know what kind of a life he wanted to have, exactly, but one thing was clear: making an ass of himself on an alkali flat wasn't part of it. His immediate priorities were clear: first, to graduate and get his diploma; second, to get married. These were concrete desires, almost facts, almost within his grasp. Nevada was fantasy, and flight was out of the question. As for peace and solitude and the life of the mind, he would work something out once he was properly graduated and married. He never had to see his in-laws again, and after they were gone it would be as though he'd made them up in order to have something funny to talk about at parties. Anyway, if people had come looking for him in Nevada, they probably would have found him right off the bat, and there would have been a lot of embarrassing questions.

Feeling drained but clear in his goals, he climbed back over Donner Pass in the gray false dawn, meeting trucks coming down at dangerous speed with headlights on and loads swaying. Below, on the rocks, lay bodies of other trucks that hadn't made it, their cabs squashed, their tires burned, their vans half-buried under heaps of smashed granite. Bad cess on them, Lowell thought. Teach them a lesson. He was going back, and he felt like being smart with everybody.

At the summit the car behind him began to honk its horn. A little fuzzy from lack of sleep and too much thinking, Lowell glanced in the rear-view mirror and sluggishly began to pull over to let it pass. Then, in a swift double take, he looked in the mirror again, floored the accelerator, and shot back into the lane with only inches to spare as the car behind hooted madly and slammed on its brakes. It was his father's car. He'd recognized it all in a flash, and there could be no doubt about it whatever: a green 1954 Kaiser sedan, the paint dull and the chrome ring missing from the left-front headlight, Idaho plates, Ada County numbers. And behind the oddly shaped Kaiser windshield, were the blurred, perplexed faces of his father and mother. Lowell drove faster.

They were over the peak now. It was all downhill, and the Ford ought to be able to outrun the Kaiser in no time. Anybody could outrun his father, no matter what they were driving. As a small boy in the back seat of the car before the Kaiser (a gray Frazer with an enormous blunt snout and a buffalo medallion), Lowell would watch with dismay as cars and pickups whipped past them with meteoric speed, even prewar Hudsons with tiny old men at the wheel. "Faster, Daddy, faster," Lowell would urge as a city bus crept abreast, then lumbered slowly ahead, its driver glaring at them. "You can't be too careful with a car," his father would reply. "There are a lot of Canyon County drivers on the road." Lowell was never able to see what Canyon County had to do with it. The important thing was that everybody passed them. A vehicle had only to make its appearance behind them—even a road grader—for Lowell's father to slow to a crawl to let it past, warily scanning its plates for the dread Canyon County insignia.

Lowell hit sixty on the curving downgrade, but his father hung in there as though their bumpers were magnetized. It was kind of terrifying and it could not end well, no matter what happened. His father honked again, two short toots and a long insistent bray, and his mother waved a handkerchief behind the windshield. Lowell hunched up his shoulders and scrunched down in the seat until his eyes were on a level with the top of the dashboard, but he couldn't see the road very well that way and presently he sat back up again. Just then his father made a desperate bid to pull up alongside. Lowell foiled this maneuver by pulling over into the middle of the road just as a huge cattle truck as wide as a house struggled into view around a curve mere feet away. Lowell ducked back into his own lane in the nick of time, nearly colliding with his father, who was audaciously attempting to draw abreast on the right. When Lowell was able to look in the rear-view mirror again, his father seemed to be talking to him through the windshield and his mother had covered her eyes with her handkerchief. Lowell took the next curve at seventy. It did him no good; his father never faltered. Lowell guessed he was really in for it now.

Far too late, large numbers of plausible explanations of his presence at the top of Donner Pass sprang into mind. For example, he could have pretended he was coming out to greet them, never mind that he was going the wrong way, he'd gotten tired of waiting; it was a little thin, but it would have done in a pinch. Or he could have said he was visiting a friend—that was always a good gambit; his parents had worried constantly that he didn't have enough kids to play with, and he was always able to get away with being sighted in strange places (such as the sewage plant or the drive-in theater) by pretending that he was on his way to, or on his way back from, a visit to a friend. His parents were usually so pleased by word of this fictitious destination that any forbidden places he might fall into on his journey were simply incidental, and they never did get wise. (Now that he thought about it, why were his parents so worried that he might not have any friends? Did they think something was the matter with him? Was there actually something the matter with him that they'd never told him about? Had anybody else noticed? In this there was much food for thought, all of it unprofitable, but now was not the time; Lowell's father was recklessly attempting to draw abreast in a truck-passing lane that had suddenly appeared out of nowhere, and Lowell had to swing busily this way and that all over the highway to keep him in his place, although what he was going to do with him there, God only knew.)

Many were the good excuses he might have made. For that matter, he could probably have gotten away with no excuse at all—his parents were mild people and not given to prying—but he was committed to his course of action now, and there was no stopping it, any more than Hitler could have called off the war. They'd caught him red-handed and guilty as sin, running away from his own wedding (actually, returning from running away from his own wedding, not that it made any difference), and they stayed right behind him like nemesis, his father and mother, tooting peremptorily on the horn every now and then, no longer trying to attract his attention, just letting him know that he wasn't getting away with anything. Lowell supposed there was always the chance that his father would run out of gas or have to go to the bathroom. Then Lowell could race back to the dorm and pretend it was actually some member of his club, a wild chap with a great sense of humor and a similar haircut. In his heart, however, Lowell knew that nothing could save him; his father, a methodical man, would have filled his tank and emptied his bladder before setting out that morning, and there was no help coming from that quarter.

Soon they were at Auburn, and the freeway began. Playing his last card, Lowell slowed down in hopes they would try to get ahead of him. If they passed him, he could dodge off at the next exit. His father, however, refused to take the bait. Lowell slowed down, his father slowed down. Lowell switched lanes and went even slower, his father followed suit. He watched them in the rear-view mirror but saw nothing that encouraged him; his father had stopped talking and his mother was smoking a cigarette, but neither of them looked very pleased. It was hard to say how they looked. Lowell stared at their faces for a long time, searching for some sign, some hint of the kind of explanation that would get him off the hook, something that would make them neither angry nor distressed in their mild way, but the prospect was not encouraging. Presently a big blue Lincoln blared past at four times his speed, its driver's fist shaking furiously, reminding Lowell that he was in the fast lane and barely moving. You could get killed that way, and although Lowell wanted things to stop, he really didn't want them to stop that much; he instantly resumed normal freeway speed. His father accelerated too, maintaining an interval so precise it was as though Lowell was actually driving the Kaiser too, by some kind of remote control.

They passed Sacramento, and Lowell still saw no way out. They climbed out of the valley and through the round, brown hills. Vacaville fell behind them, and traffic began to build up. They came to San Rafael and passed the pastel tank farms on the hills above the bay, and still Lowell's father followed him implacably. So it was that they crossed the bridge and traversed San Francisco, went down the peninsula on Bayshore, turned off at Palo Alto and crept sedately down University Avenue, beneath the magnolia trees like a duck train, and came, finally, to the parking lot of Toyon Hall. Lowell pulled into his usual spot and stopped the car. His father stopped directly behind him. Lowell sat and waited. His parents didn't move. His father's hands remained on the steering wheel, ready to resume the chase at the drop of a hat. Lowell wondered whether, if he were to get out and go into the dorm, his parents would follow him at a two-car interval, walking along behind, stopping when he stopped. He sat and waited. His parents waited too. Lowell watched them in the mirror. They watched him through the windshield. His mother lit another cigarette, waving the match back and forth like a tiny signal before putting it in the ashtray. Lowell got out of the car stiffly and walked back to them, hoping that something good would come out of his mouth when he opened it.

"Hi," he found himself saying.

His father reached down and turned off the ignition. His mother snubbed out her cigarette.

"I . . ." said Lowell. I what? I'm sorry? I'll be darned? He opened and closed his mouth several times, but nothing resembling words came out.

"I'll bet you have some good explanation for this," said his father. "I was just telling your mother, I said, I'll bet he has some good explanation."

They waited for him to come up with it, but Lowell's mind had been unproductive for two hundred miles, and nothing occurred to it now. He wished he could buy time by taking them some good place to talk, but in a campus apparently designed on purpose to contain no place where you could lay a girl but in a parking lot, there also seemed to be no place where you could have a scene with your parents except in a parking lot. He wondered what would happen if he fainted. He already knew the answer to that: they would wait patiently until he woke up.

"Your mother was doubtful," said his father.

Lowell's mother still looked doubtful. Lowell passed his hand slowly over his eyes, making things dark for a while. When he looked at his parents they were still there, waiting for some sort of an answer.

"I was running away," he said.

"That's what I thought," said his father.

"You were going in the wrong direction," his mother pointed out.

"I changed my mind," Lowell said.

"That's what I told your mother," said his father, nodding his head with satisfaction. "The boy got cold feet, I told her. Puts me in mind of his uncle, I said."

"But I changed my mind," Lowell explained.

"That's exactly what I told your mother. Get in the car and we'll go talk about it over breakfast. That was a real merry chase."

"You aren't . . . I mean . . . mad or anything?" Lowell asked weakly.

"I admit it put me out some, right there at first. Your mother and I will make up our minds about it when we have the facts. Maybe you'd like to catch some sleep first. Otherwise we could go eat. Your mother's pretty hungry."

Lowell climbed obediently into the back seat of the Kaiser and collapsed against the cushions. All his muscles seemed to have shrunk, although his bones remained the same size, and it was difficult to keep his body from suddenly clenching up in a foetal position. At the same time, he was filled with a strange, wild love for his parents that was unlike anything he'd ever felt for them before, somewhat embarrassing, totally inexpressible, and probably due to nervous reaction. His father was here, and everything was going to be all right. His father would straighten things out. His mother was here too.

They pulled away from the parking lot and hesitantly found their way off the campus. For the next ten minutes they were passed by every car on the road.

"You can't be too careful," his father said. "All these California drivers."

"Yes, Daddy," said Lowell.

He explained everything to them, although not very coherently, in a pancake house on El Camino Real. There was something wrong with his receiving mechanism—no sleep was what was the matter with it, compounded by the aftermath of panic and too much fast driving—and although he was aware that his father had forgiven him and his mother was working on it, he was not at all clear about how these good things had been accomplished. Words and phrases came to him in loud, frequently senseless snatches and then seemed to fade away with most of the light in the room, as though someone was turning his eyes and ears up and down with a kind of rheostat. The next thing he knew for sure, he was back in his room and sound asleep.

"How are you?" Leo asked Mr. Lake that afternoon when they met for the first time, peering anxiously into his face as though in search of fatal symptoms. "Call me Leo," he added. "I'm a cutter. It isn't much, but I don't know anything else and I'm too old to learn another trade."

"That's real interesting," said Lowell's father. "What do you cut?"

"As a mother," said Leo's wife, who still hadn't told anybody what to call her, "how would you say this struck you? Personally, I wash my hands, but that's only my opinion."

Lowell's mother looked at her expectantly for a moment, as though waiting for her to get on with the joke or story, but when nothing happened she blinked pleasantly and said, "I'm afraid I really haven't thought about it. I'm glad to meet you."

"You'll find out soon enough," said Leo's wife. "Mark my words."

Lowell's mother smiled wanly and backed off a little, making an agreeable mooing sound.

"Dubinsky let them in," Leo was saying. "It wasn't the employers, like some people think; it was Dubinsky. One day the war ended, and bam, there they were wherever you looked."

"I'll be darned," said Mr. Lake.

"If this keeps up much longer I'll have to take some kind of a pill," whispered Lowell.

"This isn't the half of it," said his girl, picking her cuticles. "If you think this is bad, you ought to have to live with them."

They all went to a restaurant for supper, where they were treated to a mealful of his future mother-in-law's theories on the selection and preparation of foodstuffs, some of which didn't even qualify as edible on any list Lowell had ever heard of.

"How can you eat that disgusting slop?" she demanded, pointing at Mr. Lake's Salisbury steak.

Lowell's father cut a bite of it and methodically placed it in his mouth. "It's not so bad," he remarked after he had thoroughly chewed and swallowed it. "Once you get the hang of it."

"You can't be too careful," said Leo, nodding amiably at everyone. "No sir, you just can't be too careful, you know what I mean?"

"Lowell," said his father later, when they were saying good

night at the motel. "About that little business of running away this morning."

"Yes, Dad?"

"What in God's name ever put it into your head to come back?"

Lowell tried to laugh. "Ha, ha," he said.

"Lowell," said his mother, "is there something you want to tell us?"

"If it should turn out that something isn't quite right," put in his father, "we'll back you up one hundred percent. Don't think you have to do anything you don't want to."

"We want to help," said his mother. "That's what a family's for, to help."

"Just say the word," said his father.

Lowell began to feel as though he was being worked over by the French police. He wanted sleep. He wanted all the voices to stop. He felt as though his head and body were being packed with warm, wet cotton, a handful at a time, and words came to him dully, like blows he had ceased to feel. "Nothing's wrong," he said. "Everything is fine."

"What your father and I are getting at . . ."

"I understand," said Lowell thickly. "Everything is okay. Nothing is wrong. I mean, nothing is wrong that won't be okay in a while. I mean, what I mean is . . ."

"We'll talk about it later," said his father, meaning that they would never talk about it again unless Lowell brought it up first. "I think it's time we all hit the hay."

"There's never been a Jew in my family," Lowell heard his mother say as she walked off with his father toward their room. "Has there ever been one in your family?"

"Never can tell," said his father, putting his arm around her waist.

Lowell and his wife were married by a Unitarian minister who blinked a lot and claimed to have known Woody Guthrie.

Exactly how well he'd known Woody Guthrie diminished measur-
ably each time Lowell questioned him about it, until he finally
began to avoid the subject, glancing apprehensively at Lowell
from time to time as though afraid another Woody Guthrie
question was in danger of springing from his mouth. The minister's name was Mr. Hogarth. It was the time of year when a lot
of weddings occur at Stanford, and whenever the other ministers
wanted somebody to cut a service short, they infallibly went to
Mr. Hogarth. He was both weak-willed and a fast talker, and he
seemed to suspect secretly that God didn't pay much attention
to anything Unitarians did.

"I just hope everybody arrives in time," he told Lowell, blinking, as they waited in the vestibule for the Baptists to finish.
"There's a Presbyterian service right behind us, and we're kind
of pressed for time." He gave a fatuous smile and waved to
somebody over Lowell's shoulder. Lowell turned and saw a man
donning vestments in a little room off to one side. The man
frowned at them and closed the door. "That was the Presbyterian
minister," Mr. Hogarth said.

"I wish the Pope could see this," whispered Lowell's best
man, the roommate whose tent he'd stolen. "He'd laugh his ass
off." Lowell's roommate was an easygoing Catholic who crossed
himself at table before taking food, drank prodigious quantities
of wine at club parties without ever impairing his ability to
drive, never got a grade higher than a B, and planned to be
elected mayor of San Francisco before he was forty. He was as
short and squat as a rain barrel and as strong as a bull, and he
deeply loved his father and mother, immigrant Italians who ran
a tiny bakery on North Beach, who deeply loved him back
with a devotion that was outrageous, embarrassing to onlookers,
and quite touching, like something from a maudlin old movie
come to life.

The moment Lowell took his place at the altar, a fog of terror
blew into his mind and few things sufficiently penetrated its

veil to be remembered with any clarity afterward. He hadn't been
scared a minute ago—just exhausted by events and nervous
that his voice would break or that he would fart loudly—but he
was scared now, and scared he remained. He was changing his
status in the community of man. He was in the hopper of a
great machine and he could no more get them to turn it off than
a confessed and proven murderer could change his mind about
his trial. It was Donner Pass all over again, only permanent.
The law had him and there was no way out, at least not a nice
or easy one: it was a matter for judges and courts, his wife testi-
fying about the length of his prick and the dirty things he whispered in her ear when he was drunk on Miller High Life, the
judge scolding him, alimony; he could see it all. The only other
way out was murder or moving secretly to another town, changing your name, losing all your friends, denying all your accom-
plishments, a kind of suicide (there was also the other kind). He
was really in for it now. Gone forever were the days when he
could just stop coming by her dorm. He was going to be a
grown-up now, and there was no stopping it.

It was with this sort of nonsense jangling through his head
like a burglar alarm in an abandoned grocery store that he
turned and beheld his bride coming down the long aisle of the
huge, nearly empty church, stepping on the wilted petals left
over from a previous ceremony and not swept up. She was wearing a white dress he'd never seen before. With her (and apparently being supported by her arm) was Leo in a swallowtail
coat and an immense ascot that was larger than his face, emit-
ting a smell of naphtha and old trunks that seemed to hover almost palpably in the air long after he'd sat down. Once his wife
had joined him at the altar, Lowell's mind refused to photo-
graph anything for his memory's album until the awful pause
that briefly ensued when Mr. Hogarth, blinking up a storm,
asked for comments from the audience. Lowell was certain, absolutely certain, that his mother-in-law was going to do some-

thing outrageous that would haunt him for the rest of his days. When she failed to do any such thing, he felt himself kind of collapse inside, as if they'd told him they'd decided not to shoot him after all and he could take off the blindfold.

"I almost embarrassed myself there during that pause," Leo told him afterward. "That would have been too bad, but I managed to hold it in. In case I forgot to mention it, you can call me Poppa if you want. That's what Betty calls me, Poppa. Personally, I'd rather you called me Leo, but what I'm trying to bring out to you is that you can take your pick. Call me what you want."

"Thanks," said Lowell dully, gazing almost without recognition at the bloated, stickily tear-streaked face that had risen over his father-in-law's shoulder like some kind of diseased moon. "This isn't what I wanted," he heard it say. "This isn't anything like what I wanted at all."

The reception was held at Lowell's club. All his fellow members immediately went about getting drunk, especially the sophomores and a senior from Los Angeles that Lowell had never liked. Lowell's mother and father said something to him in their fond, pleasant way, he couldn't remember what. At some time or other (he couldn't remember when) the information came to him that the white dress his wife was wearing had originally been her mother's, and this little piece of information kept turning up in his thoughts for the rest of the day like the queen of spades in a long game of hearts, but he had the good sense not to talk about it. It occurred to him occasionally in later years.

They spent their wedding night in a motel on Lombard Street in San Francisco, where they were well known. It was cheap and clean and you didn't get the feeling that the rooms were bugged with cameras and listening devices like you did at places like the Holiday Inn. Lowell had the presence of mind to stop off first at a car wash in San Mateo and remove the suggestive, obscene, and, above all, informative messages from the hood, trunk, and doors of his car, and the motel keeper was never the wiser.

First graduated, then married, Lowell finally crossed the two mountains that had loomed in his path for it seemed like years, smack in the way of having a life. Now he was over them, and he could get on with it. And what happened then was, after the bear went over the second mountain, things went downhill for a while, and then they went up a little and got flat, and they stayed that way.

2 ⌐⌐⌐⌐⌐⌐⌐

Lowell and his wife had very few friends and they entertained virtually no one in their apartment except the cleaning woman, who would occasionally be found at the end of the day curled up in Lowell's Eames chair, sound asleep with the television going full blast and a bottle of Lowell's gin beside her on the floor. She kept the apartment as neat as a pin, was utterly reliable, and did not ask for much in the way of salary; in view of these virtues, neither Lowell nor his wife considered her drinking a major failing. Once at Christmas they tried to give her a bottle of Hankey Bannister in a gift box, which offended her so much that she almost quit and was sullen for a month. It was very difficult to know how to treat her. From time to time, with every indication of pride, she would present them with some small horror or other that her son had been forced to make at school: a plaster impression of his hand, painted gold; a green ashtray made of some crumbly, flammable compound; a plaster impression of his other hand, painted red. Although Lowell and his wife dutifully displayed every gift that came, they would always return one night to find that the cleaning lady had quietly removed it from its place and thrown it away. Anyway, she didn't get drunk very often.

Lowell's best friend was the heroically moustached art director of a tobacco magazine that published in the same building where Lowell worked at plumbing. His name was Harry Balmer, and despite the evidence of his moustache he was nervous, compulsive, and wracked with small fears. He looked his best from across a wide room; the closer you got to him, the more he seemed to fall apart into a mass of twitches and gnawed fingernails and the clearer it became that his big, smart-looking moustache was a kind of bush he was trying to hide behind. Every once in a while he and Lowell would go down to McSorley's after work and get drunk together on ale. Lowell didn't really know if he liked Harry Balmer or not—his feelings about him were vaguely mingled and not very strong, one way or the other; he never spent much time with him except at McSorley's, and afterward he could never remember very clearly what they'd talked about.

"I've got it figured out," he told Balmer one night as they sat with their mugs near the old cast-iron stove.

"Good idea," said Balmer. A group of students were making a lot of noise and falling down in the next room.

"It came to me one morning," said Lowell. "I'm not having a meaningful life. It came to me just like that."

"Bachelorhood," said Balmer. "The only answer. Who needs a wife? Take it from me. Firmly committed. Firmly."

Lowell shook his head from side to side in an effort to clear it. He was certain that they'd already had Balmer's half of this conversation before, perhaps several times, and he had the queer feeling that he wasn't getting through. It was like trying to have a conversation with a tape recording.

"Marry late, live long, see life," said Balmer. "Marrying late does a lot for you. Take me, for example. Free as a bird. How come you're looking at your watch? You're worried about the time, aren't you? Got to be on time. The old wife. Not me. Did you say something?"

"I said, I'm not looking at my watch," said Lowell.

"Some fucker filled this ashtray with beer," said Balmer, picking up his hopelessly sodden, half-smoked cigarette and examining it as a nerve fluttered madly in one corner of his eye.

From time to time Lowell also went out to lunch with members of the staff, but he never drank enough to tell them anything important about himself.

Lowell and his wife had a good time living with each other, and they seldom quarreled. Their apartment was spacious and basically comfortable despite being strangely designed, and except on weekends they were never in it during the day, when you could see the place in the living-room ceiling where the plaster was badly patched and it became evident that pale green was not the color for the bathroom. Lowell generally returned home from work about half an hour before his wife, who had to take the shuttle and might decide to stop off first at Bloomingdale's. Once a week he paid the cleaning lady before he filled the ice bucket. The other four days he went straight to the refrigerator first thing after hanging up his coat. In the summertime he made his wife a whiskey sour and prepared a gin and tonic for himself. In the winter he drank whiskey and soda and set aside a glass of sherry for his wife. Then he turned on the television and watched while he waited for her to get home. For the first year after they bought the set, he was in time to watch *Gigantor, the Space Age Robot*. Then *Gigantor* moved to a new time period and he watched *Speed Racer*. He'd seen all the episodes twice. When his wife came home he turned off the set and they made supper together while they had their drinks. Occasionally Lowell would bring in a pizza or some little paper buckets of Chinese food or, very rarely and only as a special treat, a complete Pakistani meal from a restaurant down on Broadway. They took such quiet pleasure in cooking supper together that they almost never went out, and Lowell tended to become uneasy if his routine was disturbed. Whenever he brought food in, he regretted it. No sooner did he place his order than he knew he wouldn't like it, and he never did.

Once every month or so, his wife would smile apologetically and a little defensively, put on her longest skirt, and pack herself over to see her mother in Flatbush like some kind of installment-plan Eurydice. Her mother still had a nice spare bedroom ready in case her daughter came to her senses, and while there was no danger of this ever occurring—at least, not that way—the knowledge that his mother-in-law continued to nourish hope was a source of considerable irritation to Lowell, especially because he suspected that she was doing it at least partly to get his goat. As he conceived it, his mother-in-law's mind was a place of dim shadows and brooding malice, and he could find nothing in it to recommend her, but curiously his wife had made friends with her mother almost immediately after they came to New York, and they were now fast friends. They went to S. Klein's together and called each other up on the telephone and talked about people with comic-opera names like Marvin and Irving who lived in comic-opera places like Canarsie and Ozone Park—people Lowell had never met but about whom his wife unaccountably seemed to know volumes. It gave their conversations a peculiar, other-dimensional quality that profoundly disturbed him, as though his wife had a second identity that was completely alien to the one Lowell knew and cherished, a whole separate personality dwelling in another ethos that he could occasionally glimpse but never understand.

"How come you never talk to your mother about me?" he asked. "I'm your husband. I'm your mother's son-in-law. How come you never mention me?"

"It's not polite to eavesdrop," said his wife primly. "Anyway, we do talk about you, so there. You just aren't eavesdropping at the right times."

"You're always talking about a bunch of strangers."

"That's not true. They're not either strangers. I've known

Milly Norinski for years and years. What's the matter with you? Can't I talk about my friends with my own mother if I want to? Anyway, I don't even like Milly Norinski. She's nothing but an old bag and all she can talk about is money. You'd hate her, believe me. Count yourself lucky that I only talk about her to my mother. Listen, you want me to bore you? Ask me about Milly Norinski one of these times. Boy, would you ever be bored. I only keep up with her because I've known her since grade school. She never used to talk about money. People turn out funny sometimes. They surprise you."

Although over the years Lowell had heard his wife suddenly begin talking like this at odd moments, he'd never gotten used to it. Usually she didn't talk like that. Strangers talked like that, but not his wife. He just couldn't understand it. Sometimes he caught her bullying the butcher or fighting with the vegetable man, and he couldn't understand that, either. It was as though another person inhabited a little room in his wife's mind, the Hyde lurking in the Jekyll, marching forth at certain moments to take command of the situation. It always made him worry. Sometimes he felt that he didn't know his wife at all, or at least not much of her. Sometimes he had the feeling that the person he knew and loved in the evenings and on weekends was nothing but a cunning impersonation, speaking in his dialect, acting out a charade of mildness and happy marriage, and that the occasionally glimpsed person with the news vendor's voice was the real one. It bothered him how easy it would be to manage it— they were together for only a few hours of their lives, not counting the times one or the other of them was asleep. Was she somebody else the rest of the time, punching computer keys and chewing gum and winking at the office boy with her legs crossed? What really disturbed him more than anything was the feeling he had that the personality he imagined for her, though crude and devious to an incredible degree, was in a strange way more complex and plausible than the one she really seemed to have, at least most of the time.

Actually, Lowell knew that all of this was pretty paranoid and ridiculous, and normally he didn't give it a second thought once the bad moment was over. Their days went on, one piece of string tied to another, and until Lowell woke up that horrible morning soon after his birthday, it seldom crossed his mind that his little fantasies might be trying to tell him something, and not necessarily about his wife. If it did chance to cross his mind, that is exactly what it did: it came in one side and went out the other, leaving a chill little wake that was soon covered over.

Lowell tried hard to be a dutiful son-in-law, and his mother-in-law tried equally hard never to speak a word to him. If he happened to answer the phone when she called, she asked him if her daughter was there; if she was, she said, "Put her on," and if she wasn't, she said, "I'll call back," and hung up. Lowell was always very civil to her.

Part of being civil—the major and most difficult part, rather like eating a boiled sheep's eye with good grace and a tactful smile—consisted of twice-yearly appearances in his in-laws' living room, although never close to mealtime. He had the idea that he wasn't kosher or something, and exactly what purpose these dinnerless, tense, and arid visits accomplished was vague. It seemed that once every six months his mother-in-law wanted to look at his fingernails and his father-in-law wanted to talk to him about Negroes, and he dutifully trundled himself out to Flatbush so that they could do it.

Everything in their apartment seemed to be either made of plastic or covered with plastic. Even some of the things that were made of plastic were covered with plastic, such as the vases of plastic flowers that were encased in polyethylene bags and tied with big faded ribbons. There was actually very little furniture, and it was arranged like a kind of exhibit: everything faced in the direction of an imaginary observer and had been placed far apart for better viewing, which made conversation difficult without a lot of swiveling around and loud talking. The transparent plastic slipcovers made this exceedingly difficult to do. They also made it exceedingly difficult to sit still. They were cold in the winter and clammy in the summer and hard to get a purchase on no matter what the weather was like, so that some part of you always felt like it was about to slither off onto the floor, even though your back was glued in place with sweat. Beneath the plastic the upholstery was pale and washed-out, as though it had been under water for a long time. There was a very little color anywhere in the apartment, and the floor was covered with spotless pale linoleum. There were no rugs anywhere. "It's because they were born on the East Side," said Lowell's wife. "That's why." Lowell couldn't have cared less.

"Negroes look different nowadays," Leo told him. He was sitting on his electric Relaxacizor pad. It was making him vibrate faintly, as though with a mild palsy, especially when he nodded his head. "It's all this intermarriage."

"Hmmmm," said Lowell, muscles tense from the effort of keeping himself in place. He got up and sat down again. It didn't do any good. Out in the kitchen his mother-in-law's voice droned on and on like a nasal radio.

"They used to look like monkeys," said Leo. "I guess that was before your time. You can take it from me, they looked just like monkeys with big white teeth. It isn't like that anymore. How we used to laugh. They stir them up now."

There was a long pause. "Who does?" asked Lowell at last. If you watched Leo vibrate long enough, he began to go blurry around the edges, like a picture that was going slowly out of focus.

"The agitators," said Leo. "The agitators stir them up. Outside agitators. They're moving in now."

"The agitators," said Lowell. "I see." He wondered how long a man could put up with this sort of conversation before he went out of his mind.

"No, no," said Leo, leaning forward in his chair. "The agitators are stirring them up. It's the Negroes who are moving in. The agitators aren't moving in. You've got it backwards."

Out in the kitchen his mother-in-law suddenly stopped talking, as though her voice had been cut off with a pair of shears. Leo was waiting anxiously for Lowell to say something again, and there was a peculiar moment of silence that was disturbed only by the low muttering of Leo's machine. Everything, for some mad reason, seemed to focus on Lowell with crushing intensity. It was kind of unnerving. "That's too bad," he managed to say.

"Listen, they're coming in like flies," whispered Leo, as though you could hear some of them now, making a characteristic noise. Out in the kitchen his mother-in-law began talking again at exactly the same rate and exactly the same tone, as though the arm of a record player, having been raised for a second, had come back down on the same spot.

"It's been going on for years," Leo continued in the same hushed, urgent tones, with a look of mingled intimacy and fear. "Years. You know what I mean?"

Lowell agreed that he knew what Leo meant. He always felt a little drunk at his in-laws' place, and afterward he had a funny hung-over feeling, as though they had put something in his coffee. Actually, they never put anything in his coffee, and he was lucky if he got any at all. When he did get some, it came in a different kind of cup from everybody else's. He wondered if his mother-in-law kept the cup in a special place, wrapped up in a plastic bag. Drunk was not quite the way he felt; he felt like he'd watched too many girders flash past on the subway.

Lowell's visits always came to a barren end, somewhere near the fulcrum of the afternoon, when out in the real world the real people were clearing the Sunday paper off the floor and getting out the cocktail shaker and others were putting on their hats and going out the door.

"Well, so long, Lowell," said Leo in a false voice, shaking his hand as though still attached to the Relaxacizor. Lowell wondered if Leo thought he could make Lowell like him by shaking his hand that way. "I certainly enjoy these little visits of ours. I really look forward to them a lot, you can't imagine. Time sure does fly and it's too bad you have to go."

"I . . ." began Lowell as his hand was shaken faster and faster, as though caught in some sort of soft, painless mechanism.

"Don't think you have to pretend you enjoyed it," said Leo. "I talk too much. Believe me, I know my limitations like a book. I'm talking too much right now. I bet you can't wait to get out of here. This is a good time for it. The sun is still up and there's a lot of light outside. If you stayed any longer I'd run out of things to say and we'd just have to sit there. It's been good seeing you."

"Yes," said Lowell. "Good-bye," he called out to the kitchen, where his mother-in-law lurked out of sight, motionless and apparently not breathing. Nine years had passed, but she still hadn't told him what to call her, and neither had anybody else. It would have been awkward if Lowell had been trying to attract her attention in a crowd, but he didn't think he would ever want to do that. "So long," he called. "We're going now."

"I heard you," she said.

"Er, heh," said Leo, trying to shrug, smile, and look over his shoulder at the same time, giving such a look of toothy terror that there might have been an armed fugitive concealed behind the door.

"Good-bye, Poppa," said Lowell's wife.

Moving against the grain of the day, they went down the hall and got into the elevator. Out on the street, people were getting

out of cars with presents and small children, but Lowell's evening was already in the wrong place.

Lowell hadn't planned on his in-laws when he came to New
York. In a dim, haphazard way he'd known that Flatbush was
somewhere nearby, more or less the same way that he knew
there were stockyards in Chicago, but it had never occurred to
him that he would actually have to go there. Nor had it ever occurred that going there would, in a curious and disturbing way,
constitute by far the largest part of a very, very small social life.
A lot of things hadn't occurred to him. He was paying for them
now. Sometimes he wondered if he was even paying for things
he didn't know about.

"I thought we were going to Berkeley," his wife had said nine
years ago, her voice coming to him down the corridor of years
as clearly as if she had spoken to him only a moment before. It
was the instant when his life had suddenly poised itself on an
idle remark, and the hinge of fate had opened—a small moment, an utterly insignificant fragment of time that could have
passed as swiftly as turning a page in a book, but instead it had
changed his life forever. "Didn't you say we were going to
Berkeley?" she asked anxiously. "That's where I want to go. All
those pretty hills. I guess you're kidding about New York, right?
Berkeley is where we're really going, isn't it? We're really going
there, aren't we? Lowell?"

He could still hear the voice, he could still see the room, he
could still smell the old green overstuffed chair he'd been sitting
in. "Maybe not," he said. He was only teasing. Berkeley was definitely the place they were going, and the idea of going to New
York instead had just sort of wandered into his mind a moment
ago like a stray insect. No doubt it would have perished there at
once if he hadn't spoken it aloud. Now it was out in the open,
and God help them all. Even in those days his wife had an almost marvelous tendency to seize upon and circle a vagrant or dis-

tasteful idea, trying all the variations until some sort of conclusion could be drawn from it. Occasionally these conclusions took bizarre and astonishing form, such as going to New York when you really intended to go to Berkeley, but in those days Lowell hadn't had much practice with his wife's mind and he could never figure out what was afoot until affairs were well advanced, often in the direction of catastrophe. He was simply not prepared to give serious thought to the matter of pulling up his life like a bush and moving it a couple of thousand miles in a strange direction. "Us pioneers think nothing of moving around," he said with a smile. "We fought the Indians and crossed the plains."

"You wouldn't like it there," said his wife. "It's a big dirty place, and going back there is not the reason I came out here. I suppose I could stand it for a while if I had to, provided we didn't have to live in a public-housing project or some slum. I'd rather go to Berkeley. I thought you always wanted to go to Nevada. Let me tell you, New York is no Nevada."

"I never thought New York was like Nevada," said Lowell. "I know better than that."

"You don't know a thing about it. New York is like nothing you've ever seen, take it from me."

"Oh, I don't know about that," said Lowell righteously, flipping through his mind for a good example of something he'd seen that was like New York. All he came up with was mountains and dams. "Anyway," he said crossly, "you're only trying to put me down because you burned your cake."

"That's pretty typical of you," said his wife. "The underhanded blow. You're only trying to strike back because you feel inferior. You always do that. Well, it won't work this time. I never wanted to make that silly cake in the first place. I was making it for you. I hate cake."

"I never knew you hated cake," said Lowell. "I'll bet that's not true. I'll bet you're just trying to get at me in a new way. What's the matter, is it your period of something?"

"That was uncalled for," said his wife, making a thin line of her lips. "That was really uncalled for. Just because you feel like a hick."

"That's got nothing to do with it," said Lowell.

"Aha! See there, you do feel like a hick. I knew it all along, and you just admitted it."

"Now, wait a minute," said Lowell. He began to make a helpless gesture but stopped himself in time.

"Boy, would you ever hate it in New York. It's a good thing you don't have the nerve to go there. Take it from me, you would really hate it. You'd hate it more than I'm going to love Berkeley. You wouldn't even know how to ask people for directions."

"Hey, come on," said Lowell. He never knew how to react to aggression. He was always kind of stunned by it.

"I hate it when you sit in a chair like that," said his wife.

"What's wrong with the way I'm sitting?"

"It's weak. You're sitting there in a weak way."

Lowell looked down at himself, but he seemed to be sitting the same way he always did. Maybe that was what she meant. Through the kitchen door he could see the ant poison in its dish on the counter. It looked like mint jelly and it had never done a thing to stop the ants. He could see them at work now, a thin wavy line like a trail of pepper crossing the floor. A car went past in the street.

"I think maybe we really will go to New York," he said quietly.

"I wish there were some doors in this stupid place so I could go and slam one behind me," said his wife.

"There's the bathroom," said Lowell, staring at the trail of ants.

"Right," said his wife. "I hadn't thought of that. Boy, do I ever despise you." She strode past him and locked herself in the bathroom.

She remained locked in the bathroom until it was time for Lowell to depart for his job at the library. After a while he stopped staring at the ants and tried to persuade her to come out, but she refused to answer his pleas and gentle inquiries. She made no sound at all. Lowell began to worry. He wondered if people made any noise when they slit their wrists. He knew they didn't make any noise afterward, and that was exactly what his wife was doing: not making any noise. Was there any lethal substance in the medicine chest? He didn't think so, unless it was possible to kill yourself with a couple of dozen aspirin, but on the other hand, he'd never really thought about it. He considered going around to the side of the house and looking in the bathroom window, but he was afraid someone would see him; he imagined himself trying to explain to somebody, such as a policeman, that he was only looking in the bathroom window because he wanted to see what his wife was doing. He'd never get it right, and he doubted if anyone would understand him anyway.

She was still in the bathroom when he left the house, but by then he'd worried so much that he'd gotten angry and self-righteous, and he didn't care. She was in bed when he got home. He didn't wake her up. The following morning he'd forgotten the whole thing. He hated quarrels and was very good at putting them out of his mind, especially after a good night's sleep.

"When do we start?" asked his wife tersely as she loaded the ancient toaster that had come with the house. She was wearing her bathrobe. It always made her look old, and Lowell hated it.

"Start what?" he asked. He was afraid she meant their quarrel. It already seemed as though it had happened in a different world.

"For New York," she said. "We have to make plans."

"Nonsense," said Lowell. "We're going to Berkeley. Let's forget the whole thing."

"I thought you said we were going to New York. You *did* say that, didn't you?"

"Well, yes, but . . ."

"Why did you say we were going to New York if we're not? Don't let me force you into going to Berkeley. God forbid we should go to Berkeley if your heart is set on New York. Pay no attention to anything I say. You'll never forgive me if you let me talk you out of it. Eat your breakfast."

"I am eating my breakfast," said Lowell. He remembered her crack about how he sat in a weak way, and he straightened up and carried a bite of food purposefully to his mouth.

"What do you mean, we're not going to New York?" his wife suddenly demanded after they had both chewed for a while. "It was nothing but one of your little jokes, is that what you're trying to tell me? Ho, ho. Well, you just try sitting on the edge of a bathtub for half an hour and see how you like it. If you'd been half a man, you would have kicked the goddamn door down, but not you, no sir, it was only a joke and we're not going to New York after all. What a laugh."

"It wasn't a joke," said Lowell, hoping that he'd chosen a good reply. It was a little early for him, and he was kind of bewildered, although he was definitely aware that something was expected of him. He wished he knew what it was.

"Let me know when you make up your mind," said his wife. "They're only three thousand miles apart, and it should be easy to choose between them. I knew all along that you'd back down. They say that girls always marry their fathers, and I sure did."

"Wait a minute," said Lowell. "What do you mean, back down?"

"My lips are sealed."

"I remember now. You think I'm a hick."

"When you make up your mind, just holler."

"You think the reason I don't want to go to New York is because I'm afraid to. I remember now. It all comes back to me." He was terribly hungry, and there was a full meal right in front of him, toast and sausages and everything, but he had an idea that it would spoil his effectiveness if he were to snatch a bite between diatribes. It might make him look weak or vulgar. He tried to remember if she'd accused him of being vulgar yet.

"It was a joke," she said, looking off into space. "You said so yourself."

"It wasn't a joke, and I never said so. You're just trying to confuse me."

"I only want to find out where we're going, Lowell. That's all."

Lowell pictured himself dashing all the breakfast things to the floor with one forceful sweep of his arm. It only reminded him of how hungry he was. If he hadn't been so hungry, he would have stormed right out of the house, but he didn't have enough money to buy himself another breakfast somewhere, and he really wanted one. He slumped back in the chair and tried to think things out. Once upon a time he'd known what they were arguing about, but he seemed to have lost the thread. "What are we arguing about?" he asked.

"God damn," said his wife. She pushed back her chair, swept into the bathroom, and locked the door. Lowell ate his breakfast. It tasted like cardboard, and he wondered if he was chewing it in a weak way. Nobody in his family ever argued, at least that he knew about. They always agreed about everything, but on the other hand, they didn't do much. Maybe that was why.

By midmorning Lowell had decided to take the bull by the horns and announce that they were definitely going to New York. It wasn't really a decision so much as a tactic, and it was also the only thing that he could think of to do; his previous failure to decide to go to New York seemed to lie at the root of their misunderstanding and the source of all their misery. Clearly (Lowell decided) his wife was waiting for him to decide to go to New York so that she could restore her subservient female role by begging him not to. Things had gotten out of hand simply because he was so damned amiable, and also because of her secret fear of becoming like her mother. It was only elementary psychology. Lowell was glad he'd been able to think it through. He could scarcely wait until he got home.

"Okay," he announced cheerily but firmly as he stepped through the front door. A cheese-and-onion pie was baking in the oven, and the house was full of delicious odors. "Okay," he announced, "we're going to New York."

"You're going to hate it there," said his wife. "When do we start?"

And that was how Lowell damned himself out of his own mouth. There was no going back. A seamless wall descended around his life and cut him off from all paths but one, and that was the one he took. His wife was right: he didn't like it there. Nine years later he could still hear the sound of her voice, clear as a bell and true as a plumb, echoing in his mind in small, solitary moments; a wet newspaper would plaster itself to his ankle on an empty street and he would suddenly feel chilled and mortal, and he would hear her words again: "You aren't going to like it there. When do we start?"

There was no getting out of it. Afloat on a tide of events and furiously propelled by his wife, he gave notice at the library, renounced his scholarship at Berkeley, and told everyone in sight that he'd decided to go to New York, desperately hoping that someone would give him a smart-sounding and compelling reason for doing no such a blame-fool thing, but no one did. On the contrary, the more people he told about it, the more it seemed like he was actually going to go.

"I hear you're going to New York," said his ex-roommate, meeting him one morning on the quad.

"That's right," said Lowell, giving his friend a look of dumb appeal. "My wife is against it, but my mind is made up. Unless something happens pretty soon, we're really going to New York for sure."

"Look up my uncle," said his ex-roommate. "One hell of a guy."

"I'll do that," said Lowell.

One by one the familiar lights were going out in his life. He already felt like a stranger. He was no longer anybody he knew; he was somebody who was going to New York.

"I can take it or leave it," he told everybody. "If I don't like it, I can always come right back. Nothing to it. Get in the car and start her up."

"Be sure and go to Roseland," said the sub-librarian, a faded little man who was cruel to his children. "I was there once, during the war. Roseland Dance City. It was real nice."

"I might not be there very long," said Lowell. "I might not like it there."

"Wish I was going," said the sub-librarian. "All I ever had was a three-day pass. Hell of a place."

Lowell was glad that New York was supposed to be a good place to write novels in and that a lot of people had actually done so, because that was what he'd decided to do—write a novel. He wished it didn't feel like so much of an afterthought, because he'd always wanted to write a novel, he really had. He'd even started a couple of them, but although they were pretty dirty, they weren't very good and he'd gotten rid of them before somebody accidentally stumbled across them and made fun of them. He wondered what would have happened if, instead of New York, he'd said something like, "Hey, let's go to Greece. I read where everybody is going there this year." His wife would probably have told him he was out of his mind.

"I'll have to go to work," she told him. Ever since they started getting ready to go to New York, she'd been given to the utterance of sudden, sharp pronouncements, most of them ukases of one sort or another. "In Berkeley we would have had your scholarship, but in New York there's no other way."

"You won't have to work," said Lowell. "I'll get a job somewhere and write at night."

"Not on your life," said his wife. "I know all about you. You'll never write a line if you get a job. You just haven't got it in you. What kind of a job?"

"I thought maybe I'd drive a cab," mused Lowell. "Drive a cab and write at night." He saw himself driving his cab, putting down the flag and asking people where they wanted to go, storing matches in the band of his yellow-cab-driver's hat.

"Great," said his wife. "That's just great. I can't tell you how that idea really grabs me. What do you think this is, *The Jackie Gleason Show*? I want you to meet my husband the cab-driver, I met him in college? I think you've really gone out of your mind. I think you've finally flipped. I have to travel three thousand miles and work my ass off for four years in order to marry a New York cab driver? I don't think you know how bizarre that really is. I don't even believe it. I've never worn a housedress in my life. At least you could have said you wanted to be a riveter. I might have been able to take that with some kind of grace, not much maybe, but a little. Riveters make good money and there'd be a nice little pension for me if you walked off a beam up there in the sky. I liked it better when you wanted to be a cowboy."

Deep down inside, Lowell still wanted to be a cowboy, and he was not only stung but strangely saddened by his wife's scorn of his most secret places, almost as if she'd attacked him by mentioning one of the really dirty things he wanted to do in bed. "You don't understand," he said weakly, knowing that he could never explain the innocence of his purpose, the purity of his motive. "It wasn't much of a scholarship anyway," he muttered.

"Listen," said his wife, "a writer is what you're setting out to be, and a writer is what you're going to end up, not a cab-driver. What do you know about driving a cab? The man I married a couple of months ago was going to be a college professor, in case you've forgotten. If I wanted to marry a cab-driver, I could have stayed in Flatbush. I could have done better than that if I'd stayed in Flatbush. I could have married Harry Ingleman. His father owns a whole *fleet* of cabs!"

Lowell rose abruptly and went into the kitchen to make himself a drink, but the bottle was gone.

"I threw it out," said his wife. "You've been drinking too much. I had an uncle who drank too much, and I know all about it."

Curiously, although their life together was terrible and they hadn't made love in more than a week, she was wearing all his favorite clothes and her cooking had never been better.

"There's still time," said Lowell on the last morning as he settled himself behind the wheel and put the key in the ignition. "We can still change our minds." The old car was dangerously laden; for some reason, although they had relatively few possessions, they had contrived to find a great many big heavy containers to put them in. Not ten minutes ago their landlady had confiscated their deposit on the grounds that she couldn't find another tenant in the middle of the month, which Lowell knew to be a bald-faced lie even though he couldn't prove it. Otherwise everything was fine. The University of California had been informed by mail that he would not be needing their nice scholarship after all, thanks very much. Lowell had said good-bye to his friends. Sentimentally, he vowed to say good-bye to one friend a day, but he soon ran out of friends and he ended up saying good-bye to some people twice because he kept running into them on campus. He said good-bye to his roommate four times. It was all kind of embarrassing, and after a while he got the idea that people were looking at him in a funny way. "How about it?" he asked his wife, whose face was hard as stone.

"It's too late for that," she said. "This isn't the place. Drive on."

It was hard to believe that changing your life could be as easy as flipping a switch, but that was exactly what happened: Lowell turned the key in the ignition and drove away from everything he had ever known in his life. They went across the bay and over the hills and down into the valley and over the mountains, and the next day they crossed Nevada and after that they were no place Lowell had ever been or imagined he would go.

"Do you realize that I'm the first member of my family to cross this thing in a hundred years?" said Lowell as they bridged the Mississippi at Saint Louis. His emotions were strange and sinking, but not precise enough to put a name to.

"Big deal," said his wife.

They came to New York at night, hurtling through a hellish New Jersey landscape the likes of which Lowell had never dreamed existed, a chaos of roadways and exits, none of which made any sense, surrounded by smoke and flashes and dark hulking masses and pillars of real fire a thousand feet high, enveloped in a stench like dog's breath and dead goldfish.

"There it is," said his wife.

"Where? Where?" cried Lowell, bending over the wheel, uncertain of anything, his heart in his mouth and his mind in a fog. The geometry of the place was all wrong, and nothing made sense.

"Over there," said his wife.

Out of the corner of his eye Lowell caught a fleeting glimpse of something huge and calm-looking in the distance, but his perspective was shattered by neon and oncoming lights, and at that moment a sign convinced him that it was really a truck, and

§§ 54

he almost ran into a real truck that he hadn't even noticed. He swung away from it in the nick of time, only to be confronted by a fork in the roadway, each half marked with a meaningless sign.

"Which way? Which way?" he shouted to his wife.

"Beats me," she said.

And so they came to New York.

When Lowell woke up the next morning, he was astonished to discover that he wasn't in New York after all. He was in Brooklyn instead. Somehow that frightened him. He couldn't remember coming to Brooklyn. He couldn't remember anything but highways and tunnels. He felt like a man emerging from some kind of coma. The desk clerk got quite a kick out of it.

"We're in Brooklyn," he told his wife when he returned to the room. She was just waking up, and she didn't look a bit surprised, although she did look a little pissed-off.

"That's right," she said. "The St. George Hotel. What's so strange about that?"

"How did we get to Brooklyn? I don't remember coming to Brooklyn."

"We came by car and you drove us," she said, swinging her legs out of bed. "Ask me about it later."

She went into the bathroom and began running the water. Lowell sat down in the nearest available chair and felt dumb. He didn't ask her about it later.

"Let me show you the sights," his wife suggested as they finished their breakfast in the restaurant downstairs. Lowell felt the weight of the enormous building overhead. "Borough Hall is right down the street." She gestured vaguely.

"Later," said Lowell. "I never wanted to come to Brooklyn to begin with. Now we've got to go back to New York and find a place to live."

"For your information, Cholly Knickerbocker, Brooklyn *is* in New York," said his wife primly. He hated it when she did that.

"There are some very nice places to live in Brooklyn. This is the Heights. The best people live here. I'll bet you knew that already."

First Lowell had missed New York in the dark, and now he was being pressured to live in Brooklyn. Pressured was exactly it: he felt as though his brain and body were being inexorably squeezed like a tube of toothpaste. The building was above him and his wife's mouth was across the table, the first pushing down and the other sort of slapping at him lightly but incessantly. He wasn't even properly awake. He was still tired from all the driving he'd done, and every time he closed his eyes, he saw nothing but highway. "No," he said. "I mean, that's not what I had in mind. I had Manhattan in mind, actually, and I think we ought to go there pretty soon and find a place to live before our money runs out."

"Whatever you say," said his wife. "If you are determined to lie in the bed you made, far be it from me to sprinkle it with cornflakes. I have to call my mother."

She called her mother from a nearby phone booth, but she did not share their conversation with Lowell when she returned. "I told her we were here," she said, her eyes staring fiercely into some middle distance where everything was stupid. Then she guided him back over the bridge and into Manhattan, where he had made his bed.

By the end of the first day they'd taken an Upper West Side apartment that was not only very clean and too small, but far too expensive. It was in an old brownstone, and once upon a time it had been somebody's dining room, but you would never have guessed by looking at it. It looked like a room in one of the newer dormitories at school, except that it had a kitchen and was not pastel-colored. There were two windows at one end of the room and a stove and a sink at the other; off to one side was a refrigerator, and off to another was a sort of independent cubicle that seemed to have been stuck on as an afterthought and which contained a closet and a bathroom, facing in opposite directions. The whole apartment was painted stark, smooth white, and the previous occupant had not left his mark on it. Lowell examined it minutely in the days that followed, but there was absolutely no sign that anyone had ever lived in the place or done anything there. All traces of prior human occupancy had been obliterated, and there was nothing to indicate that the room had not been built yesterday. Lowell was sure that when he left the place, no one would ever know that he had been there either. It would still look like it had been built yesterday. When you were alone in it, it gave you the feeling that you weren't there. It was a kind of spooky feeling, and as time went on, it got worse, not better.

"When you're alone in the room, do you get the feeling that you're not really there?" he asked his wife.

"I'm never alone in the room," said his wife. "Whenever I'm here, you're here too. Sometimes, though, I wonder if you're really here when I'm away, if that's what you mean."

"Not exactly," said Lowell.

"How did the writing go today?" she asked.

"It's coming along," he said.

Once their life had settled down, there wasn't much to it. There was a sense of dwindling, like a slow leak in a balloon, as if all the vigor was slowly going out of their existence, all the light from the sky, all the color from the world, all the good thoughts from Lowell's head. They bought a bed and a secondhand table; they sat at the table at night, and Lowell wrote on it during the day. On one wall he hung his print of Maurice Vlaminck's *Summer Sky* and on the other wall he hung his print of Maurice Vlaminck's *Winter Sky*. He put them up with loops of masking tape, and after about a month they began to come unstuck, bulging depressingly when they weren't hanging limply by one corner. Every time they came unstuck, Lowell stuck them right back up again.

In addition to the bed and table, they had their desk lamps from college, their typewriters, their books, and a couple of wooden kitchen chairs that were weakly constructed and about twenty years old. Lowell's wife bought a set of pots at the variety store for ninety-nine cents; the plastic parts of the handles disintegrated after a little while, and you had to be careful when you picked them up. She also bought a broom and dustpan, and she cleaned the apartment from top to bottom every evening when she came home from computer training school. First she cleaned under the windows, where a lot of soot came in during the day. (It crackled when you stepped on it, much to Lowell's surprise.) Then she got down on her hands and knees and poked viciously under the bed with the broom as though trying to kill a mouse. When she got tired of that, she swept the corridor between the bed and the table and the area between the door and the closet, stabbing hard at the dust and fuzz she found. Then she got down on her hands and knees again and mopped the kitchen floor with a dishtowel. Then she started supper. They ate a good many eggs, in one form or another. Eggs were cheap.

They stayed home most evenings and weekends. Partly it was because they had so little money—Lowell's car brought a fat thirty-five dollars when he sold it to a lot out in Queens somewhere, and the cost of computer school was deducted from his wife's salary, which was pitiful enough to begin with—but the main reason they didn't go anywhere was because there didn't seem to be anywhere to go. Whenever they tried to decide what to do, they almost never came up with anything. Sometimes they went to the New Yorker and saw an old movie. More often, they only talked about going to the New Yorker, bickering back and forth listlessly. No one ever visited them, and they never visited anyone; none of their friends from Stanford had come to New York, and Lowell's wife was biding her time as far as her friends from Brooklyn were concerned. She never even mentioned them. She never mentioned her mother, either, and since they couldn't afford a phone, it was possible for Lowell to forget that she existed except as a kind of dim concept. Occasionally he saw the other people in the building—a trim elderly man, a fat Chinese with a bad limp, a prosperous young couple, and a grim-looking middle-aged woman who always wore white gloves and the highest heels Lowell had ever seen anybody seriously attempt to walk on. Lowell sometimes said hello to these people when he met them in the hall, and sometimes they said hello back, but not often.

Lowell tried writing at various times of the day to see which one suited him best. First he tried writing in the morning, and then he tried the afternoon, but the great drawback of each was that the other was left free, a procession of empty hours like so many bottles into which he was required to pour himself one by one, occupying the space for a while until it was time to pour himself into the next one. If he wrote in the morning, the barren afternoon stared him in the face; and if he wrote in the afternoon, the morning had already bored him so much that he was too benumbed to think. He tried to stimulate himself by taking long walks and observing people. Unfortunately, there were very few good places to walk, and almost no people lived in them. His apartment was on a block that had a Baptist church at one end and the playing field of an Episcopal boys' school at the other; across the street was the back of a junior high school, and on Lowell's side of the street were five or six brownstones inhabited by the same kind of people that lived in Lowell's brownstone. To the north and east everything was being torn down for a vast public-housing project. To the south were endless brown blocks with no people on them, deserted, silent, and heavy, as though everyone had either moved away or died. There was a limit, he found, to the number of times he could go to Central Park; he was trying to find something, not get away from it; he wanted to be stimulated by the city, not soothed by nature, and the park was just so much more boredom, only with leaves. Nothing whatever was happening in it that he was remotely interested in. At the other end of the scale, down on Broadway, the traffic islands were full of old people sitting on benches, the men in odd-colored shabby suits turning their faces to the sun like some kind of wizened, horrible plant life, the women with their voices like aged birds of prey and their stockings held up with bits of string. Lowell could scarcely bear to look at them; it was too much like looking inside his own mind. Sometimes he went down to Riverside Park. It was dull there too. Once he walked up to Grant's Tomb. Then he walked back home again.

When autumn came, it was as though another blanket had fallen on the heap that smothered his spirit. It was the husk of a season—darker, colder, the light weakening in the sky in proportion as his brain seemed to dim. The streets got dirtier, and all the leaves seemed to disappear from the trees in the park in a single day; he caught distant glimpses of people hurrying along the paths with their collars turned up, going about their own unfathomable business. Surrounded by millions of people, Lowell began to worry that one day he would simply forget who he was from sheer lack of recognition in the eyes of other men; nobody knew who he was, and they let it show. The boys from the Episcopal school marshaled on the playing field for games of soccer and lacrosse, and Lowell found himself pausing beyond the tall iron fence to watch them, their cries coming to him faintly across the cinder track and grayish grass as they ran this way and that. Every evening his wife would ask him how the writing was coming, and he would tell her it was coming along fine.

Eventually he began to write at night, principally because it solved the problem of what to do with his day: with a little clever management his day disappeared entirely and he no longer had to worry about it. He started working—or at least started sitting at the table—not long after his wife fell asleep, hooding the light and muting the typewriter until he realized that she slept like a stone and it made no difference what he did. He worked until he got either too tired or bored to continue, and then he went to bed and slept until the middle of the afternoon, waking briefly to kiss his wife good-bye in the morning, with numb lips. The drawbacks of this new arrangement were two. First, he woke up so close to suppertime that there was no point in eating lunch. On the other hand, he got so little exercise that he had almost no appetite. His reserves of energy fell and small tasks tired him, but he spent most of his wakeful time motionless in a chair, and it didn't really bother him very much unless he had to get up for the bathroom.

The second drawback was that, for all practical purposes, he might as well have been dead.

At the end of four months he'd finished half a novel, vaguely concerning the foundation and early settlement of Boise, Idaho. The act of writing brought him neither transport nor release; it was like slogging through acres of deep mud and had the same effect when you read it. It read like mud. Totally by accident he had contrived to fashion a style that was both limp and dense at the same time, writing page upon page of flaccid, impenetrable description, pierced here and there by sudden, rather startling interludes of fustian and vainglory that neither adorned, advanced, nor illuminated the plot, although they did give the reader a keen insight on the kind of movies Lowell had seen as a child. Characters as insubstantial and suffocating as smoke rode huge, oddly misshapen steeds over landscapes the color of lead, occasionally bursting into song or shooting one another down for reasons best known to themselves. The only reason Lowell figured he was halfway through was that the number of pages he'd accumulated amounted to about half the length of an average novel; there was certainly no way to tell from the plot, which had mostly to do with property rights and Indian raids, complicated by the free-silver question. Nine years later Lowell was astounded that he'd ever written such a thing, much less with a straight face and purity of purpose, but at the time he drove himself onward with the fixated desperation of a man trying to dig his way out of a grave. It had ceased to matter—if, in fact, it had ever mattered to begin with—whether the novel was good or bad, marketable or a hopeless bomb; he was totally focused on the act of writing it, totally obsessed with his role as the writer of it, and there existed the possibility, given optimum conditions, that he might have gone on writing it forever, or until his wife divorced him.

At the end of six months his wife systematically began to throw away his clothes. True, his clothes were showing a few signs of wear; Lowell had never been particularly interested in clothing, bought it as seldom as possible, and wore it as long as he could, often developing a stubborn affection for certain items. It was also true that his underwear was a disgrace, his Jockey shorts hanging in soft tatters and his undershirts so full of holes that wearing them was nothing but a formality; on the other hand, it was kind of startling to go to the suitcase that served him in lieu of a bureau and find that his possessions had been weeded again, the supply growing shorter and shorter as the days wore on, the time fast approaching when he would go to his suitcase and it would be empty. Worse than that, it was kind of sinister to have laid out your shirt and pants before going to bed and then wake up to find one or the other of them gone, the contents of its pockets heaped up on the table beside the typewriter. He always intended to buy replacements, but he never got around to it, and meanwhile no amount of grumbling would make his wife stop. She had a case and he didn't, and that was that; his clothes were really wearing out—perhaps not quite as fast as they were being thrown out, but that was purely conjectural and largely in the eye of the beholder, especially when it came to arguing about it—and he really did forget to buy new ones, so when you came right down to it, he had no one to blame for his impending nudity but himself. If a kinder fate had not intervened, it was altogether possible that Lowell would soon have been totally naked, hovering thin and birdlike and obsessed above the typewriter like some kind of crackpot anchorite. Although this state of affairs would have precluded ever leaving the apartment again, at least alive, that would have been all right too. A change had gradually come over him as winter approached, and instead of a desperate craving for the smallest personal contact, he had begun to fear it. He could no longer look tradesmen in the eye, and it was an ordeal to encounter another person on an empty street; he couldn't figure out what to do with his eyes, and he began to walk funny, like a person doing a bad but well-meaning imitation of the real thing. Eventually he became more afraid that he would behave peculiarly than he was embarrassed by being noticed while doing it, and he stuck more closely to the room than ever.

One day, in going over his papers, he discovered that his wife had thrown out his birth certificate. There was no proof that she had done so, but the damn thing was gone, and he knew instinctively what had happened to it. It was a blue piece of crackly paper with all of Lowell's statistics arranged in graceful script above a gold medallion and the signatures of the delivering physician, the resident, and the director of the hospital, just like a diploma. It not only proved that he had been born, but the fact that he possessed it proved that he was a grown-up. His mother had sent it to him, along with all his vaccination certificates, when she returned home after the wedding. Now it was gone. He rifled the shoebox where these things were kept, he scoured the room, searched the wastebasket and then the garbage cans outside, but it was nowhere to be found. His wife had thrown it away, just as she occasionally threw away scraps of paper on which he'd scribbled some important thought. It was gone. Lowell was overwhelmed with anger, dizzy with rage. For so many months his mental state had been a constant, curiously placid amalgam of boredom and despair—a graph of it would have shown a flat, straight line with a slight downward tilt. He wasn't used to strong emotions anymore; he was out of practice; he was assaulted by his own anger. It was as though a powerful dynamo had suddenly been switched on inside a frail shed. He couldn't cope. He had to lie down. After a while he threw up, and then he just lay on the bed inertly, smitten down, exhausted, drained, and kind of surprised, like a teen-ager who had beaten off to climax for the first time in his life. Not even the spectacle of his wife coming in the door at her usual time could rouse him from his torpor: his psyche was in limp tatters, like an old Kleenex dredged up from the bottom of a purse. He looked at her dully.

"What's the matter with you?" she said. "You look like your best friend just died." She took off her coat and shoes and prepared to sweep the floor.

"I can't find my birth certificate," said Lowell. "It's not in the shoebox or anywhere."

"What on earth did you want your birth certificate for? Are you sure it can't be found?"

"Positive. It must have gotten thrown out. There's no other explanation."

"Don't be ridiculous. Nobody would have done a thing like that. You probably overlooked it. Here, give me the box."

Lowell gave her the box, and she made a great show of looking through it, arranging the various documents on the table like a hand of solitaire, then scooping them up again. "That's funny," she said. "You're right, it isn't here. Maybe you left it out and it fell in the wastebasket. Anyway, it's no big disaster. If you ever need it, you can always send for a photostat."

Lowell agreed that he could always send for a photostat. He didn't want a photostat. Photostats were dead-looking. He lay back on the bed and decided to forget the whole thing. His wife's bluff had not convinced him, but on the other hand, he could all too easily imagine the kind of scene that would ensue if he tried to accuse her of guilt. It was a scene in which he would sound like a nut.

When he woke up the next afternoon, his wife was sitting in the chair across the room, wearing Levis and reading a book.

"What are you doing here?" he asked, the words cutting their way with difficulty through the thickets of sleep that clogged his brain. Waking up and seeing his wife there was as unsettling as if he'd woken up in a strange room. "What time is it? Should I be asleep? I mean, did I oversleep or did I wake up too soon? That's what I mean."

"It's Saturday," said his wife. "I don't work on Saturday, and I never have. You sure are mixed up."

"I'm not mixed up," said Lowell, feeling a cold little feather of panic brush the back of his neck. "It was Saturday a couple of days ago. It can't be Saturday again. It must be Tuesday or something. Where's yesterday's paper?"

Lowell always bought the late edition of the *Times* first thing when he woke up in the afternoon. He searched for it high and low, his pajama fly gaping foolishly. "It's gone," he said a little wildly. What would disappear next?

"I don't remember any paper," said his wife. "I don't think you've bought a paper since last Sunday, and I bought that one. No, wait; I remember, you bought one on Wednesday. I used part of it to line the garbage can and threw the rest out."

"Wednesday," said Lowell. Putting his mind to it, he realized that he could not, in fact, remember buying a paper yesterday; that is, he couldn't remember the act itself in the specific context of yesterday. He could remember the act well enough, but when he tried to recall doing it yesterday, he discovered that he couldn't even remember if he'd left the room except to hunt in the garbage for his birth certificate. Yet he always bought a newspaper; along with eating, going to the bathroom, and writing his book, it was one of the few things he did every day. He tried to remember if he'd gone to the bathroom yesterday. He was pretty sure he'd eaten. His wife would have seen to that. "Saturday," he said. "Yes, of course. It slipped my mind. I mean, I was sleepy. I'm okay now."

"Good," said his wife. "Why don't we take a walk before it gets dark?"

Lowell numbly put on what clothes he could find, and his wife more or less led him outside. Undoubtedly because of his earlier confusion, he had the absurd impression that several buildings had been put up in the urban-renewal area since the last time he'd looked in that direction, but he put the thought right out of his mind.

That night, nothing he wrote made any sense. It didn't make any sense at all. The forms of words had overwhelmed their functions, and his head was filled with meaningless babble. It was like pronouncing "Ethiopia" too many times, until it became an intricate but purely arbitrary arrangement of sound. It happened to every word that came into his head. Hammer away as he would, all he could get down on paper was a kind of impervious nonsense; he couldn't even decide whether to use a conjunction, a semicolon, or start a new sentence, not that it mattered much. Every new sentence was as meaningless as the last. He erased holes in his paper, he inserted fresh sheets and began again, but it was as though his mind had gotten itself plugged into some kind of shortwave band where all you could get were interminable propaganda broadcasts in obscure Central European languages, alternately faint and loud, incessant. After a couple of hours of struggle, exhausted, Lowell climbed into bed with his clothes on and fell instantly asleep. He dreamed of rocks and cold oatmeal and woke up far earlier than usual, although without the clean sensation of stepping from sleep into consciousness. It was as though his shortwave had been turned down during the night, drumming away just on the threshold of audibility while he dreamed, and now it had been turned up again. It was a horrible, swarming feeling.

His wife was in the kitchen, wearing odd bits of clothes and underwear as she went about preparing her breakfast. Lowell tried to remember the last time he'd made love to her. It seemed like months, but it was hard to be sure.

"The least you could do," she said, regarding him without pleasure or surprise, "would be to take off your shoes before you come to bed. I'm just about kicked black and blue."

Lowell looked down. It was true. He was wearing his shoes in bed. His feet felt enormously heavy as he swung them to the floor. "I'm sorry," he said, trying to tuck in his shirt while sitting down, not having much luck at it.

"You should be," said his wife. "What a stupid thing to do. How did the writing go?"

"It's coming along," said Lowell. He stood up, small change and keys falling to the floor from various folds of his clothing. He felt heavy. "What time is it?" he asked.

"Eight o'clock," said his wife. "You finally kicked me out of bed about a quarter of an hour ago. The one morning I really get to sleep. You want some breakfast?"

Lowell nodded mutely, rubbing his face with his hands. His skin felt oily and soft, like some kind of substance in a nightmare.

After breakfast he went down to Broadway and bought the Sunday *Times*. "Jesus," said the news vendor, "you sure lost weight. You been sick or something?"

"I'm fine," said Lowell.

"No offense," said the news vendor. "You sure you're strong enough to carry that paper? It's nothing to be ashamed of, a lot of my customers can't manage it, it's a big paper. Maybe you should take out the sections you don't need. You know, like travel and the want ads. Some of my customers do that. It cuts down, believe me. Here, I'll do it for you."

"I don't know what you're talking about," said Lowell, snatching up his newspaper and nearly falling over with it. It seemed to weigh as much as a bowling ball. He clutched it to his chest and staggered away, stumbling over his own feet, acutely aware of how wild and feeble he must look. He hadn't shaved, and his clothes were rumpled from being slept in.

The walk back to the apartment with the newspaper exhausted him again, and he collapsed into one of the chairs. Not only were his clothes rumpled, but the trip outside under the watchful eyes of passersby had made him conscious of how baggy they were. Even his shoes felt too big. He guessed this must be what it was like to be at the end of your rope, when you went to sleep in your clothes and they were too big for your body, when a newspaper was too heavy to carry and your brain had been taken over by a Bulgarian radio station. It couldn't go on.

"It sure can't," said his wife, giving Lowell another nasty start. He hadn't realized he'd spoken aloud. "I'm glad you're finally coming to your senses," she added, although that was not an accurate description of how he felt. He felt as though he was losing his senses, not coming to them, just kind of fading out like the pattern of a cheap fabric that had been through the wash too often. "This is awful," he said.

"You bet it is," said his wife. "I wish we'd gone to Berkeley." She sat down on the bed and opened the drama section of the *Times*. She leafed through it for a while, rattling and snapping the pages sharply. "Are you just going to sit there?" she asked without looking up.

Lowell opened his mouth, made a little sound, and closed it again for fear that nothing would come out but gibberish. His shoes began to feel funny again, and he suddenly found himself wondering if he had them on the right feet. With a strangled cry, he sprang upright in his chair and stared down at them, but thank God they were okay.

"Can I get you something?" asked his wife in a strange voice, looking at him with an expression that was hard to decipher. It came to Lowell that he had just given a convincing imitation of a person who has just seen a tiny little man dart out from beneath his chair on a wee little pony, and then dart back again. Or, for that matter, a man who suddenly wonders if he's been wearing his shoes on the wrong feet for thirty hours. No wonder his wife was staring at him like that. Had she really thrown out his birth certificate? Who could blame her if she had? "The magazine section!" he croaked desperately. "I was looking for the magazine section. I thought I saw it on the floor."

Without taking her eyes off him for an instant, his wife slowly reached behind her and wordlessly produced the magazine.

"Thanks," whispered Lowell. It had Oriental soldiers on the cover. He lifted it up and held it in front of his face.

"Don't mention it," said his wife.

They spent the next couple of hours barricaded behind walls of newsprint, warily passing fresh sections back and forth as the need arose, and doing their best not to meet each other's eyes. The last section to come before Lowell's face was the want ads. It was a moment before he realized what he was looking at. He wondered how it had come into his possession. Had he picked it up on purpose? Had his wife deliberately placed it where he could reach it? Was he absolutely certain his shoes were on the right feet?

He folded the paper and looked across the room at his wife. She immediately got up from the bed and stormed out into the kitchen, where she began to take apart the top of the stove, throwing the knobs and reflectors and prong things into the aluminum sink with a noise that went straight to Lowell's teeth. Lowell picked up his manuscript from the table. Curiously enough, although he had written it, he couldn't recall ever reading any of it, but he knew approximately what he would find. He also knew what he would think of it. The first page was awful. The second page was a little worse, and the third was a little worse than that. It was a perfect counterfoil of his life these last few months, starting with good intentions and no talent and going steadily downhill, page by page, day by day, as though someone was slowly turning down the lights and slowly turning up the sound. He regarded this fact with a feeling that was utterly flat, as if something heavy had rolled over it.

"I'm going to get a job," he said.

"It's about time," said his wife. She turned the water off in the sink with a furious motion, turned around and glared at him for a moment, and then stalked off into the bathroom, first slamming, then locking the frail door behind her.

"It doesn't have to be forever," said Lowell with the eerie and quite accurate sensation of having played exactly this same scene before, although in different clothes. This time he had the good sense to shut up and wait, and presently his wife emerged with a resolute face, and they ate a huge meal and planned their life, and both of them went to bed at bedtime.

3

"When did I grow this moustache?" Lowell asked, turning his face from side to side in the mirror.

"What did you say?" asked his wife from the bedroom.

"I can't remember when I grew this moustache," Lowell repeated. "I can't remember why I grew it, either. I don't even like it. It's the silliest thing I ever saw." Viewed closely, it seemed to be losing its hair, if such a thing was possible. It had never been much of a moustache to begin with. You could see right through it, and from a distance it gave the impression that his upper lip was hairless but a little dirty. The only reason he didn't cut it off this instant was the thought of the chaos such an act would cause in his relations with his wife and his employer. It would perplex his wife endlessly, and Crawford would be alarmed.

"I think you grew it in 1967," his wife called. "Sometime around there," she added, as if 1967 was a sort of street corner. "How come you want to know? Has this got something to do with the funny way you've been acting lately? I don't know what's gotten into you these last few days. How come you want to know when you grew your moustache? What kind of a question is that?"

"Nothing, dear," said Lowell mildly. "Nothing at all." He returned to the contemplation of his face. His hairline was receding, but instead of making his forehead look high, it made his face look as though the top of it had been cut off. His teeth were fragile, and his chin was small. His nose resembled less a majestic blade than a small, pale berry. The pure and innocent blue of his eyes had never been muddied by corrupt and secret knowledge, had never been blurred by sorrow or sharpened by command; he was thirty years old, and his eyes were still the color of flowers. He knew exactly who he looked like. He looked like a youthful Henry Tremblechin. He looked like a minor public official in a town where the Republicans have always been in power. He looked like a weakling, and you wanted to kick him right in the face.

"Are you through yet, or do I still have to wait?" asked his wife from the bathroom door. She was wearing a skirt but no blouse, and her hair was going every which way. It occurred to Lowell that except for a few minutes in the morning between breakfast and work, he never saw his wife fully clothed; the rest of the time she was either putting on garments or haphazardly taking them off. "You're not even shaving," she said. "What are you doing? Don't tell me if it's something disgusting. Please hurry up with it, whatever it is. I've got to do my hair, and it's almost time to go."

"I was looking at my face," said Lowell, stepping aside from the basin. His wife shot him a nervous glance and began to tear at her hair with fingers and comb, staring into the mirror with anxious intensity. It was not a good time for Lowell to remain around, and he gently slipped away.

In the kitchen he drank coffee until it was time for the war to be over on the radio, and then he switched it on for the weather. It didn't really make much difference what the weather was—he faced only short corridors of it, spaced at long intervals throughout the day—but he was reassured by hearing the temperature and precipitation data, and he liked to know the forecast. Then he could plan his weather gear with some care; it always pleased him to be the only man in a flash rainstorm to have an umbrella. At home his father had listened to the weather report every morning, and presumably still did; from it, he could predict with uncanny accuracy which of his friends he would meet when he drove downtown, and where he would encounter them.

The day was cold and windy and freezing rain was falling intermittently, although it was expected to turn to snow by mid-morning. The temperature in Central Park was twenty-seven degrees and precipitation probability was one hundred percent for the rest of the day and night. Lowell got out his wife's heavy coat, her gaily flowered plastic slicker, her fur hat, her red umbrella, and her tall fur-lined boots, and arranged them on the sofa in the living room. Cries of dismay rose from the direction of the bathroom, accompanied by the patter of a box of bobby pins maliciously upending itself in the washbasin. Lowell thought for a moment and then replaced the heavy, warm boots with a pair of shiny off-white English ones with a cuffed top and zipper back. Then he got out his own garb—overcoat and tweed cap, Drago galoshes and push-button umbrella, cashmere muffler and deerskin gloves—and tossed them onto the over-stuffed chair by the baby-grand piano that his wife could play but never did; it had been left by the previous tenant, no doubt because the only way to remove it was through the window by means of a derrick on the roof, at fabulous expense. The piano was just another thing that got in the way and didn't belong to him, tripping him in the dark, taking up space where he could have put his Eames chair.

Aware that he was playing the part of a very good fellow indeed but this morning taking no pleasure from the fact, Lowell washed the breakfast dishes and put them away, sponged the kitchen table, put out the garbage, and sat down with a second cup of coffee to wait patiently while his wife made them both late for work. He wondered what would happen if he were to rage and stamp about the room in his overcoat like the husband of popular fiction. He decided that he probably wasn't capable of it. He was a nice guy. That was the sort of thing you said about somebody you had nothing against and nothing in common with; you called him a nice guy. That was what Lowell was, even to himself. A nice, considerate guy.

"We're late!" cried his wife, bursting into the living room. "Oh, you *are* a darling. My hair wouldn't go right, it just wouldn't, and now we're late again. I suppose that's okay for you, you're important and everything, but I've already been late three times, and I'm going to get scolded by that old bitch again. Hurry! Hurry! You aren't even started yet."

Lowell ambled in from the kitchen wearing, he knew, an absentminded but lovable smile. His face just sort of fell into it, and then, like a wrestler's hammerlock, he couldn't seem to break its grip.

"And you did the dishes, too," said his wife in a hurried almost toneless voice, yanking herself into first one boot, then the other. "Aren't you sweet? Look at the time. Boy, I'm really in for it. Get a move on."

As they waited for the elevator in the hall, Lowell asked, "What would you think if I cut off my moustache?"

"I don't know what you're talking about," she snapped. Lowell had the impression that, combined with her hair problem and being late, his question had successfully ruined her day. It made him feel good for a while, but then he was ashamed of himself.

Lowell's cubicle at the office was slightly larger than a toilet stall, but no higher, and although the door said MANAGING EDITOR, Lowell always felt that the words had been printed there in the same spirit that moves service-station operators to paint KING on the door of the men's privy. The walls were a pale, smudged turquoise and didn't even come close to the high old ceiling, which seemed to exist up there on a plane of existence all its own, with its soot-furred sprinkler pipes and heating conduits, prepared to make the office wet in case of fire and warm in case of cold but otherwise having nothing to do with it. Lowell looked up at the ceiling a lot. He had very little else to do. Any nincompoop could run a magazine like theirs, and in fact one did: Crawford, who, fearful that anyone in the office but Lowell could do any job better than he could, ended up doing them all so that nobody would have a chance to show him up with a dazzling display of skill. About the only thing Lowell was clearly and indisputably in charge of was the advertising campaign. This consisted of inserting small boxes in the columns of like-minded publications, with the words: "Successful Plumbing Contractors Read the *Plumbing Contractor's Weekly Sentinel*." The slogan was over forty years old and never varied, nor did the size of the boxes or the publications in which they appeared; everything had all been set in smooth motion a decade before Lowell was born, and he saw no reason to tamper with it. The slogan sounded okay to him. Once a month he received a batch of bills. He initialed them and put them on his secretary's desk, and she saw to it that they were paid.

Small tasks came his way in the course of the day, mostly in the form of approving things other people had already done. He always approved things that other people had done, trusting them to know more about their jobs than he did, especially the accountant, a malicious and vituperative old pedant whom Crawford kept for the purpose of breaking the spirit of the office staff. He was also a pretty good accountant and a complete kiss-ass in his dealings with Lowell and Crawford, which was just fine with Lowell. Other people passed before his eyes in a kind of haze: young men on the way up in the industry, old men on the way down, stick-in-the-muds who had reached their level —they all strove together to put out a newspaper read only by plumbers if at all, and Lowell wished them well at their task. They came and went, but like endless ranks of soldiers, they were all the same to him. He was a string of cans, and nobody had tripped over him yet.

For nine years Lowell had nourished the pleasant delusion that his job was only temporary, a kind of stopping-off place where he was getting his breath and taking his bearings after the grim and disorganizing experience of his novel. The job had come to him, not through the want ads, but by means of his putative uncle-in-law Lester, a shadowy figure from his wife's family who seemed to be related to all of them equally and to no one specifically, any more than he had a specific occupation. He was the person you went to when you wanted something fixed up, and he fixed it up, often in ways that were puzzling; there was always something in his bag of tricks. He had an office in an old cast-iron building in downtown Brooklyn, although what he did there, aside from counsel his relatives, was vague. His name was not on the board in the lobby, and there was nothing on his door but a number. It was before this door, brushed and wearing his wedding suit, that Lowell appeared one morning long ago, having gotten lost first on the subway and then on Schermerhorn Street. It was difficult to tell whether to knock. He tried listening for office sounds, but the room was as silent as if it had been empty—a probable circumstance for a variety of reasons, chief among them being that Uncle Lester had no idea that he was coming and Lowell wasn't sure he was in the right building.

"Do something for you?" said a harsh voice in his ear, slicing through his reverie like a rusty knife. Lowell jumped as though goosed and spun around in a posture of startled guilt to confront a broad little man scarcely higher than his elbow but looking enormously strong, possibly because he was also enormously calm. "What? You're from the Board of Elections, right?" he asked, never taking his eyes from Lowell's face. They were very odd eyes. They were large, they seldom blinked, and they were extremely watchful. Behind them was no soul, only something calm and intelligent. Lowell had the queasy idea that a man with eyes like that would kill you in an instant if he thought it would do him any good, and neither enjoy it while he did it nor feel bad about it afterward.

"Uncle Lester?" he asked in a voice not quite itself.

"Go inside."

Lowell hesitated, then opened the door and went inside. The little man followed him and closed it behind them. "You called me Uncle Lester," he said.

"Yes, sir."

"How come?"

"Well, I . . ."

"Wait a minute." Pivoting so as to keep his eyes on Lowell at all times, Uncle Lester moved past him to the desk, picked up a telephone receiver, pushed a button, listened wordlessly for several seconds, and hung up. "Answering service," he said. "You were saying."

"Uncle Lester?"

"You said that already."

"Well, you see, I married your niece Betty, I mean I'm married to her, we've been married for a while," Lowell babbled while Uncle Lester gave him no help. Lowell began to feel like a first-class idiot, and his mission more and more took on the outlines of humiliating foolishness, as though he had suddenly found himself trotting beside a movie star begging to be given a break in pictures. "Well, anyway, I mean," he continued.

"How's Leo these days?" Uncle Lester asked suddenly.

"He's fine," said Lowell, wondering if this was some kind of test of his identity. He tried to think of something about Leo that would demonstrate to Uncle Lester that he knew him, but the kind of things that came to mind weren't the kind of things you say to a stranger about anyone, especially if the stranger was a relative. "Just fine," said Lowell. "Saw him only the other day. He was looking swell."

"What do you need?" asked Uncle Lester.

"Well, I'm kind of looking around for a job. I mean, Betty said maybe you could sort of give me some advice. I would have called, but nobody knew your number, so I just came over. If I came at the wrong time or something, I sure am sorry. I don't like to barge in like this. What I mean is . . ."

"What did you do before?"

"I was writing a novel."

Some slight readjustment of Uncle Lester's features told Lowell that this last piece of information had finally certified him as a member of the family. He needed a job, and he'd been writing a novel. His credentials were complete: he was another deadbeat relative.

"Can you do paste-ups and mechanicals?" Uncle Lester asked.

"What's a paste-up?" asked Lowell.

"That's too bad," said Uncle Lester. He wrote something on a pad, tore it off, and held it out. "Try this one. If it don't work out, come back and see me next Wednesday about eleven o'clock in the morning. It ought to work out."

"I don't know how to thank you," said Lowell. He wondered if he ought to shake hands, but Uncle Lester had put his hands back into his overcoat pockets, and Lowell didn't think he'd better risk it.

"It ought to work out," Uncle Lester repeated. He took a step toward the door and nodded toward it curtly. "After you."

Lowell thought it was strange that Uncle Lester was preparing to leave his office when he'd only just entered it. Maybe the office was only some kind of dummy, its doors and windows watched with mirrors and covered with guns, while Uncle Lester monitored his callers from a real office around the corner. Come to think of it, the place didn't look much like an office; there was no rug on the floor, the filing cabinet had all the earmarks of a prop, and there wasn't a piece of paper in sight. Wisely keeping his own counsel about these things, Lowell allowed himself to be herded into the hall. Uncle Lester carefully locked the door and turned to face him. "You got enough money for the subway?" he asked.

Lowell said he did, and before he could start in again with expressions of gratitude and humility, Uncle Lester turned and walked down the hall and around the corner without looking back. Lowell took the piece of paper to the address that was written on it and was immediately given a job writing copy about the doings of plumbers. His wife settled down almost as if a wand had been waved over her, bought a black garter belt, and never chewed gum again.

Having settled in his mind that his job was only temporary, Lowell was not ambitious and took things much as they came. It was easy work, and he went about it day after day rather in the same way that he sometimes wore a single suit for weeks on end. At first he and his wife had a few fitful discussions about children, but they kept putting it off, and soon their life had organized itself so comfortably that the idea just kind of petered out from lack of interest. Lowell's mother-in-law brought up the subject once or twice, driving it further back into the recesses of his mind, but eventually even she gave up.

Nine years: an endless chain of days, a rosary of months, each as smooth and round as the one before, flowing evenly through his mind. You could count on the fingers of one hand the events and pauses of all that time: two promotions; two changes of apartment (each time nearer the river); a trip to Maine, where he realized that his wife's legs had gotten kind of fat—five memories in nine years, each no more than a shallow design scratched on a featureless bead. It was life turned inside out; somewhere the world's work was being done and men were laboring in the vineyards of the Lord, Khrushchev was being faced down on the high seas, and Negroes were being blown up and going to jail, but all Lowell did was change his apartment twice, tell his wife to put on some pants, and get promoted faster than anybody else on the paper—a tiny, dim meteor in an empty matchbox. Nobody up at *Life* or on the staff of the *Paris Review* was sleeping badly and trembling for their job because of redhot Lowell Lake; he couldn't even remember the layout of his own apartment, and the doorman kept confusing him with someone named Mr. Stone who lived on the top floor. One day Lowell saw Mr. Stone. He was about fifty years old, almost bald, and had a furtive, terrified, scurrying air about him, as though momentarily expecting the pounce of an enormous cat. There was no similarity between them whatever except for the moustache, and Mr. Stone's was black, not blond, and probably dyed. The doorman was a notorious dimwit and about as useful as a potted fern, but Lowell brooded about it for weeks, and the next time Povachik called him "Mr. Stone" it was all he could do to keep from screaming in the man's face.

Seated at his desk with a sick feeling of dread in his stomach, Lowell stared at the ceiling and tried to think of something smart and meaningful that would impart a sense of purpose to his life and clothe his actions with nobility. Novel-writing was out. He'd reread his old manuscript two nights ago while drunk and last night while sober, but the perspective of years had not dimmed its overwhelming livid awfulness, and his relative condition while reading it did not alter his perception of it in the least; it read exactly the same when he was drunk as when he was sober. Over the years he'd developed a serviceable hack style that enabled him to say anything he had a mind to, provided it had to do with meetings, banquets, simple objects, and building codes; it was a style that tended to tire quickly, and something odd seemed to happen to it over distances longer than a couple of standard columns. It didn't get dull, exactly, but it started to look distinctly funny, like a man who had held his breath for too long. No doubt he could have done something about it, whipped it into some kind of shape, were it not for the fact that he had nothing whatever to write about. Every so often —although with steadily diminishing frequency—a weak urge, a kind of feeble longing, would afflict him, and he would feel the old need to get something down on paper, start another novel, work up a story, something. His ambition would burn palely for a while and then gutter out with nothing to show for itself. The truth was, he realized now, he had no subject matter. Nothing had ever happened to him. He'd grown up, gone to school, tried and failed to write a novel, and become the managing editor of a plumbers' newspaper. Written down with a straight face, his life would sound like one of those pointless Victorian morality tales, usually found in books entitled something like *Food for Thought* that his Sunday-school teacher had been so fond of reading aloud to the class. Once he'd almost been felled by a copy of *The New York Times,* and his doorman couldn't tell him apart from a fifty-year-old man. It was true that his parents ran a whorehouse, but he couldn't very well write about that; everyone in town would recognize them, and their feelings would be hurt. Anyway, except for the bald recital of the facts, he couldn't for the life of him think of how to turn his parents' occupation into a story. He was forced to conclude that the writing of fiction was definitely not his bag.

It was surprisingly easy for him to imagine what the rest of life held in store for him, short of Negro rebellion or atomic war. It did not hold much, and he would go through it sort of standing around mutely in tense attitudes reminiscent of Montgomery Clift, not particularly liking what was happening to him but totally unable to think of a single thing to do about it. He wasn't talented. It was possible that he wasn't even very smart. It seemed to him that a smart person would have gotten bored with his kind of life after a couple of months, but it had taken Lowell nine years. If his wife had had a baby right away, the kid would be in the fourth grade by now, and his daddy would only just have gotten bored. It was a frightening thought.

"Lake!" bellowed Crawford from the doorway, his voice, as usual, having a cigar in the middle of it. Lowell took his eyes off the ceiling. "Morning, Harold," he said.

"Bah!" said Crawford, snatching his cigar from his mouth, examining it with an expression of total disgust, and putting it back in his mouth again. Occasionally he would swallow tobacco juice in the middle of some forceful utterance and nearly choke to death. "Do you think you're paid to do nothing but sit around?"

This was precisely what Lowell was paid for, but he didn't say so out loud. "Aw, gee, Harold," he said instead. He gestured vaguely toward his desk.

"At least you can try to *look* like you're doing something!" Crawford barked. Lowell could tell that secretly he was happy as a clam and enormously relieved to find that his associate had relapsed into typical somnolence after two weeks of strange facial expressions and small, muted cries of anguish. Crawford had been going around as if hearing rumors that the planet was departing from its orbit, peering nervously at Lowell from around corners and across rooms. "Or is it too much of an effort to deceive people?" he went on in a delighted snarl. "The managing editor! Great Caesar's ghost, do I have to do all the work on this newspaper myself?" He snatched up a piece of paper from Lowell's desk and strode out of the cubicle, chewing his cigar like an obscene brown tongue. He was back in a flash. "WHAT IN GOD'S NAME DO YOU CALL THIS?" he roared, furiously shaking the sheet of paper under Lowell's nose.

"It's a shopping list," said Lowell mildly.

"A SHOPPING LIST?" Crawford's neck seemed to grow larger as well as more red, spilling out over the edge of his collar. "A *typed* shopping list? On letterhead stationery? Are you out of your mind?"

"I can't read my wife's handwriting," explained Lowell. "Mar-

garet can. She's a real whiz at it. She always reads my wife's
shopping lists and types them out for me. Otherwise I wouldn't
know what to buy on my way home at night. It's nothing to get
excited about."

"Lake," said Crawford, putting down the shopping list with
a kind of awesome gentleness, "if I didn't have a newspaper to
run . . ."

"I put the dummy on your desk an hour ago," said Lowell,
understanding by his superior's ritual phrase that the game was
drawing to a close.

"Spagh!" exclaimed Crawford, getting (or pretending to get)
something loathsome on his tongue. Pressing a handkerchief to
his mouth, he stormed from the room. A second later Lowell
heard him growling contentedly to himself on the other side of
the partition, where he occupied a cubicle slightly larger but in
some indefinable way more squalid than Lowell's. He was at
peace again, his paranoia momentarily laid to rest. A firm and
practicing believer in the limitless mutability of man, he nevertheless had a touching faith that the last mood he had encountered in a person was the one he would sustain for the rest of
his natural life. Lowell was a sleepy, genial blockhead again,
and a sleepy, genial blockhead he would trustworthily remain.
Crawford always had everybody all figured out.

That night on his way home from work, Lowell stopped off in
the Village and bought a 1930's-style tweed motoring coat with
a belted back and double vents. It went beautifully with his
trousers and cap, and he wore it home beneath his overcoat.

"What on earth is *that?*" his wife demanded the moment she
saw it, her voice alarmed and her eyes widening as if he'd suddenly burst into the bedroom carrying a pair of handcuffs and
an eggbeater.

"It's time for a change," said Lowell. "We've gotten in a rut,
and it's time to get out. This coat is only the beginning of a
whole new era."

"I don't understand," said his wife. "What kind of a change? Will it be expensive? Have you thought about it and weighed all the pros and cons?"

"I think you've got the wrong idea," said Lowell, although he couldn't have told her what the right idea was. He'd bought the coat on pure impulse—itself a sign that things were coming loose in his mind, although it was still impossible to tell whether they were loosening up nicely or were about to throw themselves from side to side like loose cargo in a storm at sea. He never did anything on impulse, never. No wonder his wife was worried.

The next evening he went to a shop on Greenwich Avenue and bought himself a pair of tweed trousers and a set of leather gaiters. He wore them home. Having committed himself to a policy of new-clothing purchase, it only seemed right that he should make an effort to complete his first costume, although he was beginning to feel a little reluctant. He hoped that if he could contrive to change his exterior in some smart, hip way, then some kind of smart, hip change would occur inside himself and he would see new paths before him and discover hidden potentialities that he hadn't dreamed existed. Smart and hip, however, was not exactly the way he felt as he surveyed the figure he presented in the mirror of the clothing store, clad in tweed and gaiters, with a snap-brim cap on his head. No, smart and hip he definitely wasn't; by some strange instinct, he had succeeded in turning himself into an almost exact sartorial replica of the youthful Harold Macmillan.

"You're trying to tell me something," said his wife as, thus garbed, he entered the kitchen later that evening. "I don't understand it yet, but I'm definitely getting signals."

"It's nothing of the sort," said Lowell, plumping down dejectedly on one of the chairs with his cap wadded in his hand. Secretly he'd hoped to end up looking like Dr. Grimesby Roylott, and this had happened to him instead. He didn't even know why he'd gone ahead and paid for the damned things, much less worn them home. He supposed it was a good thing he hadn't tried to look like John Kennedy; with his luck, he would have ended up looking like Richard Nixon. "A top hat," he said. "Maybe a top hat would have done it."

"You'll have to speak up," said his wife. "Either I can't hear you or you're not making sense."

"Everything is all wrong."

"Are you going to start up on that again? Listen, why don't you go see an analyst or something. I mean it. Lots of people do. It's nothing to be ashamed of. Nobody even has to know about it unless you tell them. You can go on your lunch hour. You never eat lunch anyway."

"I don't need an analyst. It's not that sort of thing."

His wife looked at him pointedly, but he pretended to ignore her, and set about getting as drunk as he could. First he made his wife a little drink, then began making his own drinks stronger and stronger; if she was a little drunk herself, she never noticed a thing. Lowell always hoped that some good idea would occur to him while he was drunk. But if any did, he was never able to remember them in the morning.

His life wasn't breaking up. On the contrary, it failed to show the smallest fissure in its bland and seamless surface. It was like the old movie scene where the hero enters a cab, only to find that the insides of the doors have no handles and the glass partition cannot be shouted through or broken. He was along for the ride whether he liked it or not, and perhaps a deadly gas would soon begin to seep insidiously from some concealed orifice and put him back to sleep forever. Strong measures were clearly called for; time was short. Lowell had an idea that people in his circumstances didn't get to wake up just every day. Already he felt himself fighting sleep, struggling against the old suicidal urge to lie back and take it easy like a good fellow. His first escape attempts had failed: it was apparently impossible, at least for Lowell, to think, drink, or clothe himself out of his situation. There was still no light at the end of the tunnel. The moment had come for a supreme effort. It was now or never, he told himself, now or never; while from some distant recess deep in his brain, a tiny voice kept whispering that if he hadn't done it by now, he was never going to do it. Lowell didn't listen to the little voice. Instead, he stared at the ceiling above his little cubicle at the office and reviewed his options, one by one.

Realistically speaking and fantasy put ruthlessly aside, these were few and discouraging. He could change jobs, find satisfying and creative labor, conquer new worlds. A good plan; too bad he wasn't trained to do anything. He supposed he could go back to college, but every time the notion came into his head, a sort of wall seemed to crash down between his eyes and his brain. He was definitely not going back to college. He was no more going back to college than he was going to spend the rest of his life on some beach in a little hut made of driftwood and leaves. Nor was he going to look for another job. The more he thought about abandoning his present job and going out to look for another one, the wider appeared the abyss that seemed to yawn at his feet. He wouldn't be throwing himself on the market; he would be throwing himself into a hole. He knew his limitations. Anyway, he couldn't think of anything else that he wanted to do. He was forced to conclude that he really wasn't cut out for capitalism. Under the circumstances, he was far, far better off where he was. Eventually he would become editor, and then—unlike Crawford—he would farm out all the work. He could see himself doing it as clearly as if he'd already done it. In the world of work, it was his destiny, and he decided to accept it. Better to accept it than to court certain fiasco.

As for the arts, they fell into the category of unrealizable fantasy. Writing was out, he'd never played a musical instrument and had no desire to learn, and the only thing he'd ever painted was the side of a house, about fifteen years ago. The very idea of artistic achievement was preposterous, bittersweet though his memories were of his lost ambitions and smothered hopes. He considered doing a research project on some subject that interested him, writing up his findings in his best journeyman prose, and sending them off to some good place like American Heritage. He thought about it for a while, but nothing interested him that much.

His whole problem, he finally decided, was simple lack of scope. His life had no scope whatever; rooms and hallways and subway cars were his portion, with an occasional street thrown in. He went in the direction he was pushed, and stood where he was told. Should catastrophe strike in his vicinity, he would participate in it in some passive way, perhaps by adding himself to the roll of the slain, perhaps as a dazed survivor, perhaps as a stunned bystander, depending on his distance from ground zero. If no catastrophe struck, he would continue on his way. When newscasters talked about pedestrians, they were talking about Lowell; on the rare occasions that he drove, he was a motorist; at least twice a day he was a subway rider; the night the power failed, he was a trapped subway rider; when one of his acquaintances sickened, he became a well-wisher; in any given situation he occupied the dead center of his role and seldom spoke to anyone. He might just as well have gone to Nevada and died of ignorance and exposure for all the good he'd been to anyone since, except as a kind of statistical entity. The whole thing was pretty depressing.

Fortunately, he thought of a good solution that very afternoon.

"You're out of your mind," said his wife. "I can't imagine what's gotten into you. I categorically will not move to Brooklyn, and that's final. What part of Brooklyn?"

"Go ahead and lock yourself in the bathroom," said Lowell.

"Nothing will stop me. It's about time we came to grips with real life and the significant issues of our time."

"You've got to be kidding," said his wife. "Listen, I've had a hard day."

"I've never been more serious in my life," said Lowell. He tried to sound manly and confident, but actually he felt defensive and edgy, as if he could easily be made to look ridiculous if the right sort of questions were asked, like the time he wanted to build a model railroad in the corner of the bedroom. "I was thinking about things this afternoon, and I suddenly remembered an article I read. Lots of people are doing it. There are all sorts of good reasons. Anyway, do you want to stay here and stagnate for the rest of your life?"

His wife turned to the counter and began slicing a potato. "I thought next we might move to West End Avenue," she said in a funny kind of voice, but her face was hidden, and it was hard to tell exactly what was on her mind.

Lowell could remember neither where he'd seen the article nor precisely what it said, but he recalled the general drift. That was all he needed. Creative young people were buying houses in the Brooklyn slums, integrating all-Negro blocks, and coming firmly to grips with poverty and municipal corruption. It was the stuff of life. It was what he was looking for. The more he turned it over in his mind, the less it became a fuzzy memory of some magazine article and the more it resembled an inspiration. In the vacuum of despair his mind had become, it took on richness and color and swelled to heroic size. In his mind's eye he saw himself striding down the littered streets like a latter-day Marshal Dillon, intimidating clubhouse politicians and inspiring his neighbors, exciting the envy of his colleagues in Manhattan because of all the rooms he owned.

"Definitely not," said his wife after a long interval during which they'd both worked industriously on the dinner and neither of them had spoken a word. Lowell was cutting up a duck with the poultry shears. "No, sir," she said. "You got me to New York, but Brooklyn is going too far. What do you know about Brooklyn, anyway?"

Her question was well-put and hard for Lowell to answer. A second or two later his wife answered it for him.

"You don't know anything about Brooklyn," she said. "Not a thing. God, how I wish we'd gone to Berkeley when we had the chance. Everything would have been so different."

"That was ten years ago," said Lowell, feeling a little stab. "This is now, and there's no going back. We've got to take the bull by the horns."

"Take your own bull by the horns," said his wife. "Unless it's the Heights, I'm staying right here. Or maybe Albemarle Road. Is it the Heights?"

Lowell didn't have any specific part of Brooklyn in mind, but he was pretty sure the Heights were not what he was after. Albemarle Road rang no bell either. The only other parts of Brooklyn whose names he could remember were Flatbush and Bedford-Stuyvesant, but he was pretty sure he would not win his wife to his cause by mentioning either of them. "I haven't made up my mind yet," he said finally. "I'm still studying the situation."

"Study it all you like," said his wife.

Lowell knew from experience that a conversation of this sort could continue indefinitely, hour upon hour of statement and retort, assertion and denial, the domestic politics of exhaustion, until the point was completely lost and the two of them began to sound more and more like a cross between *Long Day's Journey into Night* and *Father Knows Best*. They always sounded that way, and Lowell decided to put a stop to it at once before they became so firmly entrenched in their roles that only sleep would release them.

"You may be right," he said, meaning no such thing, but the

statement always satisfied her. The few problems that had cropped up between them since the days of the novel had always had to do with something Lowell had said, or with something that he had failed to say, but never with anything that he had actually done. He sometimes felt that he could do almost anything he liked provided he said the right words, even if they were downright lies. There was no time like the present to test his theory. "Yes," he said, assuming a musing tone, "there may be something in what you say. Perhaps I was hasty. I'll have to think it over in another light. I've been tired and confused lately. That must be it."

"You poor darling," said his wife, coming quickly to his side. She cradled his head against her breasts, a position he unaccountably loathed as much as she was fond of putting him in it, but which he tolerated now for tactical reasons. "What you need is a nice strong drink," she said.

Lowell agreed that a nice strong drink was just what the doctor ordered.

4

Over the phone the real-estate man advised them to come down Lafayette instead of Greene because the light was better there.

"He sounds like a fruit," said Lowell's wife. "Let's forget about it. I hate fruits."

"I don't think people call them fruits anymore," said Lowell, with his hand over the mouthpiece. They had the phone between them, and he found it hard to hear. "Hush," he said.

"Fruits or queers or whatever you call them," said his wife. "They're all the same to me."

"When you get off at Fulton Street," said the real-estate man, "go up Clinton Avenue to Lafayette. Turn right on Lafayette and walk to Vanderbilt Avenue, and *then* turn left. At four o'clock in the afternoon, Greene is *simply* out of the question," he concluded ripely, as though putting it on for the benefit of Lowell's wife.

"Thanks a whole lot," said Lowell, hanging up before more damage was done. He had a map of Brooklyn before him on the table, and he tried to decide if the borough's shape reminded him of anything. It bore a faint resemblance to a half-clenched fist, but not enough of one to count. It didn't really look like anything, which was disappointing. Lowell liked things to resemble things; it always helped him to comprehend them better.

"I guess I'll be back in a couple of hours," he said, folding the map and putting it in his pocket. "I'll just look at a couple of places to get the idea, and then I'll come right back."

"I don't trust you," said his wife. "I'm coming along."

"You don't have to do that," said Lowell. "Even if I was going to buy a house behind your back, I couldn't do it in a day. There are all sorts of papers to sign and people to see and things like that. I doubt if I could buy a house behind your back if I wanted to. Anyway, I wouldn't think of doing such a thing, and you don't have to come along unless you want to."

"Poppycock," said his wife in the voice of her mother. "I know a Blandings syndrome when I see one. I can also tell when you're lying. You talk too much and forget to blink."

Lowell realized that both his mouth and eyes were dry, and he blinked and swallowed.

"You see?" said his wife. "Nothing gets past me. Let's get started."

They took the subway. Lowell glanced at his wife from time to time, but she was lost in her thoughts, and anything could have been going on inside her head. He hated it when he didn't know what she was thinking. She was thinking something now, and he didn't have the faintest idea what it was.

"I don't like it," she said as they emerged on Fulton Street. "It's pretty bad. You can tell by looking at it."

The wide street was bordered with low brick structures, most of them dating from the last century, with boarded-up stores on their ground floors. There was a Spanish market on the corner. Outside it stood a group of men in threadbare overcoats, drinking beer from cans in brown paper bags. All of them were drunk, and one of them was throwing up.

"I don't know," Lowell said, feeling his hopes slide down to his stomach in a cold little elevator. "Maybe we should skip it. Let's go back to Manhattan, what do you think?"

"Good idea," said his wife. "There are colored people here."

"What's that got to do with anything? There are colored people everywhere in New York. Black people."

"Not in Brooklyn Heights there aren't. That just goes to show
how much you know about it. In Brooklyn there's only one
place where colored people are, and when you see a lot of them
standing around, you know that's where you are too. Let's go."

"I don't know," said Lowell, pausing with his hand on the
railing. "I mean, here we are and everything. Maybe we ought
to take a look around. We came all the way over here. Anyway,
I've got an appointment."

"You don't know?" demanded his wife. "You just said we were
going. Didn't you say that? Come on, let's go like you said we
would. Lowell, I want to go." She took his hand and pulled on
it, but when nothing happened, she released it and glared at
him. A Negro man came up the steps and went past them with a
big grin on his face. Lowell wondered if he was smiling because
he knew they were quarreling or because he'd just gotten a
good look up his wife's dress.

"I mean, as long as we're here . . ." he said weakly, making a
vague movement away from the steps but not really going anywhere.

"All right, if you won't come with me, I'll go by myself. I'm
not staying here for another minute."

"Actually, you know, that's not a bad idea. Look, why don't
you go on back home, really? I'll keep my appointment, and
then I'll hurry straight home too. It won't take more than an
hour. If it takes more than an hour, I'll walk right out on them.
Do you have enough money for a token?"

"You mean you're not coming with me? You're sending me off
by myself?"

Lowell looked at her with some confusion. At the same time,
he became aware that the men on the corner had begun to stare
at them with bright, drunken grins. Lowell was always at a loss
when Negroes stared at him. They infallibly seemed to know

what was going on in his mind, and he was a complete pushover when they asked him for money. "Can't we go someplace and talk about it?" he asked.

"You said we were going home," said his wife. "You said. I don't know why you won't do what you say. Okay, if that's the way you want it, let's go and get it over with. I really am mad and disappointed, Lowell. I really thought you were going to keep your promise. You have really made me mad."

"Promise?" said Lowell weakly.

Without another word, his wife pushed furiously past him and began striding up the street as though treading on his face with every step.

"Dear?" he said, trotting after her. It was amazing how fast she could go when she wanted to, and he had a hard time keeping abreast, especially because she seemed to slow down when he caught up and speed up when he slowed down.

"I'd give her a bust in the goddamn mouth," said one of the Negroes as they passed the store. "Straighten her out right away."

"Who asked you?" snapped Lowell before he could think.

"Better watch yourself, man," said another. "You a long way from home."

Lowell's wife turned the corner as though on rails, somehow getting directly in Lowell's path and causing him to stumble all over his feet. The Negroes got a big kick out of that. A moment later, when Lowell looked back over his shoulder, he found several of them peering happily around the corner with their beer sacks in their hands, waiting to see what would happen next. Lowell felt like he was walking into a box canyon. He hoped there was another way back to the subway.

The street was lined with tall old trees, real country trees, higher than the houses, and so big you couldn't put your arms around them; their roots had tumbled the sidewalks and cracked the curbing. Lowell wondered vaguely what kind they were, but he was preoccupied with his wife. She was steaming along with her eyes fixed on some utterly hateful middle distance, and Lowell had the impression that she wouldn't have turned her head if a bomb had dropped in the street beside her. They passed three old frame houses with deep porches and mansard roofs. One of them had been converted into a kind of church with painted windows and a big sign on its fence that said: USE THE GARBAGE CANS. THIS IS GOD'S HOUSE.

"Look at that sign over there," said Lowell. His wife said nothing and kept on walking.

It was a pretty strange street they were on, and Lowell would have paid a great deal of attention to it if it hadn't been for his wife's behavior. She didn't behave like this very often, and he never knew what to do when she did, possibly because he got so little practice. That was the trouble with having a nice life; you never knew what to do when things took a bad turn.

"This sure is an interesting street," he suggested, not very forcefully, as though struggling to open a conversation with a forbidding stranger. That was exactly what his wife was right now: a forbidding stranger. He had no more idea of what she was going to do or say than if he'd never met her before in his life. "Who'd ever think we were in New York?" he suggested, but although his wife blinked, she still refused to take up the thread.

Actually, the strange thing about the street was that there was nothing strange about it at all: with its tall trees and old houses of brick and clapboard, it was the kind of street he'd grown up expecting he would live on; it was the kind of street everyone lived on when he was a kid. It was older and closer together, but not enough of either to make any difference, and anyway, he'd forgotten most of the details of how things looked back home except for very close up or very far away, the way a child sees things. It was the same way, distracted by his wife and Negroes, that he was seeing things now, as ambience instead of objects, interspersed with brief, vivid glimpses of things he really wanted to see, like bark and brickwork and turrets with sharp conical roofs. Once he'd read a Ray Bradbury story about some men who went to Mars and discovered a Midwestern town. It had given them quite a turn. That was the same way Lowell felt now. The street wasn't supposed to be here, but here it was, and he couldn't decide what to do next.

"Shit," said his wife. "Shit, shit, shit."

Lowell deemed it best not to respond to this. A moment later he said, "I think this is the corner we're supposed to turn."

"Not this one," said his wife with repugnance and loathing. "It's the next one. This is Greene. The light was wrong here, remember? Can't you even read a street sign?"

There seemed to be considerably more wrong with Greene than the light, but Lowell was too abashed to pay much attention to it beyond noting that it was obviously another part of the colored-people place.

The real-estate office, when they finally doubled back to it, proved to be housed in a building that was in the process of being either torn down or repaired. Half the cornice was missing, all the upper windows were broken out, and although ladders and brickwork were visible in some of the rooms, others appeared to be filled with bags of garbage and broken television sets. There were, in fact, several burst bags of garbage stacked up in the lee of the stoop, along with the remains of a pair of tubular kitchen chairs and a V-8 engine block. The double front doors were off their hinges, the ceiling was coming down, the walls were painted a dingy lavender with a shiny substance that appeared to be compounded equally of mucus and glue, and there was a dirty loaf of bread lying on the floor. The place was such a complicated mixture of the decrepit and the sinister that Lowell couldn't decide what was more likely to happen to him if he entered it: falling through a weak place in the floor or being knifed from ambush. A kind of dark vapor seemed to hang over it (the adjoining building had tin over its windows and looked comparatively tidy), and as Lowell turned to his wife he heard, from somewhere within, the sound of hammering followed by a noise like sand and pebbles being poured down a drainpipe. It was impossible to tell what part of the house it came from or what it was all about.

"You were right," said Lowell. "Let's go home. I'm sorry about the whole thing."

"It's too late for that," said his wife. "You dragged me here, and we're going in."

"If I was by myself I wouldn't go in," said Lowell. "I'd go home. I see the light now."

"You're not by yourself," said his wife, starting toward the gate beneath the stoop.

The basement was inhabited, after a fashion. Its windows still had glass in them, and in the left-hand one there was a dime-store sign that said REAL ESTATE. Below the sign was a notary decal that had mostly flaked off. Lowell's wife marched up intrepidly and began to haul away at the locked gate, while Lowell remained limply behind on the sidewalk with a miserable expression on his face. After a while the rattling and clashing was answered by a blond young man who looked about sixteen years old. "Most people ring the bell," he said, indicating a boldly lettered sign that said RING THE BELL and pointed to the button with an arrow. Lowell had seen the sign but had not been able to find words to tell his wife about it. "At least you didn't tap on the window with a quarter," said the young man, unlocking the gate with considerable bad grace. "God, I can't tell you how that bugs me. Taptaptaptap. Sweet Jesus."

"May I speak to your father?" said Lowell's wife.

"I am my father," said the young man. "I fought in the Korean war and I'm old enough to be your uncle. Everybody makes the same mistake, and frankly, I don't care if you believe me or not. Come into the dining room."

The room he led them to was an office with a desk and filing cabinets; it didn't look in the least like a dining room, and Lowell expected momentarily to be led somewhere else, but he wasn't. The preternaturally elderly young man went behind the desk and sat down moodily in a swivel chair. He was wearing tan chinos and a bulky-knit yellow turtleneck, both of them much cleaner than Lowell's clothes ever seemed to get. It seemed incredible that he'd been in the Korean war. He looked scarcely old enough to shave.

There was a loud thud somewhere in the upper reaches of the house, and a little shower of pulverized plaster sifted down through a crack in the ceiling, just like in a war movie. The young man paid no attention to it. He folded his hands on the desk and looked steadily at Lowell's wife.

"I can't remember what you came for," he said. After a pause to let this information sink in, he added, "Houses or apartments?"

"I came for the ride," said Lowell's wife. "It is my husband who has a purpose."

Lowell was certain she was imitating some actress, and it bothered him that he couldn't figure out who. "Houses," he said. "Are you the real-estate man?"

"Good," said the young man. "Apartments are a pain in the ass. How much money have you got?"

Lowell reluctantly admitted to having about two thousand dollars, although not with him. "Who was the person I talked to on the phone?" he asked.

"That was my associate," said the young man. "That's not enough." He looked at Lowell wearily. Lowell allowed as how he might have a little more. He might even have another thousand, in a pinch.

"That's more like it," said the young man. "I'll bet you've got even more than that. They always hold out on you."

"*Three thousand dollars!*" squeaked Lowell's wife, her face aghast, indignant, and astonished in roughly equal measure. "We don't have three thousand dollars! If we had three thousand dollars we could have gone to France last summer! We could go to Aruba right now! Where did we get three thousand dollars? Saint Thomas! We could go to Saint Thomas! We just don't *have* that kind of money!"

Actually, the real-estate man was right and Lowell's wife was wrong. He was holding back, not exaggerating. The true sum was $8,322 and some odd cents. He had his bankbook right in his pocket. Except for food and rent and clothing, they never bought much of anything, and Lowell had been packing away the surplus for years. God knew why. It was just part of his monthly schedule. Anyway, this was the first he'd heard about a trip to France, much less Aruba. He wasn't even sure he knew where Aruba was.

"I guess we can look at something now," said the real-estate man briskly, as though the squeaking and sputtering of outraged wives was all in a day's work. He picked up some file cards, flipped through them, and selected one. "Asking twenty, take eighteen, with a third in cash and a five-year balloon at seven and a quarter," he said. "The more cash you've got, the lower the price."

"I don't understand," said Lowell, trying hard to sound forceful instead of bewildered, but not succeeding. "You're not the person we talked to on the phone, right? I mean, I'd just sort of like to get things straight in my mind."

"That was Raymond," said the young man. "He's working upstairs and can't be bothered to change his clothes, although I don't know what that's got to do with anything. Let's go." He shrugged on his coat and herded them out the door.

"Don't even think about balloons," whispered Lowell's wife. "Balloons are a trap."

"What's a balloon?" whispered Lowell.

His wife drew in her breath with a sharp sipping sound and

refused to say more, leaving him feeling like a spy who'd given the wrong countersign. It was all gibberish, and he didn't understand a thing.

An early twilight was falling through the trees as the real-estate man led them toward Washington Avenue. Numbers of Negroes had gathered in silent, cold-looking groups outside the houses, apparently for the sole purpose of showing Lowell's wife how many of them there were, because they certainly didn't seem to have come outdoors for any other reason; they weren't even talking much. There was almost no place you could look without finding someone looking incuriously back at you from it. It was kind of eerie. The sky seemed unusually large and full of pollution, and there was no rest for the eye up there, either; it was growing grayer as the light failed, making everything look limp and dreary and drained of color, as if the whole neighborhood and all the people in it had been underwater for years. It was November. Over in Manhattan, Lowell never thought of it as being any special month—you just had winter, and you were glad when it was over, and then it got hot—but this was a real November he was feeling now, for the first time in years. It was a bad month in a bad season in a poor part of town. A cold wind was getting up and naked light bulbs had begun to shine from behind curtainless windows. Lowell wanted to go home.

"The neighborhood slummed up after the war," said the real-estate man in a cadenced, unreal voice. "Before that, it was by far the most fashionable part of Brooklyn, and only millionaires could afford to live in it. Just look at these houses. The vast majority, including the one I'm about to show you, are in sound basic condition and only need minimal repair, if I make myself clear."

"Maybe you'd better go into it," said Lowell's wife. "I wouldn't want anything left unclear in my husband's mind."

"Well, you can't make a definite statement about that kind of thing," said the real-estate man. "It varies a lot from house to house. You can't expect every house to be the same. Am I right, sir?"

"Guess so," said Lowell. "I wasn't listening very closely."

"Don't take my word for it," said the real-estate man. "Look around for yourself. Look in all the rooms. I'm only here to help you, don't take my word for a thing."

"Don't worry about that," said Lowell's wife. "Not that it makes any difference. I'm just humoring my husband by coming out here. We have a marvelous apartment on the West Side, and I'm perfectly content to stay there for the rest of my life. How much commission do you make on a deal like this?"

Lowell walked beside them, a thoughtful outcast. It was clear what his role was: he was a kind of conversational convenience, to be used as a foil when the need arose, and the rest of the time to be apostrophized as a way of clarifying his wife's feelings. On the whole he was glad that nothing more was required of him—it was an easy part to play, it would be over soon, and then they could go home and forget the whole thing—but at the same time it made him feel worried and jealous. It was like the times in his childhood when the big kids would leave him out when they talked about sex, except that his wife and the real-estate man were talking business. Lowell knew about as much about business as he used to know about sex, and his wife's apparent grasp of the subject was disturbing. Not only did he wonder where she'd had an opportunity to learn about it, but it upset him to hear her discussing it with another man. It was as though she'd started talking to someone else about strange bed positions he'd never heard of. "Isn't it getting a little late?" he suggested.

"Here we are," said the real-estate man, stopping before a mansion of such surpassing opulent hideousness that Lowell could scarcely believe someone was actually offering to sell it to him. It was just the kind of place he'd always really wanted with a powerful subconscious craving that defied analysis. "The townhouse of Darius Collingwood, foremost corporation lawyer in the Northeastern United States," said the real-estate man. "Built between 1800 and 1885 of Philadelphia brick, brownstone, terra-cotta, and Runcorn stone, whatever that is."

"Darius Collingwood," said Lowell.

It had a turret and a mansard roof with a wrought-iron railing in a design of vines and flowers. The façade jutted forth in a great bay like the prow of a mighty ship, its windows decorated with panels of stained glass, its waist defined by a wide course of ornamental brickwork, interspersed with terra-cotta panels displaying a relief of urns and human faces. There were flat windows and curved windows, rectangular windows and oval windows with belts of stone. There was a lightning rod on the turret. The main entrance, on the right as you faced the house, and some twenty feet to the rear of the great aggressive thrust of the bay, was reached by a flight of wide brownstone steps and was framed by thick brownstone columns that supported a kind of porch or miniature fortress. The front door itself was deep in shadow.

"It's a rooming house," said Lowell's wife.

"Delivered vacant," said the real-estate man. "Very observant of you."

Lowell hadn't known that it was a rooming house. He looked at it closely, but he still couldn't see why it was a rooming house.

"What's the C. of O.?" asked his wife.

"Class B roomer," said the agent.

Lowell didn't know what they were talking about.

"The house on the right," continued the agent in his reading-it-off voice, indicating a three-story frame structure in bad repair, "is occupied by a number of elderly Irish ladies."

As though alerted by a concealed microphone, an elderly Irish lady appeared at an upper window and regarded them suspiciously.

"Hump," said Lowell's wife.

"The place on the left," continued the agent, pointing to a narrow brick house that was separated from the mansion by a narrow alley piled high with discarded beer cans and burst bags of garbage, "is owned by an old man. Shall we go inside now?"

The real-estate man led them down the walk toward the porch. Halfway there he stopped, picked up a weatherbeaten mop handle that was leaning against the house, and banged loudly with it on the window above his head. "Henry!" he called. He paused with a look of impatience and then banged again. "Henry! Henry, you home?"

An elderly Negro man in a tattered undershirt pushed aside the curtains and sleepily heaved open the window. His eyes were bloodshot and foggy, and his face beneath the grayish stubble of beard had a kind of bruised, soft look, like some kind of dark, spoiled fruit. He looked down at the agent and swayed a little. "Man can't get no sleep," he said.

"These people want to look at the house, Henry," said the agent.

"I do my job," said Henry. It was difficult to tell how he did anything at all, his eyes were so cloudy; the brown irises seemed to be dissolving. "Got a nice apartment. Fix it up all nice. Work all fucking day long. You come back tomorrow. I got to sleep."

"You can sleep later, Henry. Mr. Grossman wants you to show these people the house now."

"Shee-it! You go tell Mr. Grossman he can goddamn well go and fuck his goddamn self. I ain't no fucking horse. I got to sleep, I'm a working man. Now, you just get off my sidewalk and leave me alone."

"We'll see you at the door, Henry," said the agent. "We go through the same scene every time," he explained to Lowell and his wife. "It's just a big act."

"Don't you go doing that!" shouted Henry. "Don't you go talking about me when I'm standing right here! Ain't you got no fucking manners? Shee-it! I done told you before, you got something to say, you say it to me. Ain't never worked a fucking day in your life, waking up a man like that, talking about him when he standing right here, goddamn it, you stay away from that door, hear?"

"Let's go in," said the agent, climbing the steps. He took out a ring of keys and began trying them in the lock one by one. Other windows had gone up in the house, and Lowell saw faces peering down at them indistinctly in the dusk.

"I think maybe . . ." he said.

"You all get away from there!" shouted Henry, leaning perilously out of his window and waving his arms clumsily. "You hear me? I said get away from the goddamn door! People is trying to eat their supper!"

"Here it is," said the real-estate man, turning a key in the lock and pushing open the door. It had once been inset with a tall oval of glass, but a sheet of battered tin covered the place now. "Don't pay any attention to old Henry. He always carries on like that. He'll be here in a minute. Perhaps you'd like to take a look at the back parlor while we're waiting for him."

"Why not?" said Lowell's wife brightly. "Let's look at everything."

They were standing in a kind of lobby. The floor was filthy and the walls had been patched frequently but not well with huge handfuls of plaster. A staircase wound up into the darkness on the right. On the left were a pair of tall doors, and a short corridor behind Lowell's back terminated in a pair of equally tall doors, presumably the ones through which Henry would issue when he put on his shoes and got out his knife, or whatever he was doing. Everything in sight had been painted a peculiar and utterly depressing shade of pale green, which had then apparently been thickly sprayed with a mixture of soot and old cobwebs. They were the dirtiest walls Lowell had ever seen, and he instinctively shrank from touching them. The floor was so dirty it was impossible to tell what it was made of—a sheet of slightly flexible cardboard over an abyss, it felt like—and the only light came from a dim fluorescent ring high up on the ceiling, flickering off and on and nearly buried in another crude plastering job. There were water stains everywhere, and dim racks and banks of pipes went this way and that, up the walls and across the ceiling, festooned with a gray fur of dust and soot. The air smelled strongly of stagnant water and burned wood. Upstairs someone opened a door and spoke a word, then closed the door again. Somewhere a toilet flushed.

The real-estate man knocked on the door to the left. An attempt had been made to fit it with a peephole, but the hole had been drilled too large and the device hung out of it like an eye gouged from its socket. A woman's voice called, "Who?"

"Landlord," said the real-estate man. "Open up."

There were bustlings and whispers inside the room, and a heavy object was moved about on squeaky casters. It sounded to Lowell like they were barricading the door with a chest of drawers. On the other hand, he supposed they could just as plausibly be unbarricading it. Whatever they were doing, they soon stopped. A moment of silence followed, and then someone began to wash dishes.

"Damn that Henry," said the agent, looking very cross indeed in a very prim way. He banged on the door with his fist. "You in there!" he barked. "Open up!"

"Don't you think we should come back tomorrow?" asked Lowell, uncomfortably aware that several heads had poked over the railing above them. At any moment Henry might come charging out of his room with a weapon of some kind and raise the house against the intruders. Lowell wondered what he would do if someone came at him with a knife; all his life he'd been afraid of knives, and he was always a little worried when he was in a room where they were being used. He imagined himself being backed into a corner by a knife-wielding resident of the building, trying to explain that all he wanted to do was leave in peace, not being understood because his attacker didn't understand English.

Before the agent could answer him, the door was opened by a tiny brown lady in the kind of loose cotton dress Lowell could vaguely remember his grandmother as wearing: it was faded and had flowers printed on it. She smiled at them hopefully, looking from one to the other as though in search of the one who was nicest. "Yes?" she asked.

"It's all right," said the agent. "The landlord wants these people to look at your apartment. You understand? The landlord."

"Who?" she asked, still smiling but not as hopefully. Her hair was tied back with a piece of string, and Lowell noticed that she was wearing an old pair of men's carpet slippers.

"I hope we're not disturbing you," said Lowell's wife, rising on tiptoe to get a better view of the room.

"I no espik no Inglis. Please?"

"That's what they all say," said the real-estate man to Lowell. "It's okay," he said to the tiny lady, gently taking her by the arms and steering her back into the room. "*Es bueno. El casero dice.*"

"Ain't either all right," said Henry, suddenly appearing in the hallway behind them. "God damn it, what I tol' you, you ain't got no right busting in on people like this. People gotta sleep, they gotta eat."

"Now, then, Henry," said the real-estate man, turning to the superintendent after having steered the woman to a chair, making a kind of hole for Lowell and his wife to enter the room by. The little old lady folded her hands on her lap, put her knees together, sat up straight, and gave them her entire attention.

The room was long, high, and narrow. It had been painted pink, including the ceiling and fireplace, but not very recently. Tall windows rose from the floor almost to the ceiling on two sides of the room, the bottom third screened with cardboard and

the middle third covered with thin cotton curtains of an astonishing turquoise color, held together with sagging lengths of
string. Tall mirrors stood above the fireplace and between the
rear windows, their massive, pink-painted frames carved in a
design of flowers and seashells. The pink ceiling, deeply cof-
fered, centered on a heroic central medallion of what appeared
to be lettuce leaves in a nest of worms. Every coffer had a five-
o'clock shadow of dust and soot.

"Don't you go talking about no Mr. Grossman to *me*," Henry
was saying in an aggrieved high voice that sounded embarrass-
ingly like a white man's imitation. "*I* run this building, and
what *I* says goes."

"They always paint the marble mantels," said the real-estate
man, apparently to Lowell. "God knows why."

A candle guttered in a tall glass in a dim corner of the room,
which was furnished only with a sat-upon-looking bed, a couple
of end tables made of some kind of pressed synthetic material
that was veined and painted brown to resemble wood, a kitchen
table of the same substance (one leg of which was tied together
with a strip of cloth), and a couple of old tubular chairs of the
sort Lowell had seen discarded on the street. At the table was
sitting a small brown man. For some reason, possibly because
he was sitting utterly motionless and was the same color as the
furniture, Lowell had failed to notice him before. It gave him
quite a turn.

"Allo," said the little man, smiling and nodding with desperate pleasantry, as though he expected Lowell to shoot, arrest, or
strike him at any moment. "How are you today?"

"I hope we're not disturbing you," said Lowell, looking
around the room, so barren of sources of enjoyment or activity,
and wondering what in the world he might have disturbed them
at.

"No, no," said the little man, smiling more broadly and nodding more rapidly than ever. "Please."

On the end tables were a pair of lamps with plastic bases in the form of black panthers, their muzzles red with blood. On the left-hand table there was also a vase of faded plastic flowers, covered with a dusty polyethylene shirt bag, and on the right-hand table, also covered with a bag, was the statue of some saint. Against the other walls were a beaverboard bureau for clothes, and a tiny, ancient, and unspeakably filthy gas range with a sort of brown halo behind it. In a tall alcove that must once have been intended for books, a kind of cardboard hut had been constructed, no doubt to conceal a toilet. The linoleum on the floor was peeling in strips, and someone had taped a loaf of French bread to the wall by the door; it looked like it had been there for a long time. Lowell wondered what they'd been pushing across the floor before they opened the door.

"It's a slice of life, my dear," said his wife.

"This is the back parlor," said the real-estate man as he detached himself from Henry. He indicated the front wall, where a plasterboard partition, its edges not matching and its nails badly driven, filled a wide, arched doorway. It was painted a different, more disturbingly fleshlike shade of pink than the rest of the room. A roach was crawling on it. "There may be sliding doors under there," said the real-estate man. "Originally there were, but there's no way of telling. Sometimes they have silver doorknobs and panels of stained glass. If there was a hole we could see." He seemed to regret that there was no hole. Lowell wondered what the tiny Puerto Ricans thought of all this. He found himself hoping that they really didn't understand English.

"Look at that molding up there," said the real-estate man, pointing at the worm-and-lettuce medallion in the middle of the ceiling. "You can chip that paint right off."

"Thank you very much," said Lowell to the Puerto Ricans. "I'm sorry to have intruded. Thanks again." He felt a compelling, incomprehensible urge to go on saying variants of "thank you," smiling idiotically, and nodding along with his host, until he was either dragged from the room by force or somehow managed to convince them that his soul was pure.

"No, no," said the little man, rising from the chair with a desperate grin. Apparently he had fallen prey to a similar urge as Lowell's but was less capable of restraining it, no doubt because of his Latin temperament. "No, no, ess okay, yes? Ess okay, ess okay." Smiling and bobbing his head, he followed Lowell to the door, patting him very lightly on the arm as though wanting to reassure him but afraid that this might not be the way Americans did it. "Good-bye," he said, somehow contriving to smile even more broadly. He ushered Lowell and his party out into the hall, then closed the door slowly, smiling through the narrowing aperture. "Good-bye, good-bye."

"Good-bye," chimed the little lady from her chair as the door finally closed. Lowell felt drained.

"This was the sewing room," said the real-estate man, taking Lowell's arm in the same place where the Puerto Rican had patted it and turning him around in his tracks. Lowell found himself facing another door. They were all jammed together so tightly in the hallway that Lowell could smell his wife's powder and the liquor on Henry's breath and the sour odor of his own clothing. The real-estate man seemed to have no smell at all.

"Shit, man," said Henry. "That Bowman Parker's room. It ain't no sewing room, no kind of sewing room at all. What's the matter with you, anyhow? Don't go knocking there, he work nights. I said, don't go knocking there."

The real-estate man put his hand on the door and silently pushed it open. The room was deep but no more than seven or eight feet wide, and it ended in another tall window. A thin Negro man was sitting hunched over on the unmade bed, wearing nothing but a pair of pants and a set of what appeared to be Army dogtags. His feet and hands seemed far too big for his body. The light was off and the room was very dim in the twilight. The man looked up at them and then looked back at the floor. On a small table at the head of the bed was an alarm clock and a pack of Pall Malls.

"Probably there was a door in that wall," said the real-estate man, "connecting this room with the one we were just in. Actually, this place hasn't been cut up as badly as some. Originally there were twenty-one rooms, and all of them are still more or less intact."

"Twenty-one rooms?" said Lowell's wife. "Who needs twenty-one rooms? What would you do with them all? How would you keep them clean?" Lowell could tell that she was impressed, but it was difficult to guess in what way. He looked down at the man on the bed and wondered what was going through his mind and how he occupied his days. "Servants," said the real-estate man. He gently closed the door and cut the man off from view. Lowell wondered if he knew they were gone. "All right, Henry, we'll have a look at your room now."

To Lowell's surprise, Henry turned and led them down the hall to his door, muttering about how some people didn't have no fucking respect. Lowell allowed himself to be carried along. The deeper his reluctance to continue this farce bored into his spirit, the less will he seemed to have to resist.

Henry's room was almost totally dark. There seemed to be no lights, and the windows were covered with all manner of things: old roller blinds, shredded at the bottom, perhaps by a cat or a child with long fingernails; scraps of old bedsheets, swaybacked and rumpled on limp strings; taped-up yellowing newspapers; pages torn from magazines; squares of Woolworth oilcloth; rags; cheap lace curtains, far too short, very old, turning to dust. Every window had a separate and distinct history, like the exposed strata in the face of a cliff, thickest at the bottom and growing thinner toward the ceiling, the layers never completely overlapping. Stray emanations of twilight filtered in through the chinks. It was hard to decide whether Henry feared the sun or simply hated the sight of the street; perhaps he suspected spies and peeping toms, and Lowell couldn't imagine how he'd gotten through to the sash, much less opened it, when the real-estate man had knocked. Maybe he had a technique.

Enough light came through the open door so that shapes were visible, although not very clearly. Boxes and cartons and great looming things were heaped around in the gloom, in some cases all the way up to the ceiling, taking up half the floor space and containing God knew what—dead rats and old rags by the smell of them. Pictures and notices were taped haphazardly around wherever the walls were clear, but except for a Kennedy portrait clipped from the *Daily News* and a headline that said REJOICE, Lowell couldn't make most of them out too well in the dimness; he had a vague impression that most of them were about cows or religion. A pot of grits was boiling on the stove, stirred by a woman who seemed to be clothed in the same general sort of material that the windows were covered with, but he couldn't see her too well either, and it was hard to be sure. Her hand and the spoon stood out in the strange weak light from the burner, but her face was hidden in shadow. She seemed to watch them the whole time they were there, her hand slowly stirring. It was difficult for Lowell to look away from it.

"The occasional parlor," said the agent. "A room usually kept closed except for receptions, parties, important visitors, and major family holidays. The ceiling is pretty elaborate, and there are two big fireplaces in here somewhere. Why don't you put on the light, Henry?"

"Power failed," said Henry.

"That's too bad. I'll have to mention that to Mr. Grossman when I call him up this evening, along with your cooperative attitude."

"Be sure and do that," said Henry.

They left the room and went upstairs, the agent leading, followed by Lowell's wife, then Lowell, and finally Henry, who hadn't spoken a single word, either of greeting, introduction, explanation, or farewell to his wife, or whoever she was.

"Soul food, huh?" said Lowell utterly at random and completely without forethought. He'd been searching for something pleasant to say, and it just sort of popped out.

Henry responded with an expression of implacable hatred. Lowell began to feel nervous about walking ahead of him.

"Last year alone," intoned the agent as they climbed the winding and apparently interminable staircase, "last year alone, twenty-two houses were sold in the area for renovation. That's not counting respectable old families who've been persuaded to stay on. You might say we've turned the corner," he concluded just as, in fact, he turned a corner onto a landing and passed from Lowell's sight.

"Respectable families my ass," muttered Henry. "Ain't nobody going to sell no fucking house to nobody till I gets my two thousand dollars. No, sir. Two thousand dollars, and I ain't seen a penny of it. Doing plaster. Painting. Climbing fucking stairs. Shee-it!"

Lowell fell into a daze. He reached the landing, and they looked at more rooms. The more rooms they looked at, the more dazed Lowell felt. No longer embarrassed, scarcely feeling a thing, he stared blankly through the open doors of other people's lives, and turned away without a word.

"The master bedroom," said the agent, gesturing into a room inhabited by strings of laundry and a young Puerto Rican couple, who had been interrupted either while making love or thinking hard about it. The girl, wrapped in a sheet beneath which she was rather obviously nude, turned her face to the wall and kept it there, furiously, throughout Lowell's visit, while her shirtless and shoeless husband (who was, nevertheless, wearing a beret that was more natty and smart-looking than any headgear Lowell had ever owned) followed them about the room with his arms folded across his chest and an extremely pissed-off expression on his face. There was a fireplace in the room, but it was different from the one that was downstairs.

Another room was in the turret. It was about ten feet tall and not much larger in diameter than the inside of a barrel, and it had no walls to speak of. Instead of walls, there were two enormous curved windows. "How do you do?" said the little old white man who lived there. He was wearing a bathrobe over a pair of long johns. He was also wearing shoes and stockings held up with old-fashioned garters, which had the effect of making his feet look both huge and quaint. "I'm the bat in the belfry," he told them. "This is the belfry. I'm the bat. A bat in the belfry and spooks in the cellar. I'm not as crazy as I sound. You try living with colored people sometime and see how you like it."

"That's okay, Charlie," said Henry fondly, the way you might speak to a favorite old dog. "That's okay. You get on back in bed now, hear?"

The rear bedroom was occupied by a drunken Negro woman who was attempting to cook something amid dense billows of smoke while three small children, none of them wearing anything below the waist, played on the bed with old baby bottles and a couple of empty beer cans. Next door was another sewing room. It was darker than Henry's place, smelled powerfully of cigars, and was occupied by a crone who remained in the shadows, her presence barely visible but powerfully felt, like the emanations of a witch who had almost, but not quite, succeeded in turning herself invisible. Upstairs in the largest room a family of Puerto Ricans was eating supper at a big, plastic-looking table; they became utterly motionless the moment the real-estate man and his little party trooped in, and they remained utterly motionless—knives and forks in their hands, untasted food growing cold in front of them, jaws not moving, throats not swallowing, an absent smile playing about the lips of the head of the household—until the little party trooped back out again. They reminded Lowell of some French painting or other, but he couldn't remember which one.

"I think maybe we've seen enough," he suggested, it seemed for the dozenth time. "I mean, it's getting kind of late and everything."

"There's still the servants' quarters," said the agent firmly. "Also the dining room and kitchen. You'll want to see them, surely?"

"By all means," said Lowell's wife. "Also the cellar. My husband is very knowledgeable about furnaces and pipes."

They climbed to the old servants' quarters in the top of the house—a series of little rooms incredibly close together, clustered around a central foyer—but although the odor of some ghastly boiled foodstuff hung heavily in the air, no one could be persuaded to open their door. Lowell was glad.

"This was the old dumbwaiter," said the agent, indicating a gap in the paneling that was filled to the brim with crumpled papers—cups and wads of what appeared to be used toilet paper. He'd gotten very cross as he knocked fruitlessly on door after door, and Lowell had the impression that he pointed out the dumbwaiter from some spiteful private motive.

"Dumbwaiter my ass," muttered Henry.

They marched back downstairs. Lowell was somehow next to last again, with Henry behind him. He wondered if he should try to make some explanation about his soul-food remark, but although the urge to do so was powerful, he couldn't think of any good-sounding mitigating comment. Fortunately it took less time to go down the stairs than it had to go up them, and he managed not to blurt anything out before they reached the bottom, where the real-estate man asked him if he'd noticed the banister.

"Was there something special about it?" asked Lowell.

"It had a *very* graceful curve," said the real-estate man, fixing him with the same kind of look that he had bestowed on the doors that had refused to open. "It's one of the principal features of the house."

"Oh," said Lowell, hoping that he wouldn't be made to run back to the top of the house and look at it.

"Let's see the furnace," said his wife.

"There's solid mahogany under that paint," grumbled the real-estate man as he turned and led them down another flight of stairs, a dark one that seemed to descend into a cave of night. Lowell couldn't see where to put his feet, and his balance became uncertain, but he didn't want to support himself with the walls for fear of what they might have been smeared or impregnated with. No light whatever filtered down the stairway from the hall above, and his eyes were filled with swarming shapes. "Solid mahogany," said the disembodied voice of the agent from somewhere ahead of him and below. "All it needs is a little paint remover."

A door was thrown open at the foot of the stairs, a dim rectangle of light in the impenetrable tissue of the darkness, and although Lowell was still unable to see where to put his feet, he could now see where he was going. The knowledge made him feel better, but not for long. A great warm wave of new horrible odors, different both in degree and intensity from the old horrible odors that he'd almost gotten used to, rolled up over him and nearly knocked him flat. It was like the first whiff of the atmosphere of some alien planet: heavy, warm, barely breathable, seemingly compounded of urine and stale oatmeal in equal measure. Any astronaut in his right mind would have closed the airlock and gone straight home, but Henry was still behind Lowell, and he pressed on.

"I think I'm going to be sick," said Lowell's wife as they emerged into the light. "No, I guess not."

The hallway where they had emerged was low, narrow, and painted some dark color that once might have been a kind of green; now it looked black, but not exactly, and gave the impression that the walls weren't really solid but composed of some substance that would yield and engulf anyone unwary enough to lean on them. Somewhere a television set throbbed with a hollow sound, as though speaking from the bottom of a deep, narrow pit. Dozens of suits of men's clothing were hung from the sprinkler pipe on metal hangers. It was hard to move around without becoming entangled in them, a situation that was not improved by the fact that none of them were very clean and most of them were very old; it was like being embraced by a bum's ghost.

"Mrs. Blouse?" called the agent, pushing his way through the suits with a show of considerable bad grace. Evidently he was still mad about the banister. "Mrs. Blouse!" he called again, banging on a door whose surface was patched in several places with squares of battered tin. In a moment, to the accompaniment of strident muffled shouting, it was opened by a little Negro girl of five or six. She regarded them expressionlessly.

"You just keep on like that, Rory Fitzgerald," said a shrill woman's voice from somewhere in the room, apparently on the verge of hysteria. "You just keep on like that and I'm going to slap your goddamn little face right off. You just keep on like that. Just keep on."

The little girl remained motionless in the doorway. The real-estate man leaned past her into the room, holding the jamb with both hands. "Good evening, Mrs. Blouse," he said to someone. "I've brought some people to see the place."

"Pebbles!" shrieked the woman's voice. "You get in here and let them people by! Rory, you get up on that couch! Pebbles!"

"Good," said the real-estate man as if he had done something rather clever and difficult, such as picking a lock. "We can go in now."

The room wasn't as dark as Henry's or the old lady's, but it was considerably lower, as though something had sat on it. The windows were covered with old towels and the walls looked like they had been constructed by throwing handfuls of mud and cow shit at a framework of ancient lath until most of it was covered. The little girl and an even smaller boy were seated rigidly side by side on an enormous, spavined, yellowish sofa that was much and questionably stained and which stank to high heaven with an odor that resembled a superhumanly protracted fart. It was a wonder the children weren't overpowered where they sat, but overpowered was not what they looked like: they looked petrified. Their feet stuck straight out in front of them, their hands were folded on their laps, their backs were rigid, and their faces were impenetrable masks. On the opposite side of the room, next to another of those damn fireplaces, was an unfocused television set, its sound turned down to the threshold of audibility. On its screen Robert Vaughn, pursued by his ghost, ran down an alley paralleled by the ghost of an alley, while frantic chase music murmured like a love song from the speaker. It was a rerun of *The Man from U.N.C.L.E.* Lowell had seen it before, but he found it difficult to keep from watching. It was what he'd be watching if he were home right now, instead of out here on this fool's errand. *The Man from U.N.C.L.E.* was one of his favorite programs, and he was sorry the series had ever been discontinued.

"You just sit right there!" shrieked the woman's voice from somewhere to his left, jerking him from his reverie with a nasty start. "Don't you move a muscle! Don't you dare! One move and I'm gon' bang your little ass against the wall until it *stick!*"

Lowell watched with astonishment as a cronelike creature, preceded by this storm of senseless abuse, picked her way through a doorway that Lowell had assumed led to a closet of some sort. Her hair was dyed a rich shade of dark orange, which, in combination with the uncertain light and a faded green sweater, made her skin appear olive-drab. She was dressed in shapeless heavy clothes of the sort found in bins at church bazaars and Hadassah thrift shops, and she was evidently quite drunk in a kind of generalized way, as though drunk was the way she always was, just as some people are always sober. One of her stockings was falling down, just like in the racist propaganda.

"This is Mrs. Blouse," said the real-estate agent. "Mrs. Blouse is always very good about showing us her apartment. She has the largest apartment in the whole building."

"That's right," said Mrs. Blouse in a slurred voice, gazing at them with congested, unfocused eyes. "The biggest one."

"How do you do?" said Lowell, immediately getting the feeling that it was a foolish thing to say, although he couldn't decide why.

Mrs. Blouse looked at him as though she thought it was a pretty foolish thing to say, too. Suddenly she wheeled in the other direction and shrieked: "SIT!" The little boy, who had allowed himself to slump a little, sat back upright and shook himself. "Little fucker," said Mrs. Blouse, apparently to Lowell.

"The kitchen is this way," said the agent. He led them through a doorway into a large room that contained a stove and refrigerator in worse condition than any Lowell had seen abandoned in the street. Between them was an enormous two-basin sink, half of which was clogged and filled to the brim with black goop.

"It's too bad it's gotten too dark outside to see the garden," said the agent.

Lowell's wife went to one of the windows and peered out between cupped hands. "I can see it," she said. "It's filled with bags of garbage."

Lowell joined her. Sure enough, the garden was filled with bags of garbage. Not a patch of earth was visible, just garbage.

"Ain't enough cans," said Henry. "People afraid to come down after dark. I'm going to clean it up. I'm going to clean it up tomorrow. Just ain't enough cans. I'll clean it up."

"Shit you will," said Mrs. Blouse.

"Shut your mouth," snapped Henry.

"Well, I guess that's about all," said the agent, taking Lowell by the arm and pointing him toward the door.

"We were going to take a look at the furnace," said Lowell's wife.

"Don't you go telling me to shut my mouth, Henry Gruen," said Mrs. Blouse.

It appeared that the basement lights had burned out, but Henry said that he kept the bulbs upstairs in his room to prevent theft. He went up to get them, and Lowell and his wife and the agent stood around among the suits until he came back. Every so often Mrs. Blouse would appear in the doorway and stare at them, each time with a different expression, as though trying out the various ways her face would go. "I bet you got a real good job," she said to Lowell during one of these visitations, but she disappeared again before he could think of an answer.

Presently Henry returned with a couple of encrusted fifteen-watt bulbs, and they went downstairs to inspect the furnace. It was a great, antique leviathan of a thing, sheathed with rotting asbestos and displaying more arms than you could shake a stick at. It looked big enough to power a steamboat, but if Henry's mutterings were to be believed, it was scarcely adequate to warm the house. While they watched, an electric switch clicked somewhere in its bowels and it sprang to life with a muted roaring.

"There was a wine cellar over there," said the agent, pointing into the bottomless shadows that extended beyond their feeble circle of light. He seemed fidgety. "Well, I guess that's all. Let's go back upstairs."

He started toward the steps. At that very moment a toilet was flushed somewhere in the upper reaches of the house and a few seconds later its contents were deposited on the basement floor with a great gurgling and rushing of water. This event occurred more or less behind Lowell and his wife, their attention having been riveted in the direction of the invisible and possibly specious wine cellar. Quite a sight met their eye when they turned around. They were standing not more than ten feet from the edge of a shallow black pond, its agitated surface flashing dully. It extended into the shadows toward the rear of the house, and it was impossible to tell exactly how large it was, but it was clearly pretty big in an obscene sort of way. Something pale, perhaps fungus, seemed to be growing on the walls and pillars back there, but Lowell couldn't bring himself to look too closely; he felt as though his eyes might become polluted, and there was a funny metallic taste in his mouth. He'd heard that people with radiation poisoning got metallic tastes in their mouths, but he knew he couldn't have radiation poisoning. He didn't feel particularly disgusted, just a little worried. He supposed the reason he hadn't noticed the smell before was because he'd already smelled so many bad things today that he'd stopped paying attention.

"Waste line got a crack in it," said Henry. "Some stuff gets out through it, and some stuff don't."

"I see," said Lowell.

"Been like that for a couple years," said Henry. "A couple years at least."

It was dark when they finally returned to the street, much darker than in Manhattan, as though the night lay more heavily on Brooklyn. A cold wind was tossing the branches of the trees back and forth with a stiff, ungainly motion, not like trees at all, like people whose joints were locked by some disease.

"Of course, a thing like that can be fixed," the agent was saying, somewhat too rapidly. "It can be put in the contract."

"I'm all turned around," said Lowell, watching the dark trees struggle with the wind. "Which way is the subway?"

"I thought we could go back to the office and have a chat."

The idea of going back to the office had never entered Lowell's mind, and the prospect of going back there and having a "chat" made it sound positively repulsive. It sounded like some kind of fag thing he would never want to do as long as he lived. "I don't think so," he said.

"We could look at some other places. Perhaps something not quite so grand?"

"Not today," said Lowell.

"Tomorrow?"

"I'll give you a call."

"I guess you aren't really serious," said the agent peevishly. "I can usually tell when people aren't serious by looking at them, but you two had me fooled. I thought you were serious. I thought you were the kind of people who really get involved. I don't do this for a living, you know. I do it as a service."

"I'm cold," said Lowell's wife before the agent could go on and tell them what he really did for a living.

"I think we'd better go," said Lowell. "My wife is very sensitive to the weather." He put his arm around her and turned her in the direction he presumed the subway lay, which also happened to be in the teeth of the wind. "Women have poor circulation," he heard the agent say, or thought he heard the agent say, but he didn't look back, and for all he knew the agent continued to stand there, staring after them with a cross expression on his face, until they vanished from sight. Nobody had ever told Lowell he wasn't serious before. Usually people told him he had no sense of humor.

The street was dark and very empty, and the stiffly tossing branches of the trees made strange, uncertain patterns against the lighted windows of the houses. It wasn't a pleasant emptiness; it was the kind of emptiness that suggested that if someone else was moving in it too, he probably didn't mean you well. It was a thief's emptiness, the emptiness of a street in a city occupied by a hostile power. No one who was out of doors belonged there, least of all Lowell and his wife, who weren't even the right color. He'd had the same feeling on certain streets on the West Side, but they were only a few blocks long and this street seemed to go on for miles, the street lamps falling away in the distance for as far as the eye could see. He'd never thought of how big Brooklyn was or how enormous a slum in it could be, low and all spread out and unconfined. It didn't make him feel fortunate in his wealth and comforts; it made him feel powerless and small and infinitely fragile. There were so many of them; he'd never realized before how many of them there were.

In a short while, fighting the wind, they reached Fulton Street. None of the remaining stores were open, although it was only about seven o'clock, and the absence of trees had the peculiar effect of making the street seem more sinister, not less. Pulverized glass glittered on the sidewalks like handful scatterings of hard tiny jewels, and broken storefronts and burned buildings were everywhere. It wasn't even possible to buy a loaf of bread. Everyone with money had gone away when the sun went down, and everyone else had gone indoors.

"Man!" a voice burst on them when they were only a few steps from the subway. "Look at that white motherfucker hustle along!"

"Shit, man," said another voice, "you got something the matter with your eyes? That ain't his mother."

They went down the stairs almost running and then felt sheepish about it when they got to the bottom and no one else had followed them. They were back in the familiar world again, the grimy station and the harsh lights, the people standing on the platform sourly wrapped up in their thoughts: it was New York again, ugly, shabby, and thirty years out of date, familiar, safe. Lowell felt the same way he used to feel on the infrequent occasions when he'd made it home before the bullies caught up with him. He also felt dirty all over, as though he'd been dipped in some loathsome fluid and not a single part of him had escaped. He wanted a bath.

"I need a bath," he told his wife.

"Me first," she said. "I see that you've come to your senses."

"Something like that," said Lowell. Then the train came.

That night he dreamed of sewage and suffocation. Nothing unusual happened to him the next day except that an old man keeled over dead on the corner of 92nd and Broadway and Lowell joined the crowd in time to see the swaddled body being put into the ambulance. He knew that he'd tell his father-in-law about it the next time they met; his father-in-law was the kind of person you told about things like that. When he went to bed that night he had a dream so dull that he woke up from sheer boredom and sort of stumbled around the apartment until he got tired enough to go back to sleep. The next night he got so drunk that he forgot to take his underwear off before putting on his pajamas. "Darius Collingwood," he said to himself as he sat in his office that afternoon. "Darius Collingwood." It was a good name. It was the kind of name he wished he had.

His wife noticed the direction he was taking and did her best to stem the tide. "Let's do it differently tonight," she said. "I'll be the man and you be the woman, how about it? If that doesn't suit you, we could do something else. We could do anything you want. Anything. What do you say?"

But Lowell was too drunk to talk and it was quite a job just getting him into bed, much less doing something with him after he got there.

Then she bought a new wardrobe of mini-dresses, but she forgot to purchase enough panty hose to go with them, and garters and stocking tops were alarmingly visible about half the time when she sat down. Garters and stocking tops were not Lowell's thing, but he knew they were a big deal to other men, and he worried about it a lot and became a nag, which was not exactly the kind of result his wife had hoped to produce. She tried hiding the gin. When Lowell discovered what she'd done, he didn't say a word. There was a fifth of crème de cacao in the liquor cabinet, and he drank it instead. He drank the entire fifth, sitting in front of the television set; it didn't make him very drunk, although the stickiness caused his speech to thicken badly, and it completely spoiled his appetite. The next night his wife put the gin back where it belonged, and Lowell made himself a martini as he watched a rerun of *The Patty Duke Show*, which ironically enough was set in a townhouse on Brooklyn Heights. Lowell did not comment on the fact.

The following morning Lowell called up the public library and asked them for information about Darius Collingwood, prominent Brooklyn attorney in the last century. The girl was gone from the phone for a long time, and Lowell sat there with his hangover, wondering exactly what he thought he was doing.

"There's an awful lot of stuff on Collingwood, sir," said the girl when she returned, for some reason sounding surprised and breathless and much cleaner and less hungover than Lowell had felt for years. "Articles and Ph.D. theses and things like that, and then there are the usual biographical sources, and then there's his own book, *The Autobiography of a Scoundrel*, published in Caracas in 1892. He's also mentioned in a lot of places." She sounded pretty pleased with old Darius in a helpful sort of way. Despite himself, Lowell began to wonder if anyone had ever really socked it to her, ever taken her and really stuffed it in. He wondered how clean and young and breathless she'd sound *then*, by God. In a minute he was going to start panting hoarsely into the receiver. He wished he knew what size breasts she had, and he was on the verge of asking her when he remembered that he'd given her his name and his paper's address. He also remembered who he was. He couldn't imagine what had come over him. He never had thoughts like this, at least not very often. It must be the hangover. He'd always wondered what kind of a man would pant over a telephone, but it had never occurred to him that he might actually be one of them. He'd never wanted to pant over the phone to anybody in his life, not even Jane Fonda, and he'd absolutely never thought of asking any girl the size of her breasts.

"If you want to see them, you'll have to come down to the library," said the girl, frightening him out of his wits and almost eliciting a hysterical response, he scarcely knew what, before he realized that she was talking about the reference materials. "However, there is a kind of incomplete biographical sketch that I could read to you over the phone if you want me to."

"Go ahead," said Lowell in an unnatural voice. He wanted the information, he told himself; the information. Forget the voice. The information. Not the voice. The information. Yes.

" 'Darius Collingwood,' " said the girl, as chipper and pert as could be. " 'Born; Brooklyn, Long Island, 1841, child of Tunis Collingwood, merchant, and Catherine Joralemon Collingwood, youngest daughter of . . .' I guess I forgot to tell you, but this comes out of the *Proceedings of the Old South Brooklyn Historical Society*, 1923, published by Livingstone and Cooper, Brooklyn, 1924. Do you want me to repeat that so you can write it down or something?"

"That won't be necessary," said Lowell.

"I'm not usually such a scatterbrain, but this is my first day on the job, and I'm not used to it yet."

"That's perfectly all right," said Lowell. "Just go right ahead."

"Golly, it's sure good of you to be so tolerant and everything. Now, where was I? Darius Collingwood blah blah blah 1841, son of Tunis blah blah blah blah, youngest daughter blah blah blah, here we are. I found it, sir. Are you ready? 'Attended the Busby School, displaying a remarkable precocity. Graduated from Columbia in 1859 at the age of eighteen, admitted to the bar the following year, meanwhile standing unsuccessfully for Brooklyn city alderman on the Republican ticket. Engaged in real-estate speculation, 1859–60. Declared bankrupt, May, 1861. In June of that year, following his father's death by apoplexy, he joined Walker's Gowanus Zouaves (later the Seventeenth Brooklyn) with the rank of lieutenant. Elected lieutenant-colonel, winter, 1861–62. Mentioned for conspicuous gallantry at Antietam. Wounded at Chancellorsville and invalided home. Commanded a detachment of Special Constables during the Draft Riots, July, 1863. Returned to the army the following month. Breveted colonel of volunteers, November, 1863. On detached duty to the Department of War, January, 1864–January, 1865. Personally congratulated by President Lincoln for gallantry ("Collingwood's Ride") preceding Jubal Early's abortive attack on the capital. Present at Lee's surrender, although it is unclear in what capacity. (See K. Hedingger's painting: Collingwood appears as third officer from the left, mistakenly depicted in the uniform of a brigadier general.)

" 'Following the war, Collingwood established a practice in San Francisco. Records are vague about his activities there. Returned to New York, August, 1871. Established an office on Wall Street the following month. Denounced in the Senate by Carson Pike, 1877. Termed "Jay Gould's Gray Eminence" by the New York *Herald,* March 21, 1879. An attempted assassination on the floor of the Stock Exchange by the Irish anarchist Fergus O'Dowd, April 5, 1879, failed due to the pistol's misfiring and the intoxicated condition of the assailant. Declared bankrupt for the second time, January 1, 1880. Commenced building a substantial home on Washington Avenue, Brooklyn, sometime during the following three months. Married Felicia Hargrove, fifteen-year-old daughter of Dr. Erasmus Hargrove, pastor of the Military Garden Dutch Reformed Church, in June of that same year. Named as co-defendant in the Nebraska Grain Case (State of Nebraska vs. the Texas and Midwestern Railway, et al.), September, 1881. Appointed Consul at Venice by Chester Allan Arthur, October, 1881, amid further protests on the Senate floor. Traveled widely through Europe, 1881–84. Rumored to have been close to the Prince of Wales. Children: Albert, b. London, 1882; Humility, b. London, 1883; Tunis, b. Berlin, 1883; Edgar,

b. aboard White Star liner *Carithnia,* two days out of Southampton, Sept., 1884.

" 'Following their return from Europe, the family took up residence in the Washington Avenue mansion (Oct., 1884). In March, 1885, Collingwood fled to South America one day before the collapse of the Far Western Trading Corporation (the "Montana Bubble"), leaving his associate, Lester A. Birdcoat, to bear the brunt of public censure and legal prosecution. (Note: Birdcoat, a man of high principles and unquestionable probity, was subsequently cleared by a high court. He died shortly thereafter.)

" 'Collingwood's whereabouts remained shrouded in mystery until May, 1887, when he appeared at the Conference of Buenos Aires as the official representative of the now defunct Republic of San Pedro, then under the control of the dictator Felipe Ryan. Appointed San Pedro's Minister of the Interior, June, 1887. Divorced his wife by decree (in absentia: Mrs. Collingwood naturally having remained in America), June, 1887. Married the following month (July) to Ysibel Rivas y Mondonza, thirteen-year-old daughter of a wealthy landowner, subsequently known as "La Piranha." Fled with his wife to Caracas during the revolution of 1887 (November 3–7), in which Ryan and the majority of his followers perished. Lived quietly in Caracas for five years, writing his memoirs. May have traveled to England sometime in 1894. Vanished from Caracas residence in March, 1895 (exact date uncertain). Reappeared April 15, 1895, at Cucuí, Brazil, with a band of sixty armed men, principally Americans secretly recruited in the dives of Seattle and San Francisco. They were accompanied by the enigmatic False Emperor of Brazil, João Antonio de Sousa e Bragança (the so-called João VII), whose claim to be the nephew of Dom Pedro II and legitimate heir to the Brazilian throne has largely been exploded but whose true identity remains uncertain. He may have been a Scotsman named McCormack. Whether he was a tool of Collingwood's or whether, as it was rumored, they were both pawns of British ambitions in the Orinoco Basin, are largely matters of conjecture. The truth will probably never be known.

" 'Raising the Imperial Standard at Cucuí, Collingwood moved toward Manaus, trapping a government column in a sharp bend of the Río Negro called "the Hinge of Fate" and virtually annihilating it. Town of Barcelos surrendered without a fight, May 2. On May 3, Sousa e Bragança telegraphed his famous list of demands to the government (the "Declaration of Barcelos") and publicly assumed the name João VII. On May 21 Collingwood's forces were swelled by a second contingent of adventurers that appeared at Cucuí as mysteriously as the first. June 17, audacious night attack on Manaus repulsed by garrison and inhabitants. June 18, second attack on Manaus fails. June 19, Cucuí occupied by Venezuelan troops, cutting Collingwood's line of supply and reinforcement. June 23, Barcelos abandoned in riverboats and escape attempted up the Río Branco. July 5, Catrimani captured. João calls for royalist insurrection ("Plea of Catrimani," July 7, 1895). Catrimani abandoned, July 10. Failure of northern breakout, July 18, in Maxim gun ambush of the boats by Bôa Vista garrison. Collingwood divided his forces the following day and returned to Catrimani with the wounded and fever-stricken. July 26, surrender of Darius Collingwood to Col. Alves of the Manaus garrison. July 30, Collingwood tried by a military court, condemned, executed by firing squad, and, over the strenuous protests of the American consul, buried without honors in an unmarked grave. The fate of "João VII" is unknown.

" 'On February 3, 1894, a band of four men, led by Collingwood's wife, the redoubtable La Piranha, reached Fort Napier, British Guiana, where they surrendered their weapons to the District Commissioner. (For details, see *With Collingwood in Brasil* by Archie [sic] Burritt, a survivor, whose book, while shedding absolutely no light on the mysteries surrounding the episode, gives a gripping and truly harrowing account of the overland trek of the last contingent of the so-called Imperial Brazilian Liberation Army. It would perhaps be more accurately entitled *With Mrs. Collingwood in Brasil.* New York, 1901.) The second Mrs. Collingwood subsequently remarried and at the moment of this writing lives in Tampa, Florida. She has four children and two grandchildren.

" 'Darius Collingwood's watch and Brazilian journal, together with his Civil War memorabilia, may be viewed at the Society's headquarters, 37 Dean Street, Brooklyn, on the fourth floor between the hours of noon and four p.m. Ring the bell.' "

5

"I wish to God you'd stop harping on it," said Lowell's wife, standing in the middle of what had been Henry's room. She had a broom in one hand, and the other was holding a crumbling shoebox filled with what appeared to be petrified human shit. She took it over to the barrel in the middle of the floor and dropped it in. The barrel was filled with all manner of things that Henry had left behind, very few of them identifiable and all of them worthless. "Old what's-his-name only lived here for a couple of months. Henry lived here longer than that."

"Six months," said Lowell, peeling off another huge patch of linoleum from the floor. It was more brittle and somewhat cleaner than the last layer, and he broke it into pieces before throwing it into the barrel. Lowell couldn't guess how many more layers there were, each one cleaner than the last; they seemed to go down for inches more. Henry's layer, the top one, hadn't even been a layer, properly speaking; it was a sort of jigsaw puzzle of chunks and strips and squares, usually of linoleum but almost never of the same pattern, frequently filled in with some alien substance like burlap or bathroom tile, all of it haphazardly affixed to the floor with something that appeared to be a mixture of roofing tar and vomit. Lowell had been forced to

wear a handkerchief soaked in camphor over his nose as he
pulled it up; he nearly suffocated, but it really cleaned out his
sinuses. When he finally got the first layer pulled up, he put it in
the garbage cans. The garbage men refused to take it. Next he
tried to burn it in the backyard, but the stench was so horrible
that he extinguished the fire even before the police and firemen
arrived and served him with various summonses. It was still out
there now, with a big charred pit in the middle of it where the
fire had been, like some kind of squat volcano. He thought
maybe he would bury it or something one of these days, but he
had so many other problems that he never got around to it. He
gazed at it from time to time from one of the rear windows.

"Six months," he said. "October to March. I don't think I'm
harping on it. I think it's interesting. Don't you think it's interesting?"

"No," said his wife. "I don't."

"Bankrupt at nineteen. A colonel at twenty-three. A part of
history?"

"Who cares?" said his wife.

Lowell shrugged pleasantly and went about his work. He had
a long row to hoe, but he was industriously hoeing it. His marriage was a shambles and the house was a mess beyond his wild-
est dreams, but the odd thing was that, though surrounded by
wreckage, he felt he was actually getting somewhere for the first
time in his life. Where exactly he was getting or what he would
do when he got there were matters for conjecture, but there
could be little doubt that he was on his way at last. He was
struggling against forces and odds. He was pulling a load. He
was thinking. He was actually thinking. Using his brain, he was
attacking problems that were not only relatively coherent but in
some cases capable of rational achievement. He'd actually
solved some of them. It was amazing, looking back, to realize
how little of his life he'd spent thinking, especially when you
contrasted it with all the things he was doing now. Meanwhile,

of course, his marriage was going down the drain. He supposed
that was bad, but he didn't think about it much, one way or the
other. He just stood there and watched it go. It made him feel a
little strange; not unhappy, exactly, but strange.

The old dim pleasantness had departed from their dealings as
completely as if there'd never been any to begin with, but a peculiar side effect of this development was that Lowell found
himself interested in his wife's personality. He couldn't remember a time when he'd been so interested in it, not even in college, when what had principally interested him had been her
ass, if the truth had to be told, although he had also concerned
himself with her personality at least to the extent of finding out
whether she had a good one or a bad one. He'd decided that
she had a good one. Since then he'd thought about it very little
except on the infrequent occasions when something seemed to
go awry with it, but it always seemed to get fixed pretty
quickly, and then it was all okay again, like a table whose wob-
ble had been repaired. The rest of the time it just sort of stood
there, a good and serviceable object whose height, width,
length, shape, color, and approximate density were assumed to
be known. You could always count on it; it was exactly the same
when you returned as it was when you left, never mind those
phone calls to her mother and the midnight crying fits in the
bathroom. It was a good little piece of furniture. For nine years
Lowell had been married to a table.

The true villain, he realized now, was not his wife, and no
doubt she would be glad to hear it, if only she would allow
Lowell to talk about it one of these days; he would have to
choose his words carefully. The true villain wasn't Lowell, either, although his part in the affair could scarcely be described
as distinguished. The real villain was their marriage. Lowell
saw it all now. Starting as a contract haphazardly entered into,
their marriage gradually evolved into a kind of conspiracy to
protect Lowell and his wife from the unpleasant shocks of what

passed with other people as normal life. Soon it became bigger than both of them; it absorbed and simultaneously diminished them to the point that, finally, they lived almost exclusively on its terms, like citizens who have inadvertently voted a tyrant into office. It defined their roles in relation to each other, which meant that it also defined in large measure the roles they would play in relation to the world even when they were apart, preventing them from getting themselves into situations where outside forces might come into play and make them excited or discontent or something. They weren't married to each other, and it was doubtful if they ever had been, at least for long; they were married to their marriage. It was a wonderful thing. It was the most sensible arrangement imaginable. So long as you abided by its terms and never questioned its premises, all paths were made smooth and all questions were answered, principally because you never tried to go anyplace that was hard to get to and you never asked any questions if you knew what was good for you. In the end you just sort of withered away like the state. No wonder they never had any children.

Now Lowell had kicked over the whole structure with a single rash, intemperate, and totally uncharacteristic act, and their marriage no longer stood between them. A fat lot of good it did him. His wife just sort of stood there, looking bewildered and a little sad. Sometimes she got cross, but most of the time she just moped around and did as she was told. There was no fight in her at all, and he could not seem to get through, no matter how hard he tried. He didn't want his wife to mope and do what she was told. He wasn't exactly sure what he did want, but that sure wasn't it. He brooded about it a lot as he stood in one or the other rear window and gazed out at his linoleum volcano, but nothing useful occurred to him, which only made him brood more.

At least one problem in his life was solved. He no longer had to worry about what to do with his time. He no longer had enough of it. Every evening he came straight over to Brooklyn from the office, changed his clothes, and started right to work, demolishing partitions and cardboard closets, ripping extension cords from the baseboards, obliterating all the fragile artifices of his impoverished predecessors with a fine unholy glee. By special arrangement with Mr. Grossman, he was allowed to commence his work of destruction before the final closing. "Yeah, go ahead," said Mr. Grossman over the phone. "Bust up anything you like, none of it's worth a shit anyway. Might persuade some of them holdouts to leave. Save us a little money, know what I mean?"

Lowell did not know what he meant, and it disturbed him that he'd never met Mr. Grossman face to face, but he was still pleased to have permission. He got together his tools and went right over.

It appeared that everybody was a holdout. No one was preparing to move. Henry wanted his two thousand dollars and Mrs. Blouse didn't seem to understand what was expected of her, but the motives of the others remained obscure, at least to Lowell. He could understand how poverty and lack of education drove people to live in such accommodations, but he simply couldn't conceive of them getting so attached to their miserable rooms that they would refuse to leave if someone asked them nicely. Rationally he could understand it—or at least, he could understand the literature about it—but he had no capacity for imagining it; and although he kept explaining over and over to himself that there were a lot of good reasons why these ignorant, deprived people refused to abandon their squalid habitations, in actual practice he went ahead and helped kick them out with scarcely a second thought. The people had to go just the same as the partitions before Lowell could start putting things back the way they belonged, and that was that. They were probably just after money anyway, just like Mr. Grossman said. Lowell was not pleased to discover that he agreed about something with Mr. Grossman, although that didn't make him change his mind. On the phone Mr. Grossman had the kind of voice that made you feel he was standing too close to you, holding on to some part of your clothing. Maybe Lowell would feel differently about him if only he could meet him. At least, maybe he would feel better about agreeing with him. He hated people who stood too close to him and held on to his clothing, and he had always taken pains to avoid them.

Henry refused, incoherently but emphatically, to help Lowell in any way, attempted to order him from the house, threatened to call the police, and finally went into his room and slammed the door. Left to his own devices, Lowell wandered upstairs with his brand-new box of tools. He poked around here and there until he finally found an empty room. Its door hung open, and dust balls lay thickly on the floor; apparently no one had lived in it for a long time. It was difficult for Lowell to imagine anyone living there at all. It was the kind of room where normal people kept their empty cardboard boxes: low, narrow, badly lighted, and curiously shaped, serving no purpose in the overall plan of the house except to make the other rooms on the floor come out square. Along one wall, on an iron bedframe of such brutal massiveness that it seemed intended to support some kind of heavy machinery, lay a filthy, misshapen mattress that looked as though someone had been tortured to death on it. Against the opposite wall were a metal closet and a water-stained cardboard bureau. Lowell decided to start with the bureau because it looked easy to crush. First he changed into his work clothes, doing so without sitting down or touching the walls with any part of his body. It was a procedure that necessitated a great deal of hopping around, first on one foot, then the other, and pretty soon someone began to bang on the ceiling of the room below with a broomstick, which made Lowell self-conscious but did not make him stop. After all, he owned the place, or at least he would soon. He only hoped that nobody would come in and try to talk to him. Even if they spoke English, it was like a foreign language, and he had a feeling that he didn't want to hear anything they might want to tell him.

He didn't notice when the banging stopped, but it had definitely ceased by the time he'd emptied the old rags out of the bureau drawers and had stamped and kicked the bureau itself into flinders. He made bundles of the pieces and tied them up neatly with twine. The metal closet contained a single suit, which looked like a refugee from Mrs. Blouse's collection in the basement. Lowell wadded it together with the rags from the drawers and rolled them up in the mattress. Next he dismantled the immense bedframe and carried it down to the garbage piece by piece. Then he carried down the metal closet with the mattress inside it, being extremely careful neither to fall to his death nor to make any more marks on the walls. When he returned to the room for his bundles of cardboard, he found a Negro man standing in the doorway. He was about sixty years old and stooping in a way that gave the impression that his hands were too heavy for his body. His face was hard to read.

"Can I do something for you?" asked Lowell.

"My furniture," said the man tonelessly.

"Your furniture?"

"My good suit of clothes," said the man, staring into the room. "My underwear."

Though Lowell now understood what had happened, he was understandably reluctant to comment on the situation. He had a feeling the old man was about to become either unpleasant or boring, and he wished he could think of some way to get rid of him both swiftly and quietly. There did not seem to be such a way. "The door was open," he remarked gruffly, assuming an expression that he hoped would intimidate the old man without making him mad. "You'll find your property downstairs by the garbage cans."

"My bed," said the old man like Rachel reciting the names of her children. "My cabnit. My chester draws."

"They're all downstairs," repeated Lowell in a loud, firm voice. "They're downstairs by the garbage cans. Help yourself."

"Downstairs. By the garbage cans."

"That's right," said Lowell. "Now, if you'll excuse me."

The old man stood there as though rooted to the spot. Lowell waited for him to ask for money or have a fit, but nothing happened. Lowell thought about going back to work on the room, but somehow he didn't think he could do it with the old man watching him like that. He was pretty sure he couldn't do it. He knew he couldn't do it. "Listen," he heard himself saying, "I'll give you a break." He wondered why he'd said that. He didn't have anything special in mind, and he found himself looking at the old man for some kind of clue as to the nature of the break he ought to give him.

"That's okay," said the old man in a sad but soothing voice. "Don't you go worrying about me. I can always sleep down at the mental hospital if nothing else comes up. That's where I work at, the mental hospital. I expect they'll let me have one of the empty beds. They do that sometimes."

Lowell scarcely knew how to reply. "That's nice of them," he said lamely.

"I got a good job there," said the old man, motionless as a rock, his huge hands still hanging limply at his sides. "Pays good money. Ain't much to do. Just fucking the dog. That's all, just fucking the dog. Food's good too. We eats just what the crazy people do. They eats good."

Fidgeting and embarrassed, Lowell wondered how long it would go on, but he suspected that the old man was capable of standing there, droning on and on like a radio recounting the bleak details of some utterly crushing national disaster, much longer than Lowell was prepared to wait for him to stop. He pictured himself grabbing the old fellow by the shoulders and trundling him down the stairs like another piece of furniture, but he didn't think he could really bring himself to do that. The old man probably wouldn't let him, anyway. He decided to go and look in his toolbox in hopes that it would distract him or give him a good idea; he couldn't imagine what. He bent over it and threw back the lid.

"See you around," said the old man suddenly. He was gone like a shot, leaving Lowell to stare after him with some surprise and a great deal of relief. He guessed he'd never figure out these people, but then he turned back to his toolbox and experienced a moment of insight.

The old man had stolen his brand-new drill, his brand-new drill that he hadn't even used yet. Lowell hadn't even taken it out of its plastic case. The old man had stolen the plastic case, too. Nothing else was missing, and the old man had left the toolbox a good deal tidier than he'd found it. Lowell stared into the box mutely for some seconds. He wished he'd gotten to use his new drill at least once. He'd really been looking forward to it. Then he closed the toolbox and carefully locked it and hurried after the thief, knowing in his heart that he was already too late. He kind of hoped so; he had no idea what he would do if he caught him, and he was pretty sure there would be a scene.

To Lowell's secret relief, the old man had vanished. There was no one in the hall (at least, there was no one in the hall in front of him; behind him, doors were opening like a kind of wake), and out in the street everyone was a Negro. A few of them were skinny old men, but it was impossible to tell if one of them had stolen anything. Lowell had never believed that every Negro of a certain physical type looked like every other Negro of the same type, but he was willing to concede the point now; they all sure looked alike to him. One of them might even be the thief, for all he could tell. He supposed he could pick one at random. He thought about it for a minute, and then he decided not to. One thing continued to bother him: he could not for the life of him imagine how the old man had managed to hide the damn thing on his body. It was as big as a bowling ball, and you would think that at least there would be a bulge or something.

He returned to the little room, preceded by the sound of gently closing doors. They were always just ahead of him, like soft drum messages pacing an explorer through the jungle. He entered the front hall, and all the doors on the first landing closed; he reached the first landing, and all the doors on the second landing closed; he reached the second landing, and all the doors on the top floor closed. It was sort of like being in a haunted house, except that the house wasn't haunted, it was inhabited; that was the whole trouble. For all he knew, the thief might be hiding in one of these very rooms, plastered against the wall with every sense alert, like a partisan sweating out a Gestapo search. Lowell might be passing the very door even now. Big deal. He reached the empty room and sat down on the sill, and for a while nothing moved in the entire house. Then a door opened far below, someone spoke, and a child raced down the stairs, rattling a stick against the spindles of the banister. Gradually, at first with a kind of wariness and then with increasing confidence, the house came back to life and went about its business. Lowell sat on the sill a while longer, but now that he'd demolished all the furniture in the room and thrown the clothing in the street, there was really nothing left for him to do today. He hauled the bundles of broken bureau downstairs, and then he returned to the room and changed his clothes and took his toolbox and went home.

For some reason that Lowell didn't understand and that no one seemed able to explain, the accidental eviction of the old man had the same effect on the other tenants as the removal of a keystone. Soon everyone in the building was on the move. The elderly Puerto Rican couple were the first to go, nodding and smiling and refusing to be helped as they carried their furniture and possessions out to a U-Haul trailer that had miraculously appeared at the curb, apparently without benefit of car. Lowell put on his work clothes and watched them from the window of the old man's room, scarcely able to believe the stupendous burdens they were able to carry, or the boundless, wizened energy with which they scurried back and forth, mattresses and chairs held aloft, occasionally pausing at the curb to chat with a passing acquaintance. Lowell was glad that they apparently bore him no ill will. Once they caught sight of him in the window and waved. Lowell waved right back. Suffused with benevolence, he stood there and watched as they stole the stove and refrigerator from their apartment and heroically manhandled them into the trailer; it was no skin off his nose, and they were welcome to whatever they could take, provided it wasn't something he wanted. He wondered if, when they were finished loading, the old man would simply pick up the tongue of the U-Haul and trot off down the street with his ton of furniture and plunder like some kind of superhuman Spanish coolie; nothing seemed impossible. Presently a rust-splotched and fender-crumpled 1959 Chevrolet raced dangerously up the street, squealed to a halt in front of the house, screeched back and forth a couple of times with a smell of burning rubber, and eventually, with a good deal of horn blowing and happy shouting, took up a towing position of sorts at the head of the trailer. The doors opened and a half-dozen young men spilled out, all of them more or less drunk and apparently members of the same family. The trailer was hitched up with much *machismo* and to-do, the old people were somehow squeezed into the car, and they all roared off to wherever they were going, shouting and laughing, the tappets clattering, and a cloud of blue smoke rising in the air. Lowell heartily wished them well. He wondered who would come to help him move when the time came. He imagined Leo coming to help and getting in the way, carrying a pair of salt shakers and unable to figure out how to open the elevator door without putting one of them down on the floor. The image made Lowell feel sorry for himself, but not very much; anybody who had a father-in-law like Leo was bound to feel sorry for himself whenever the fact was called to his attention, and he'd gotten used to it over the years. It was too bad that he didn't have a big drunk Spanish family at a time like this, but he supposed you couldn't have everything.

The vacated apartment was empty and tidy if not very clean, and they had been careful about turning off the gas before removing the stove. Unlike many apartments, including Lowell's, the place looked like it had really been lived in by people, and he felt a little reluctant to start working on it so soon after they'd left; it still felt faintly inhabited. Lowell hesitated, but he reminded himself that he was there to do a job, not ponder, and presently he began his work of destruction. For a while it was like he was smashing someone else's dishes for no good reason, but soon he made enough of a mess that he didn't feel that way anymore.

The other tenants moved out shortly thereafter, although neither as amiably nor as colorfully. They moved out like people being evicted from their homes, sluggishly, resentfully, and destructively, smashing holes in the walls, scarring the hallway with their furniture, breaking the banister in two places, knocking out a couple of windows, stealing the brass pipes from the plumbing, and breaking off their keys inside the locks so that it was impossible to get into the rooms without taking off the doors. There was quite a little fad of key breaking, and sometimes Lowell wasn't able to get the pins out of the hinges and was forced to kick a door in, shivering the frame often knocking out a panel. He complained about it to Mr. Grossman, who told him that it was no goddamn problem of his in such a way that Lowell got a good idea of what it must be like to rent an apartment from him.

Every time someone moved out, Henry emerged from his

room and watched them silently with his arms folded, like the general of a defeated army brooding over its retreat. One day, when all the rooms upstairs were empty, he went too. Lowell came back from work one day and he was gone, leaving his enormous collection of junk and offal behind, as if he'd been collecting it all these years for no other purpose than to give Lowell a hard time getting rid of it. A few days later Mrs. Blouse wandered upstairs to visit somebody, found nobody but Lowell, looked around at the heaps of rubble with the same expression she always had, and moved out the following afternoon. As for the crazy old white man and the silent Negro with no shoes, Lowell never did find out what became of them. It was a long time before he could bring himself to enter their rooms, but when he did, he found no sign of either of them except for a crumpled, dusty Pall Mall pack under one of the beds.

Nor did he ever get to see Mr. Grossman, who was represented at the closing by a lawyer of such intimidating respectability that he made Lowell feel like some kind of meek crook whenever he spoke to him. Sometimes Lowell wondered if Mr. Grossman existed at all, if he wasn't the creation of real-estate interests, doing voice imitations over the phone in order to collect rents and fight off city agencies and sell houses to people like Lowell. Anything seemed possible, even probable. Sitting there in the lawyer's office above Court Street with sleet rattling on the windows, money changing hands, and a great deal of incomprehensible but threatening nonsense going on all around him, he felt like a mental defective on trial for rape and witchcraft: he couldn't understand a word of it, but he had the distinct feeling that it would not end well. Papers were produced and signed; Lowell wrote checks, and they were taken from him; men conferred in glum, hushed voices with their heads close together, continually referring to Lowell as "him."

"What's going on now?" he asked his lawyer at one point when things seemed held up. He hadn't written a check or signed a paper in five minutes, and the men at the other end of the table were involved in a lengthy intramural discussion that required them to pass a great many documents back and forth, indicating passages to each other with the ends of pencils.

"I don't know," said Lowell's lawyer, turning up his palms in a gesture of helpless ignorance. He was a weak little man who was some kind of relative of Leo's. Lowell had hired him for want of a better idea, never having needed a lawyer before and therefore knowing none. He would have dismissed him long before now, but the man inspired his pity, and besides, he knew he would never hear the end of it from Leo if he did. "I think it's some bank business," the lawyer suggested after a moment, not with much confidence. "They usually do bank business about this time. I think that's what it must be. Bank business." He began to rifle frantically through his briefcase as though the answer might be found there if only he could lay hands on it, meanwhile throwing Lowell nervous, ingratiating glances over the tops of his glasses. "Heh, heh," he said.

Lowell looked out the window. The sleet was coming down worse than ever.

Eventually matters got unstuck at the far end of the table, no thanks to Lowell's lawyer, and the affair ground on to its conclusion. Lowell wrote more checks and signed more papers.

"That's the city man," whispered Lowell's lawyer, indicating a person who had just come into the room and seated himself without taking off his hat. A mumble of greeting flowed around the table. The city man handed the bank man a document, and the bank man handed it to Mr. Grossman's lawyer, who studied it. Lowell noticed that nobody ever seemed to hand his lawyer anything. "You have to give him five dollars," whispered his lawyer.

"Who?"

"Shh. The city man. You have to give him five dollars. Get it ready."

"Why do I have to do that? Suppose I don't have five dollars? Can I write him a check?"

Lowell's lawyer signaled frantically for him to lower his voice and met his last suggestion with a look of horror. "No! No!" he whispered hoarsely. "You don't understand. Just give him the five dollars and forget about it."

"You mean this is a bribe?"

Silence fell, and everyone seemed to stop moving for a second. No one looked at Lowell. The city man was still wearing his hat. Another second passed, and then, as though a spell had been lifted, they all went back to doing whatever they'd been doing when Lowell spoke, just as if he hadn't spoken at all.

"I'm not paying any bribe," he whispered to his lawyer, indignant but also a little daunted. "It's against everything I believe in. I've never paid a bribe in my life."

Every time Lowell uttered the word "bribe," his lawyer winced visibly, as though Lowell was flicking fingers at his face. "Mr. Lake," he whispered. "Mr. Lake, please, please, you don't understand. This is a very sensitive topic. Listen, if you like, I'll slip him the money myself. It's not usual, but I'm sure he'll understand. The usual thing is for the buyer to slip him the money."

Lowell looked at him stonily. "What will happen if I don't give it to him?"

"People always give it to him. It's part of buying a house. He always gets it. I've never known a time when he didn't get it. It's usual."

"Are you trying to tell me you don't know what will happen if I don't give him his five dollars? Is that what you're trying to tell me?"

"I'll give it to him myself," pleaded the lawyer, casting desperate looks toward the other end of the table. "Please, out of my own pocket I'll give it to him. My own money. Just stop talking about it. Please just stop talking about it. Please?" He dug out his wallet and looked into it miserably.

"Okay," said Lowell. "I'll pay him."

His lawyer sort of collapsed a little with relief and swiftly put his wallet away. "You'd better get it ready now," he told Lowell. "Any minute now he'll come over here to shake your hand."

"Get it ready? What do you mean, get it ready? I'll give it to him when he gets here."

"No no no no no no no," begged the lawyer. "Please. There's a way these things are done, a way. They're always done that way, and you have to do it, otherwise it won't be right and everything will be wrong. You have to fold the money up in a little pellet and slip it to him under the table. That's what you have to do, you have to fold it up. Hurry, hurry, he'll be here in a minute. Oh, God."

"Why do I have to fold it up? Doesn't everybody know about it?"

"Everybody knows about it, everybody knows about it. You just have to do it that way, don't ask me why. Just do it." The lawyer gave a little whimper.

Pondering the fact that he was not only going to have to bribe a city official but do so in secret although everybody at the table knew he was doing it and perhaps would not sell him his house if he didn't, Lowell slowly drew out his wallet and removed a five-dollar bill. He supposed it was some kind of a comment on American culture and morals, but for the time being he wasn't worrying so much about morality as he was about whether or not he was doing something dumb. Just because he'd never paid a bribe before didn't mean it wasn't procedural, he supposed; he'd never bought a rooming house before, either. Suddenly he found himself wondering if people like him did indeed ever buy rooming houses. What if he was the first one? He hadn't even checked. The thought didn't make him feel any smarter, and he gazed dully at the money in his hand.

"Hurry, hurry!" begged his lawyer. "They're shaking hands. Fold it up!"

The city man was getting to his feet, chuckling conspiratorially with the bank man and Mr. Grossman's lawyer. Lowell knew instinctively that the city man wouldn't chuckle with him or his lawyer; they weren't the kind of people city men chuckled with. This knowledge made him feel small and unhappy. He folded up the five-dollar bill.

"Fold it up more!" whispered his lawyer. "Fold it up smaller! Get it out of sight, get it out of sight! Here he comes!"

Considerably unnerved by his lawyer's frantic excitement, Lowell rose to greet his bribee. He was surprised to discover that he was nearly a foot taller, even when you counted the hat. For some reason, this discovery didn't make him feel any better; it only made him feel thin. The city man was smiling tightly and with confidence, his eyes twinkling with amused contempt. Lowell knew he would never be able to smile like that, not even if he were to practice in front of the mirror for the rest of his life. There were no tight smiles in him at all. He wished that at least he'd learned to ride a horse when he was younger. He didn't know why, but somehow he thought it might have made him feel better at moments like this.

"Well, Mr. Lake," said the city man, sticking out his hand. Lowell looked at it without comprehension. From what his lawyer had said, he was pretty sure he wasn't supposed to put the money in it, but for the life of him he couldn't think of anything else to do. He'd been thinking so hard about doing one thing that he simply wasn't equipped to think about doing another, although he was aware that the room had fallen strangely silent.

"Shake his hand, shake his hand!" whispered his lawyer in a squeaking voice that was apparently close to tears. "For God's sake, shake his hand!"

"Oh," said Lowell. He shook the city man's hand. "How do you do?" he asked.

The city man, still smiling tightly, looked at him steadily. "Pretty well," he said. "How are you?"

"Oh," said Lowell, "just fine." He had the bribe pellet in his other hand, but he'd been given no instructions beyond "slip it to him," and he couldn't figure out how to do it. Maybe there was a special time, or maybe they had to do something else first, who knew? He continued to shake the city man's hand, awaiting developments, although he'd already shaken the city man's hand longer than he'd ever shaken anybody's hand except for his Aunt Maudie's, who was crazy as a bedbug and occasionally had to be gently pried loose from someone she'd latched on to.

"Give it to him!" croaked Lowell's lawyer in a voice that must have been audible to everyone in the room. He poked Lowell's bribe hand to emphasize his point. "Why don't you give it to him?"

Wishing that he knew what he was doing, Lowell started to sort of sidle the bribe across the space between himself and the city man, but his muscles were all tensed up and he found it hard to move with either accuracy or purpose. His lawyer gave him another punch in the arm, and the bribe fell from his lifeless fingers. "Oh, my God," said his lawyer, burying his head in his hands.

"I think you dropped something," said the city man. "Here, I'll get it for you if you'll let go of my hand for a second." Feeling like a mechanical toy, Lowell forced himself to stop shaking the city man's hand. The city man bent over and searched the floor. "Nope," he said. "I guess you didn't drop nothing after all."

"Huh?" said Lowell.

"Nope," said the city man, straightening up. "If there was anything down there, it's gone now. Forget about it." He slapped, then squeezed Lowell's shoulder. "It gets easier after the first time, kid. See you around." He told the others he would see them around too. Mr. Grossman's lawyer and the bank man nodded gravely. Lowell's lawyer took a pill.

The rest did not take long. Everyone sat around for a second as though in silent prayer, and then there was a good deal of throat clearing and paper shuffling, and Lowell was asked to write another check. In a few minutes he was handed his deed. He'd been handed so many things in the last few hours that it was a while before he realized what he was holding, and then it didn't seem like much.

"Well," said his lawyer in a voice weak from strain, "that wasn't so bad, was it?" He mopped his face and watched Lowell write out a check for his fee with a queer expression of anxious yearning, like someone who was trying to stop smoking watching another person light up a cigarette. "Whoo," he said when Lowell handed him the check. "Oh, boy, what a day. I swear to God, no more favors for the family. I swear this is the last time, positively."

"You got paid," said Lowell.

"That's not it," said the lawyer, picking up his briefcase. "You don't understand."

"How do you feel?" asked the bank man, peering at Lowell with the kind of mixture of sharpness and anxiety that is usually reserved for prostrate accident victims and women who have just had a baby. "Everything okay?"

"Just fine," said Lowell.

"Congratulations," said Mr. Grossman's lawyer in the perfunctory manner of a grocer asking a shoplifter if he can help him.

Lowell told them good-bye. He put on his hat and coat and went home. His wife was waiting for him in the living room, and although it was only three o'clock in the afternoon it was evident that she was pretty drunk. She was sitting in the Eames chair, watching the sleet. "Aruba," she said when Lowell entered.

"Well," said Lowell in a tone of forced good cheer, "we own a house."

"I don't own any house," said his wife. "It belongs to you and old Cyrus What's-his-name. Leave me out of it."

"Darius," said Lowell. "Darius Collingwood."

"I could have been in Jamaica by now," said his wife.

"At least you could get his name right. You're only trying to get at me. I can tell. Otherwise I wouldn't care. It's the principle of the thing."

"Sure," said his wife. "That's right."

"You're goading me again," said Lowell, looking around for the bottle and mixer. He found them in the kitchen and made himself a drink. "Darius Collingwood has nothing to do with it. I mean, of course Darius Collingwood has something to do with it, but not the way you think he has. He has something to do with it in another way."

"Seven thousand dollars," said his wife. She watched the sleet. "Cyprus."

"Darius," said Lowell automatically.

"I didn't say Cyrus," said his wife. "I said Cyprus. Not Cyrus. Cyprus is a place. Cyprus is real."

"Where's your glass? I'll make you another drink."

"I don't have a glass," said his wife. She got up suddenly and left the room. Lowell looked around after she was gone, but it was true: she hadn't had a glass. If she hadn't had a glass, she couldn't have been drinking. Lowell knew his wife wouldn't have drunk out of the bottle. But if she hadn't been drinking, what had she been doing? It did not take Lowell very long to hit upon that one, although he was not very pleased with it when he got it. She'd been crying. She cried so seldom that he'd almost forgotten what she looked like when she did, and that was why he'd assumed that she was drunk. The two states did not manifest themselves in dissimilar ways. Lowell made himself another drink. Soon he had a third one, and presently it was possible to forget about the whole thing until he went to bed. His wife did not return, and he had leftovers for supper. When he finally joined her, she was pretending to be asleep. Lowell could tell that she was pretending—under the sheet her body was as rigid as a fencepost, and her eyes were squinched tightly shut as though against the glare of a powerful light—but he was a good fellow about it and pretended not to know that she was pretending. Shortly thereafter, without anything further having developed, he drifted off himself and slept soundly all night long.

Fortunately he had nothing resembling a plan, so he didn't have to worry about things not working out according to it. He simply let them happen, unable to make up his mind whether he was losing his judgment or finally developing some perspective. He didn't have much time to brood about the matter; for the first time in years so many things were happening to him that he actually forgot some of them. Even his hours at the office were full, phoning architects and contractors, making appointments to interview them, studying the building code, and reading up on the history of Brooklyn. He bought a half-dozen books full of helpful tips for the home handyman and went through them thoroughly, taking notes and making lists, the majority of which he misplaced. He was amazed at how little he knew about the simplest things. He didn't even know how to fix a leaky faucet. For years he'd listened to jokes about people who were so dumb that they didn't know how to fix a leaky faucet, but it had never occurred to him before that he was one of them; there were a dozen leaky faucets in his house and he couldn't have fixed them if his life depended on it. He didn't even know how to begin.

Lunches with Crawford and trips to McSorley's with Balmer soon became things of the past; a slice of pizza was his portion at noon as he hastened from hardware store to hardware store, trying out tools and being sold things that his books said he ought to have. It was great fun. In the evening he took his day's purchases over to Brooklyn and tried them right out, or else he carefully put them aside in his apartment until the time came to put them to work; in some cases the opportunity never came, and there were one or two exotic-looking tools whose exact functions he actually forgot, not that he cared.

He was suddenly famous. In a building where he had labored five days a week for nine years without a single person asking him what he did, he suddenly found himself cloaked in a highly conspicuous new identity: he became known as the Guy Who Moved to Bedford-Stuyvesant. He tried to persuade them that he hadn't moved yet and that it wasn't Bedford-Stuyvesant, but nobody listened to him, and he thought that it was symptomatic of the feeble grip he'd taken on the memories and imaginations of his colleagues over the years that nobody ever referred to him as the Managing Editor Who Moved to Bedford-Stuyvesant. He found it difficult to care.

As for his wife, she left him.

She left him at the end of the second week and went to her mother's. During the two weeks she had steadfastly refused to join Lowell at the house, not even to keep him company, and they even stopped having supper together. Lowell usually picked up a ham sandwich at the bodega on Greene Avenue and washed it down with beer; he had no idea what his wife ate, or where. They continued to eat breakfast together, after a fashion: they sat at the same table and devoured food, with the radio tuned to WNCN. It was a curious situation, but it seemed perfectly natural to Lowell at the time. He spent his nights dreaming of rooms and hammers, and he woke up full of plans. During breakfast he thought about them. Occasionally his wife made attempts at conversation, but he couldn't keep his mind on what she was saying, and after a few minutes she just sort of ran down for want of response. In fact, he more or less forgot about her for long periods of time, and when he came home one night and found the bed empty and unslept in, there was a moment when he couldn't remember whether she'd been in it last night, either. Anyway, the point was that she wasn't in it now. Her clothes were also gone, as were her cosmetics. Lowell wasn't sure what he ought to do about it. At least he knew that you didn't call the police. You only did that when people were missing, and his wife wasn't missing, she was only gone. Lowell supposed he ought to search for a note; on television they always left a note when they walked out on you or killed themselves. He looked around the room for a while, but when he found no trace of one he decided to go make himself a cup of coffee instead. He wondered if it was significant that he always ended up in the kitchen when there was a crisis in his life.

The note was propped up against the coffeepot; Lowell reflected that another woman, with another kind of husband, might have rolled it up and put it in the barrel of the family gun. On the whole, he supposed he would rather be a coffee drinker, although he doubted that it made much difference in the long run.

"I have gone to my mother's," the note said simply, exactly like the little missives they used to leave for each other when they went down to the newsstand or the delicatessen when the other one wasn't home. For a moment the laconic, familiar wording made him think that it was all a mistake that she'd only gone for the evening, at most the night, and would be back soon. Then he remembered that she'd taken all her clothes, and his little spark of hope went out like a light.

When his coffee was ready, he took the cup to the phone and dialed his mother-in-law's number. His mother-in-law answered. "Is my wife there?" he asked.

"That depends," replied his mother-in-law in a voice so flat that it had lost all trace of an accent.

"On what?"

"On who you are," said his mother-in-law.

"Don't be ridiculous. You know very well who I am."

"Do I?"

"Stop playing games. This is Lowell, and I want to talk to my wife."

"Lowell who?"

Angry but not confused, Lowell opened his mouth to speak, not the rest of his own name, but hers; to utter it like a rebuke and at the same time remind her of the bond that existed between them, whether she liked it or not. His mouth remained open for some seconds, and then it closed on empty air. He didn't know her name. Maybe he'd known it once—he must have known it once, it wasn't possible that he hadn't known it once—but he sure didn't know it now. He didn't even know what letter it began with. It was a ridiculous situation, and partly his own fault, but this insight did not help him, at least not now. It probably wouldn't help him later, either. There was still one solution. He could call her "Mother." Lots of people did it. It would stop her in her tracks. He had only to utter the word, and victory was his. Unfortunately, the very thought of doing so stopped Lowell in his tracks, too. He was hoist by his own petard, and there was no way down. He sensed that he wasn't doing very well. Meanwhile, the silence lengthened.

"Listen," Lowell said at length with as much snap as he could muster, which was not as much as he would have liked, "I'm your son-in-law."

"Is that my fault?" asked his mother-in-law. "Believe me, if I had my way, you'd be nothing but another name in the phone book, but I ask you, who listens to a mother? What's a mother?"

With difficulty Lowell restrained himself from answering her question. "See here," he said.

"*I'll* tell you what a mother is!" his mother-in-law suddenly shouted. "A mother is someone who was *right!*"

"Are you going to let me speak to my wife or not?" demanded Lowell without putting the phone back to his ear.

"Don't take my word for it, ask any psychologist. Ask the biggest men they got. You know what they'll tell you?"

"Jesus Christ."

"LISTEN TO YOUR MOTHER!" his mother-in-law bellowed faintly as Lowell hung up the receiver. "That's what they'll tell you!"

Somehow, as he threw on his coat and made sure he had his keys, Lowell had the feeling that she hadn't been taking to him at all.

"Good evening, Mr. Stone," said the doorman as Lowell raced past him in the lobby. Uttering a strangled cry, Lowell hurled himself into the night.

It was incredibly dark. Something had happened to the street light again, and the sensation of emerging from the soulless fluorescent glare of the lobby into profound darkness was like suddenly being afflicted with blindness while drunk. For a moment Lowell was simply unable to think. He'd never imagined it could get this dark in the city; he couldn't even remember it getting this dark in the country. There was always a moon or something. Although he was standing on his own street, in front of a building where he'd lived for years, there was a moment when he couldn't remember where anything was, and all at once he thought: *My God, what am I doing here?* It was almost as though someone else had spoken in his ear. Then he lunged off in the direction of Broadway, with his hands held slightly before him, like a blind man who had lost his cane.

All the cabs on Broadway seemed to be going in the wrong direction. Lowell stood and watched them for a while, and then he decided he didn't want a cab tonight anyway; he was not in the mood to hear about what the mayor and the Negroes had done wrong this time, either separately or in collusion, although he supposed that in a certain sense a New York cab driver would be an appropriate prelude to the kind of visit he would no doubt have with his mother-in-law. It was like a 1930's urban movie gone mad, the same characters but a different script, a whole myth turned vicious and the actors believing every word. Lowell didn't want to be part of a movie. He never had. He stood and watched the cars go past for a few more minutes, and then he turned and walked toward the subway. If concrete took a print, he supposed he could have seen the path he'd made over the years from his building to the station. He'd be willing to bet that it wouldn't have been more than three feet wide, at the widest.

He waited on the platform for half an hour. When the train came it was full of smoke. He got on it anyway and rode to Brooklyn.

At night his in-laws' neighborhood looked like nobody really lived in it. Lights burned behind most of the windows, but they seemed to have been turned on only to create a realistic effect, like the lights in the windows of the little buildings on a model railroad. Lowell walked the streets without encountering another person, surrounded by a kind of bleak municipal tidiness where the sidewalks were cleaned and the shrubs trimmed and the grass cut by people who did it solely because it was their job and they got paid for it, like steelworkers. The cars were neatly parked at the curbs, the people were neatly tucked away in their rooms where they belonged, and there wasn't a speck of litter or a scrap of imagination anywhere to be seen. It made Lowell feel exceedingly strange and completely out of place as he raced along to rescue his wife, almost as if activities of that sort were not allowed here and he was going to get away with it only as long as someone didn't spot him.

"There's not a psychologist in the world who doesn't have a mother!" announced his mother-in-law when she opened the door of her apartment, momentarily stunning Lowell with a sense of warped time and insanely fixated purpose, although she was actually speaking over her shoulder to someone in the room behind her. "What do *you* want?" she demanded, suddenly turning on Lowell with suspicion but without much apparent recognition. It was like being addressed by a creature from another dimension, and for a moment Lowell was at a loss for words.

"I want my wife," he finally said, somewhat less forcefully than he would have liked.

"I think we talked about this before," said his mother-in-law.

"Never mind about that," said Lowell. "I know my wife is here and I want to see her."

Down the hall the door of another apartment opened a crack. Lowell was aware of being watched from a new quarter. It was not a good feeling. All his life he'd hated being conspicuous, and he would often deliberately lose an argument to avoid making a scene. He could scarcely do that now.

"Why don't we talk about it inside?" he suggested.

"We can talk about it out here," said his mother-in-law. "I'm not particular."

"I want to see my wife."

"So you said."

"Now, you listen to me . . ." said Lowell.

"There's no need to shout," said his mother-in-law, calmly folding her arms. Although almost two feet shorter than he was, she somehow gave the impression that she was looking down at him. No doubt this was what other men meant when they said they felt emasculated, but Lowell didn't feel emasculated, he felt as though he'd never had any balls and his mother-in-law had just found out about it. Down the hall another door opened and a man came out in his stocking feet and stood beside it nervously. He was about fifty, and he succeeded in neither looking directly at Lowell nor taking his eyes off him for a minute, a feat which gave him a severe facial tic. He conveyed the impression that he was ready to spring back into his apartment at the slightest provocation and place an anonymous call to the police, disguising his voice and putting a handkerchief over the receiver. Lowell found it hard not to hate him on sight, especially because the man's appearance only proved that he really had been shouting. "This is crazy," he heard himself saying. "Absolutely crazy."

"*This* is crazy?" said his mother-in-law in tones of mild amazement. "Am I hearing right? This is the opinion of the big-real-estate tycoon, the Zeckendorf of Bedford-Stuyvesant? *This* is crazy?"

"Mother," said Lowell's wife from somewhere in the apartment. Lowell was glad to hear her voice. It meant that something different might begin to happen—not necessarily something better, but different. It might even get him out of the hall.

"That's enough, Mother," said his wife. Her face, determined and cool, suddenly appeared over her mother's shoulder. She stared intently at her mother's profile. Her mother, meanwhile, continued to look hard at Lowell, who was gazing supplicatingly at his wife. They stood there like that for a long moment, their eyes not meeting and totally different expressions on their faces, a sort of invisible Möbius strip of conflicting but strangely congruent purposes. Then, without warning, his mother-in-law began to back into the room like a bank robber backing away from the scene of a crime, alert, slow, ready for anything, her eyes never leaving Lowell's face. Lowell followed right along, closing the door behind him. His wife and mother-in-law continued to move backward at a stately pace, until they reached the middle of the living room, where they stopped cold. Lowell's wife was looking at him now, too. God knew how long they might have stood there like that, each of them waiting for one of the others to make a move; if it had been up to Lowell, they would have stood there all night. He couldn't think of a thing to say. He was even afraid to open his mouth for fear that the movement would be seized upon as a pretext for something.

"What do you say, let's have some coffee?" broke in Leo's voice with a quavery, fearful brightness. Lowell looked over and discovered him sitting in his chair with his feet far apart and his hands resting limply in his lap, like he was paralyzed from the neck down and an unimaginative nurse had arranged his limbs for him. He looked inoffensive but not very lifelike, and there was a weak, hopeful little smile on his face. "How about it, what do you say? Coffee? Nice hot coffee for everyone? Maybe with a little cake?"

"If you want it, go make it," snapped his wife without taking her eyes off Lowell's face. Leo got up from his chair as though afraid his knees were about to suddenly bend backward like a flamingo's. He made a hesitant movement in the direction of the kitchen, looking around the room to see if one of the others would call him back. When no one did, he sort of sidled jerkily away, as though being manipulated by an unusually clumsy puppeteer.

"Maybe we ought to sit down," suggested Lowell when Leo was safely out of the room.

"Not on your life," said his mother-in-law. "You might decide to stay."

Lowell's wife went over to the window and stared out of it. Lowell looked at the narrow hunch of her shoulders, her bowed head, and he felt the last remnants of fight go right out of him. He hadn't known he had any left. "Will you come home with me?" he asked.

"Home!" cried his mother-in-law, causing Lowell to start violently. "Home? Where is this home you speak of? An apartment without a husband in it? A falling-down rooming house in Bedford-Stuyvesant? These are homes? And you could have married Ira Miller!" she continued, apparently to her daughter. "Look where Ira Miller is today. A Park Avenue practice and a home in Forest Hills, *that's* where Ira Miller is today! One of the biggest men in his field, and you had to turn him down. Who cares about a few pimples? Anyway, they cleared up. I ask you, would Ira Miller have moved to a slum? You should live so long, believe me. Ira Miller has spent his whole life moving *out* of slums. I forget if I mentioned that he lives in Forest Hills. Tapestry brick."

"Huh?" said Lowell, both stupidly and despite himself.

"Tapestry brick," repeated his mother-in-law. "His house is made of tapestry brick. Only yesterday his mother was showing me some pictures."

"Oh," said Lowell.

"Listen, you want to know something about that neighborhood where you bought a house with my daughter's trip to Antigua?"

"Do I have a choice?"

"Don't get smart. Our people moved out of that neighborhood twenty years ago. Twenty years!"

"I don't think your people were ever allowed to live there," Lowell heard himself say musingly. He hadn't known he was going to say anything like that. It just sort of came out of its own accord, like "soul food." It was followed by a lengthy silence during which Lowell and his mother-in-law looked at each other almost speculatively, like a pair of philosophers mulling the implications of a fresh concept.

"So," she crooned at last, smiling poisonously. "So, now it comes out. Finally, it comes out. How long it took. Nine years."

Lowell opened his mouth to speak, but once again closed it without uttering a sound. Denial would be useless, and explanation would only be viewed as a cover-up. His mother-in-law had made up her mind and planned her scene, and she could no more have been deflected from her purpose than fate. She'd lived for this moment for too many years. It occurred to Lowell that if he'd overheard their conversation as an outsider, he probably would have been on her side, but the thought did not make him feel very bad. He regarded the bag of shit that was about to fall on him with a kind of fatalism. He'd always known this was going to happen. He'd always known it was going to be his fault. He only hoped they could get it out of the way quickly so they could get on with their real business.

"Listen," said his mother-in-law, putting on a face of great compassion and understanding, "believe me, I know how it is. I mean, nine years with a nice Jewish girl, having a good home and eating the best of food, it gets bottled up. God knows why you married a nice Jewish girl, I don't. Don't say a word, I don't even want to think about it."

"I wasn't going to say anything," said Lowell.

"Nine years," his mother-in-law went on, ignoring him except as a kind of rhetorical device. "Nine years is a long time. Don't think you had me fooled for a minute. Many's the time I've said to my husband, 'Leo,' I said, 'it's got to come out. It's not natural it should take so long. Leo,' I said, 'Leo, mark my words,' I said. Look at it my way, it's fate. You can't fight it. It was bound to happen. Just tell me one thing before you walk out of my life forever. One thing."

"One thing?"

"What did I do wrong?" she almost whispered. "Where did I fail? How come my daughter married you? What happened to all those years of good upbringing, all those virtues I tried so hard to instill? Where was my mistake? Just tell me where my mistake was and I will go to my grave in peace."

"Shut up, Mother," said Lowell's wife.

Lowell had forgotten she was in the room. He had been hypnotized by the gentle, melodious tones of his mother-in-law's voice, totally engrossed in the unfolding of this latest chapter of his dreary and utterly predictable destiny, and she had completely slipped his mind. It was depressing to know everything that was going to happen to you in your life, but sometimes it could be pretty engrossing to watch an episode unfold, especially if there were unexpected variations in the script. Lowell had always assumed that his mother-in-law would rant and

scream when the time came, and the fact that she had chosen to
croon instead—crooning, in fact, the exact words he had always
imagined her shouting—made the whole thing a good deal more
interesting, like watching someone being tickled to death when
you had expected that he would be shot. On the other hand,
when it was over, he was just as dead. Lowell was especially
glad now that he'd bought his house. He didn't know a thing
that would happen to him in it.

"Come on," said his wife. "Let's get out of here." She stomped
over to the corner and began to wrestle with two enormous
Samsonite suitcases Lowell had never seen before. They were
brand-new.

"Where did you get those suitcases?" Lowell asked.

"On Fifth Avenue. I used the Master Charge."

Lowell went over and took the suitcases away from her. They
were as heavy as if filled with damp sand. He couldn't imagine
how his wife had ever managed them. It only went to show how
mad she was. Slope-shouldered and red in the face from strain,
he tried to look into his wife's eyes to get some idea of what was
going on behind them, but she kept her face firmly in profile,
her nostrils pinched and her mouth set in a thin line. Her
mother remained in the middle of the room with her mouth
open. From it came a faint, barely audible sound, somewhat like
the noise Alka-Seltzer makes when dropped in water.

"Close your mouth, Mother," said Lowell's wife.

Her mother's mouth snapped shut like a puppet's, and the
sound began to come out her nose. When he was little, Lowell
used to make an airplane noise like that. It was different from
the airplane noises other children made, unlifelike but much
harder to do. Making her noise, his mother-in-law pivoted
slowly as they went toward the door, as though something had
happened to her spine and it was the only way she could keep
them in view.

As they passed the kitchen door, Lowell caught a glimpse of

his father-in-law. Leo was sitting at the kitchen table. He was staring off into space, and for some reason he'd taken off his shoes. The coffeepot had never been turned on.

"Good-bye, Leo," grunted Lowell in as amiable a tone as he could manage what with the suitcases.

"So long, Lowell," said Leo in a strangely cheery voice, moving only his mouth. The rest of his body seemed not to have heard. "Take care."

Lowell's wife held the door for him and followed him out, closing it softly behind them. His mother-in-law did not choose to speak.

Later, in the cab that was taking them back to Manhattan, he said, "I'm glad you decided to come back."

"I couldn't have stayed there a minute longer," said his wife grimly, staring straight in front of her. "It was like being in the middle of a Jewish radio program."

"I didn't know there were any Jewish radio programs," said Lowell.

His wife did not reply, and they finished the trip in silence.

卍回卍回卍 6 卍回

Lowell's wife joined in the labor of cleaning the house the following day. She worked industriously if not exactly with zeal, cleaning and mopping while Lowell was smashing and hauling. Occasionally they found themselves in the same room, whereupon they felt obliged to speak to each other. For this reason they usually managed to stay in different parts of the house. It was not particularly hard to do with twenty-two rooms to choose from, all of them in need of much work. They worked and thought. At least, Lowell was thinking. He hoped his wife was thinking too. Every once in a while, on one of his toting and hauling expeditions, he caught a glimpse of her in some room or other, standing at the window and staring at it with unfocused eyes. He assumed that she was thinking.

There were two conditions to their reconciliation, if that was the word for it. The first condition was seemingly minor: his wife would work in the house only during daylight hours, and only if Lowell would personally escort her to the subway station when night fell and wait with her on the platform until the train came. It cost Lowell an additional thirty cents to wait on the platform, a small enough burden, but one that he deeply and secretly resented. He tried to make a deal with the token seller, but nothing came of it. He had to pay thirty cents every single time, despite the fact that he never took the train. It was a rule.

(His wife also said that she wasn't going to live in the house when they finally got it ready. She was going to stay in the apartment. Lowell could do what he liked. He decided to cross that bridge when he came to it.)

The second condition didn't cost him a penny: he was no longer allowed to have any sex. In their old life they'd never made love, properly speaking; love had very little to do with what they did, except to establish a kind of moral precondition. They made fun, especially if they were either very drunk or very sober. It was about the only time in their lives when they did something just for the hell of it. Being generally content with placidity rather than fun, they didn't do it very often, but they really cut loose when they got around to it.

The fact that Lowell was no longer allowed to make fun came as something of a blow, but in the long run it didn't bother him nearly as much as the thirty cents. It wasn't as if they'd talked the matter over or anything, he just wasn't allowed to do it any-more. He just came home at night and didn't get any, and that was all there was to it. It didn't make any difference whether his wife was awake or asleep, he was not allowed to do it. She didn't want any fun, and that was that. He probably could have raped her; in fact, he almost certainly could have raped her. He knew exactly what she'd do if he tried it: she'd lie there like a corpse and let him go ahead. Screwing corpses was not his style, nor, when you came right down to it, was raping his wife, al-though there was a time when he liked her to wear high heels in bed, but he got over it.

Actually, it wasn't too hard for him to do without his fun be-cause he was working himself to exhaustion. He came home a filthy mess every night. Sometimes he was so tired that he went to sleep in the bathtub. One night he nearly drowned when a cake of Ivory floated under his nose while he dozed. He'd never

worked so hard in his life. From time to time he would stop by
the window in the back room and stare down at his linoleum
crater and wonder what was going to happen to him next, but
he never came up with an answer, which was okay with him.
He wondered about the window too. Why was it so clean? It
was strange and possibly significant that the person who had occupied this room, alone of all the dozens of people who had occupied this house, had kept his window clean both inside and
out. Why had he done that? Lowell tried to remember what he
looked like, but all he could remember was a pair of bare feet
and a vague, bent form. He couldn't remember the face at all.
The only things he knew for certain about the man were that he
sometimes sat in his room with his shoes off, and he kept his
window clean. And that his name was Bowman Parker. It made
Lowell feel a little peculiar to know things like that about somebody whose face he couldn't remember.

"I bought the old Collingwood place out in Brooklyn," he told
people when they asked him what he was doing with himself
these days. "The old Darius Collingwood place. I'm fixing it up."
He was a bore on the subject. He could talk about it for hours
and frequently did. What he didn't know about Darius Collingwood you couldn't find in a book; Lowell had already read
every book in existence that contained the faintest reference to
the man. He could also give you a complete rundown on the or-
igins and meaning of the word "filibuster," and he knew more
about architecture in the Brown Decades than almost anyone
cared to know. He found that people had quietly begun to
avoid him, falling suddenly into animated conversation with the
nearest available third party whenever he approached, and frequently he and the nutty girl from the secretarial pool who read
palms were the only persons in the cafeteria who enjoyed private tables during coffee break. It didn't bother him a bit. He
was just as happy to be alone with his thoughts.

The Old South Brooklyn Historical Society had passed out of

existence, and its building on Dean Street was occupied by a Puerto Rican trucking company. What had become of Darius Collingwood's watch and Brazilian journal was anyone's guess, but Lowell had come into possession of what he was reliably assured was one of the few surviving copies of *The Autobiography of a Scoundrel*. He found it in a bookstore on Nevins Street, and it cost him $12.89. It smelled powerfully of mouse shit, and its pages were the color and consistency of stale Finnish flat bread. Mechanically it was not an easy book to read. In some cases, whole pages disintegrated as Lowell scanned them, as though the weight of his gaze was too much for them to bear. The book told Lowell little that was new as far as mere facts were concerned; indeed, in some cases Darius Collingwood had covered up facts that Lowell already knew about. It was interesting for other reasons. For one thing, it revealed that Darius Collingwood was no titan of literature, whatever else he might have been; the best you could say for the book was that it was vigorously written. For another thing, it was mistitled. Darius Collingwood revealed himself on its pages as no mere scoundrel. He was one of the most perfect pricks that ever lived.

"They say," he remarked in a typical passage, "that the Jews are taking over the country. What a joke. The country was taken over twenty years ago. The Goulds and the Huntingtons and the Fisks and all that crowd did it, and nobody ever found out. Nobody's ever going to find out, either. We'll always be able to pin it on the Jews or the niggers or somebody." In another place he wrote, "You might think they caught me, but I was ready to go. All those years of living with that saintly woman, my wife, had taken their toll, and I was glad to get shut of her. I only married her in the first place because she was a preacher's daughter and made me look respectable to the neighbors. Take my advice and let them denounce you on the Senate floor, but keep your next-door neighbors happy; they can make life a living hell. Anyway, it was Birdcoat who took the rap—an honest simpleton if I ever saw one—while I went south and had myself a whale of a time with Phil Ryan. What do you think of that, dear reader?" Lowell got a big kick out of it.

"The Irishman O'Dowd," Collingwood revealed in another chapter, "tried to plug me at the Stock Exchange because he found out that I was cohabiting with his wife. Now, there was as tempting a little baggage as you ever saw. He went to the gallows protesting that he was not an anarchist and a drunkard but a Democrat and a cuckold, but nobody believed him. It is common knowledge that all anarchists are liars, as are Irishmen." Lowell thought that was pretty funny.

In order that there should be no doubt in anybody's mind why he was writing the book, Collingwood explained himself with typical arrogance and candor on the very first page. "I could have remained silent," said Collingwood. "Others have. You may be wondering why I have chosen to speak. The reason is simple. I got away with ten million dollars of other people's money, and I did it so slick that if I didn't tell you about it, you'd never discover it. In California I had three men murdered for a pile of Confederate gold and the love of a beautiful woman, and I got away with that one, too. Once I cornered the national market in household nails. I got away with so many things that I am in danger of being ignored and forgotten, and we wouldn't want that to happen, would we? There's no sense in being clever unless you get admired for it."

Lowell admired old Darius quite a bit. He hadn't read anything as entertaining since Horatio Hornblower. It was made even better by the fact that it had really happened, but so long ago that he didn't have to feel upset about it. Scandal and chicanery, bribery and extortion, swindles, boondoggles, low cunning, and naked greed passed in colorful parade before his eyes, and he loved every minute of it. Perhaps the nefarious Montana Bubble had been plotted in his very parlor. Anything was possible, and Lowell owned it all. He couldn't get over it.

The only part of the book he didn't like was the chapter about the Civil War. Collingwood had acquitted himself with honor and modesty, and he told about it with uncharacteristic diffidence, almost as though the story was being drawn from him somewhat against his will. He'd been frightened at Ball's Bluff. The waste of life appalled and saddened him throughout the war. He wept like a schoolgirl when his horse was killed beneath him at Antietam. Lowell didn't like it one bit.

"I opened the door and discovered the President standing there," said Darius Collingwood. "In some confusion I attempted to withdraw, acutely conscious of the mud and dried foam that befouled my uniform, but he stopped me with a gesture. 'Arbuckle has told me the news,' he said. 'I believe we are deeply in your debt, Colonel. That was a fair piece of riding.' He shook my hand and retired by the opposite door. I remained standing there for some moments." Lowell thought the President should have gone straight out and washed his hand.

By and large, however, the rest of the book remained satisfactorily in character, and the next time Darius Collingwood shook a President's hand (Chester Alan Arthur's) it was in the course of another kind of transaction altogether. Antietam and Abraham Lincoln notwithstanding, there was not the faintest scrap of evidence anywhere else in the book that inside the Weasel of Wall Street there was a twenty-three-year-old lieutenant colonel struggling to be let out. At least there was none that Lowell could see. Anyway, it had all happened a long time ago.

When he was finished with the book there was little left of it but the frayed binding and a pile of brittle brown flakes that got smaller and smaller the more you handled them. It was as though the book had a primitive self-destruction mechanism worked into it, like the tape recorders in the spy programs on television. Lowell put the relics in a manila envelope and placed it in his safe-deposit box at the bank, where he kept a replica of his birth certificate, his lease, his deed, and five canceled bankbooks. He was reasonably certain that he knew more about Darius Collingwood than anyone else alive. It didn't bother him that he bored people. He was like a man with a peculiar but utterly banal fetish—earrings, umbrellas, or newspapers, for example—that he was compelled to talk about incessantly, although no one but himself found it either dirty or remotely interesting. He was really talking to himself. He was so intrigued with his own thoughts that he simply had to speak them aloud whether anyone was listening to him or not, although he usually preferred to have someone standing in front of him when he did it. He even managed to bore people who had started out interested in what he was saying. It didn't matter; it was the act of speaking that counted, not the reaction it drew. For the first time in years he had something on his mind. No longer did he spend his days idly looking at the pipes in the ceiling as he waited for some bit of ephemera to come stumbling into his head like a crippled butterfly. Now he knew what all those pipes were for. He owned some just like them himself, and whenever he looked at them these days, it was with professional interest. He wanted to know how they were put together. Lowell had a great many plumbing problems, and he was glad of any hints. Every pipe in his house was either rotten or in the wrong place.

As it turned out, a good many things in his house were either rotten or in the wrong place. The mansion had fallen on evil days since Darius' first wife, Felicia Hargrove Collingwood, had passed on to her reward. (A virtual recluse, her children scattered and out of touch, she died in the master bedroom late in April, 1947, and was discovered early in May.) The house was not only a mess, it was falling apart. Down in the cellar the great main beam that supported the bearing wall was as soft as cheese; you could drive a butter knife into it up to the hilt with scarcely any effort at all. Several of the pillars supporting it had turned to punk, as had the floors of most of the closets upstairs and a disturbing number of beams and stringers. Lowell had the uncomfortable feeling that at any moment the place could come popping apart like a cardboard cutout whose tabs and slots had given way, and it was bemusing to think that if the house ever caught fire it would smolder instead of burn.

Lowell was depressed but not deterred by these discoveries, and he went right ahead with his work. He only hoped the house would hold together long enough for him to get it cleaned out, so he could start rebuilding it. The longer it took, the more distant was the moment when he and his wife would have their final reckoning. At this rate, it might be years before they got around to it. He wondered if they could stand that.

It was shortly after their reconciliation (or whatever it was) that Lowell met his neighbors for the first time. The weather turned fine and brilliant with the biggest sky Lowell had seen in years—a huge sky, tall and milky and bright and intimidating, the kind of sky you could lose yourself in. Lowell had gotten used to Manhattan skies, cozy and small and full of smoke. He didn't like the Brooklyn sky at all. It made him feel cooped up when he was inside the house, and when he went outdoors it made him feel utterly exposed, like a beetle on a sidewalk.

He took the opportunity to examine his linoleum crater. It had been rained on and frozen and thawed a couple of times, and it was not in good shape; it had kind of dissolved and run together in a particularly horrible way. At least it no longer stank to high heaven. It merely smelled bad, sort of like a mixture of Clorox and fusel oil. Somehow a couple of empty Goya food cans had appeared inside it, almost as though they'd generated themselves spontaneously. Their labels were coming off, and they gleamed in the sun. Lowell bent over pensively and picked them up.

"Trash," said a voice that seemed to fall from the sky, as though by way of explanation. It was the kind of voice a small, very nasty angel would have, a spiteful angel that had recently been passed over for promotion. Considerably startled, Lowell looked up and discovered a small, very nasty-looking old lady in the yard next door. She was staring at him fixedly with narrowed eyes, as though he was a long way off and she was trying to make him out. She wore a nubbly black coat of the sort Lowell's mother had owned and constantly worn when he was a little boy, back in the middle of the Second World War. It even had the same kind of fur collar. In one hand she held an ancient rake, although for what purpose was obscure. The dirt in the yard where she stood was as hard and as barren of vegetation— either living, dead, or dormant—as a naked tabletop.

"How do you do?" said Lowell politely.

"Trash," she repeated, making a short, aggressive gesture with the bleached handle of the rake.

Lowell gave her a cautious look. He had never gotten over how many crazy people there were in the city, and he always had a hard time disengaging himself once they got started with him.

"Puerto Ricans!" she croaked, as though calling to some of them.

Lowell smiled agreeably and took a step toward the door.

The old woman began to sput and jerk about like a person on the wrong side of a window, in the last furious throes of frustration because she could make herself neither heard nor understood. "Puerto Ricans!" she said, mouthing the words exaggeratedly. "The coloreds! Trash and garbage! Can't do nothing with them!" Lowell realized at last that in some way she was referring to the origin of the cans in his hand. He looked down at them witlessly and couldn't think of a thing to say. He gathered that it was somehow okay for him to have a big rotting linoleum crater in his yard, but it was not okay for Puerto Ricans to throw cans in it; but it wasn't the sort of thing he wanted to get into a conversation about. He took another step toward the door and then stopped, arrested by a look of dumb pleading in the old woman's face.

"I'm Lowell Lake," he said heartily.

"Lake," said the woman. "Lake." Her eyes were pale blue, and they looked out upon the world with a kind of panic-stricken innocence, as though everything she saw was strange and possibly the source of some concealed and incomprehensible menace. "You ain't been living here long?"

"I just bought the house."

"A nice young man like you."

"I'm going to live in it," he said.

"You should have seen this neighborhood forty years ago," said the old woman. "It was some swell place."

"Yes, indeed. Well, it was nice meeting you."

"Hey!" a voice suddenly roared behind him. They were cropping up everywhere. "Hey! Are you the gas meter?"

Lowell scarcely knew how to answer that, if at all, but he was no longer surprised by anything. He turned and discovered an old man standing in the other yard.

The old man was far older than the old lady, and it was obvious that he was also much crazier. He was bald, purplish, and completely toothless, his mouth like an obscene flabby asshole stuck into the middle of his face, and despite the coldness of the day, he wore neither a shirt nor an undershirt. His shoulders were rounded, and his chest was caved in as though he no longer had any vital organs, and his muscles were as shriveled as if they'd been drying out in the sun for weeks. All in all he was a pretty horrible sight as well as an alarming one. Lowell glanced around at the other yards that were visible from where he stood, half expecting to see more old people proliferating in various degrees of madness and nudity, like some kind of ghastly, pale fungus brought forth from the sterile soil by the sun, but there was no one else to be seen. There weren't even any sounds.

"Hey!" roared the old man again, cupping his hands to his mouth and leaning forward. Lowell swore that when he was old he would always wear his false teeth, always, even to bed. "I ASKED YOU! ARE . . . YOU . . . THE . . . GAS METER?"

"That's Captain Macaulay, he drinks," said the old lady. "His mind is gone, drink took it. He thinks you're the meter man, he makes no sense, it's because of the drink. Pay no attention to him, you'll only encourage him. He was such a fine figure of a man in his prime."

"HEY!" bellowed the old man again, as though a hundred yards of storm-tossed sea lay between them instead of fifteen feet of frozen yard. It was amazing that such a small chest could produce such a volume of sound. "I SAID . . ."

"I'm not the meter man," said Lowell.

"YOU THERE!" the old man roared. "YOU! PAY ATTENTION! ARE YOU THE GAS METER, OR ARE YOU NOT?"

"Captain Macaulay!" barked the old lady in a voice that was both sharp and strangely sane. It was as though a door had opened suddenly in her mind, and she was speaking through it from twenty years ago. "Amos Macaulay! Go inside this instant and put on a shirt! I won't speak to you again!"

The old man's mouth suddenly collapsed in a gummy pucker that was horrible to see, and his eyes lost all their sense of purpose. For a moment he stared at Lowell and the old lady as if he couldn't imagine who they were or how they got there, and then he slowly looked down at his chest. When he looked up again, his face was hard to read. "You old bitch," he said, in one of the most malevolent voices Lowell had ever heard outside of a radio. Then, with a grimace of pure hatred, he turned and shuffled slowly back into his house.

"He drinks," said the old woman. "It was drink that took his mind. He thought you were the meter man. He does so look forward to their visits. It's strange to think of, when you consider that he simply can't *stand* the Witnesses. You'd think if he liked the meter man, he'd like the Witnesses too, wouldn't you? Maybe it's because there isn't any kind of logbook he can keep for the Witnesses, I don't know."

"Well, it's certainly been nice talking to you," said Lowell. He held up his Goya cans to show her he had an errand to do.

"Nineteen-nineteen," she said.

"I beg your pardon?"

"Nineteen-nineteen," said the old woman, looking off into space. "He started drinking in nineteen-nineteen, that was the year it was. Nineteen-nineteen. He lost his wife in the epidemic, she died while he was at sea, dead and buried before he set foot on shore, his wife and his little boy, it was the epidemic, he started drinking then and never stopped."

Lowell scarcely knew what to make of that. If it had been a movie, he probably would have been moved by it, but it was reality, and he was a little bewildered and kind of irritated. It was as though some kind of claim was being made on him. He didn't mind the fact that elderly people were old and strange, but he really hated it when they tried to act like people.

"I'll be darned," he said, or some such thing, and hurried into the house, scarcely conscious that the old woman was no longer even looking at him.

He was depressed for the rest of the day. When evening came he went home with his wife, got moodily drunk in a very total way, and silently failed to arrive at any conclusion about what was wrong with him, either at the present moment or at any other time in his life. He was still engaged in his quest when his wife went to bed, and shortly thereafter he passed out in his chair.

7

As though meeting the old people had been some kind of signal that his good times were about to be over, everything suddenly started to go wrong. It didn't go wrong all at once or with any kind of drama. It went wrong in a very Lowell way—by dribs and drabs. Sometimes he was almost able to convince himself that nothing was really going wrong at all. Other times he told himself it was only a phase. The rest of the time he tried not to think about it.

It was a great disappointment to Lowell that no one who was hip and smart and dynamic—even as hip and smart and dynamic as he was, which God knew wasn't asking for much—had bought a house on his block and begun their fight with urban problems. Lowell wasn't sure what the local issues were or where to go to find out, and he was kind of hoping that somebody issue-conscious would buy a house nearby so he could talk to them and find out. Even if he managed to sniff out the issues on his own, there wasn't much he could do about them by himself. He couldn't very well run out on the street with a sign or hire a hall. People might pay attention to him and either laugh at him or demolish his arguments with close reasoning. Lowell needed to be led but he was all by himself, a willing Indian in the cause of virtue, with a leaky tepee, an ambiguous marriage, and no chief in sight.

It was not for lack of trying. There were a few interesting-looking people in the neighborhood, and Lowell had done his best to make friends with them. He started with a hippie couple. They were blond, willowy, ethereal, and physically as similar as a matched pair of bookends. Lowell frequently saw them in the street, dressed in blankets and cowboy clothes, walking along with distant eyes and serene smiles, as though lost in contemplation of another world where everything was much nicer. Lowell had the idea that hippies were easier to approach than other people, in addition to knowing where it was at, and he introduced himself one evening when he met them down in the grocery store while buying beer. "I'm Lowell Lake," he said.

"You sure look it," said the boy hippie dreamily, and before Lowell could think of a good reply, they gathered up their groceries and cigarette papers and departed into the night with a faint ringing of bells.

"Heepies," said the proprietor merrily. He was a round little man from the Canary Islands who seemed to have been born with a feather up his ass. As a result he was very popular, although not with Lowell, who disliked merry people and always suspected that there was something wrong with their heads. "Heepies," giggled the proprietor again. "Heeheeheeheehee. What you say, eh?"

Lowell couldn't think of a good reply to that one, either. He gathered up his beer and left, feeling as though he was the object of some kind of minor conspiracy that was designed to make him look funny and feel bad without ever finding out what it was all about.

The next person he tried to befriend was a pretty young mother, relatively smart-looking and apparently not spaced out, whom he occasionally encountered on one of the major avenues, laboring under an incredible number of groceries and two small children. It seemed impossible that anyone so small and pretty would have to carry so many packages so frequently, but she did. There was something odd about it, something not quite right. Lowell supposed it was because she didn't have a car. On the other hand, neither did Lowell, and *his* wife never went around loaded down like a packhorse. Neither did the wives of any of the people he knew, most of whom did not have cars either. Under normal circumstances Lowell would have dismissed the whole thing as another little urban mystery that was best left alone, but these were not normal circumstances. Lowell needed a contact, even a strange one, and the girl was obviously part of the world he was trying to get into: she lived in a freshly painted, pumpkin-colored house on Greene Avenue, with a newly planted tree at the curb, a tiny but beautiful front garden, and a shiny brass number plate just like the one Lowell wanted to get for his own house. Anyway, if she really was a weirdo, he could always drop her after she introduced him to her friends. One thing could be said for all those sacks and bags and kids: she would be easy to catch.

Spurred on by his encounter with the hippies, he approached her the very next time he saw her, one bright day on Lafayette Avenue, where he'd gone to buy a box of brads. She was struggling with a full shopping cart and an immense bag full of canned vegetables and condensed milk. She carried one child in a backpack and dragged the other one along by means of a length of clothesline that joined her waist to his, like mountain climbers use. Her hair was in her face, and her eyes were kind of wild. Both kids were crying to beat the band.

"How do you do?" said Lowell in his most manly voice, stepping up to her with a confident smile. "I'm Lowell Lake. I just bought the old Collingwood place on Washington Avenue. May I help you?"

She looked at him as though he'd just offered to buy one of her children. Her pace quickened and she swept past him without a word, narrowly missing his shin with the hub of her shopping cart. "Mommmmeee!" screamed the older child. "We're going too *fast* again!"

Lowell gave chase and soon overtook them. "Are you sure I can't take your package?" he asked.

"I'm all right," said the girl, her eyes darting about a little wildly. "Everything is okay. Everything is fine." She began to walk even faster, the shopping cart fishtailing behind her. The older child fell into a stumbling trot beside her, and the baby in the backpack looked around with an expression of astonishment. "But . . ." said Lowell. He made a feeble gesture, as though hopelessly begging for help instead of hopelessly offering it, and then he gave up. He just stood there on the sidewalk in the full blaze of noon and mutely watched the girl double-time off into the distance with her kids and freight like some weird kind of urban Mother Courage. He decided that she was crazy, and he never tried to talk to her again, although in the days that followed he occasionally sighted her in the distance, struggling along like some kind of ant. She was probably a tenant at the neat-looking house on Greene Avenue. She probably didn't have anything to do with the way it looked at all.

He occasionally saw the hippies on the street too, looking around them as though the world had turned some delightful new color. Sometimes they looked at Lowell. They seemed pretty pleased with him too, but not in any human way. After a while Lowell began to check the street before he left the house, to make sure they were nowhere in sight. He didn't like being looked at like that.

Lowell thought the matter over and decided that the situation was not normal. In the weeks since he'd first come to the neighborhood, he'd met a fag real-estate agent, two senile old people, a pair of stoned hippies, and a nut. (He'd also met, albeit briefly, a substantial number of Negroes and Puerto Ricans and one goofy grocer from the Canary Islands, but they were not the people he was looking for, and they didn't count.) Clearly such a collection couldn't be a reasonable cross-section of this or any other neighborhood. Therefore he had managed to meet the wrong people. Undoubtedly an opportunity for meeting the right people would arise in due time. Meanwhile, he decided not to worry about it. He'd worry about it when he got done with the house, and he went right upstairs with a couple of six-packs and set to work, attempting to pull a nest of old wiring out of the wall without electrocuting himself, shorting out the house, burning it down, or a combination of the three. Presently he began to sing "The Battle Hymn of the Republic," or as much of it as he could remember, which was quite a lot more than he could remember when he wasn't drinking beer. It established a good rhythm for his work, made the time pass quickly, gave rise to thoughts of Darius Collingwood, and was fun. He was aware that he'd forgotten to eat again. It was a good thing beer was so nourishing.

"*I said, the downstairs door was open.*" roared a voice from somewhere as Lowell was trampling down the vineyards for the third or fourth time. Lowell broke off and peered around him as though squinting through a dirty windshield. He discovered a short, Assyrian-like man in the doorway, regarding him with a belligerent expression suggestive of unredressed grievances and unpaid bills. He had greenish-brown skin and comic-book blue hair, and his suit appeared to have been tailored for an oil drum. Lowell had never seen him before in his life and could only stare at him drunkenly, a bundle of live wires clutched in his hand.

"I wouldn't do that if I were you," barked his visitor.

Lowell examined his wires. They looked all right to him. "Why not?" he asked.

"Leave the door open," said his visitor with obvious exasperation and contempt. "I wouldn't leave the door open. That was what I meant. I meant the door."

"Oh," said Lowell.

"My name is Warsaw," the man went on. "I'm a lawyer."

"How do you do?" said Lowell, wondering if he was about to be presented with a summons. He couldn't imagine why, unless his wife was divorcing him, and she hadn't said anything about it. "I'm Lowell Lake," he added. "I'd come over there and shake your hand, but I have this bunch of wires."

"We bought our house on Saint John's Place six years ago," Mr. Warsaw snapped out. "That was three years before anybody." He jabbed toward Lowell with his index finger. "What have you done?"

Lowell searched his mind frantically for something he might have done.

"What rooms have you finished?" demanded Mr. Warsaw, allowing Lowell to know what he was talking about while keeping his reasons for asking the question hidden. Lowell wondered if Mr. Warsaw's conversational style had been permanently effected by cross-examining recalcitrant witnesses, but he couldn't decide whether they were having a conversation or not. Maybe he was really being cross-examined. "I can't remember," he said. "I mean, we haven't finished any. No rooms are finished. Not one."

"I see," said Mr. Warsaw.

"I'd show you around," Lowell explained, "but I have this bunch of wires." He held them up.

"In that case, I'll look around by myself," said Mr. Warsaw, turning abruptly on his heel and striding up the stairs like a policeman. A moment later Lowell heard him walking around overhead. Lowell suddenly felt very silly, standing there in the empty room with his wires. He also felt wrong. He decided maybe he'd better go upstairs too. That seemed best. He carefully put down his wires and went upstairs.

Mr. Warsaw was darting from room to room like a man desperately searching for a lost wallet, flicking on lights as he went.

Lowell stood on the landing and watched him. Soon all the lights were on and all the doors were standing wide open, even the closet doors. Mr. Warsaw came out of the last room, looked around in a harassed and disorganized fashion, did not seem pleased by what he saw, and hurried down the stairs, brushing past Lowell with no more regard than if he were some kind of especially uninteresting piece of hallway furniture. Lowell followed at a discreet distance, marveling.

"That's a coffin niche, did you know that?" said Mr. Warsaw suddenly, indicating a recession in the wall where the staircase took a turn.

"No," said Lowell. "I didn't." He wondered why it was called a coffin niche and what it had been used for, but he decided not to ask about it.

Mr. Warsaw reached the bottom of the stairs and immediately scurried into the parlor. He popped back out of it a second later. "What's the matter with the lights?" he demanded. "The lights won't go on; what's the matter with them?"

"I'll bet you got the wrong switch," said Lowell. He went into the parlor and turned on the right one. Mr. Warsaw dashed past him again and immediately took up a central position.

"My wife and I," he began, striking an attitude, "bought our house six years ago." He'd asked so many questions that this utterance of a simple declarative sentence sounded extremely strange, as though he'd begun to read aloud. "No one else had bought in the neighborhood when he arrived. We were the first. Our house was built in 1873. The Pouch family owned it. Some of the original furniture was still in the basement."

"That's interesting," said Lowell. "Our place was built by Darius Collingwood."

"I see your parlor has two fireplaces," said Mr. Warsaw. "So does ours. It was a common feature of the larger houses." He was looking at Lowell with eyes that did not seem to register another human presence. It was as though he'd been told that there was an audience in that direction, and he'd decided that his voice would carry better if he faced them. "You'll probably find that yours are Carrara marble. Ours are slate, which is extremely rare. Carrara marble is difficult to keep clean. It stains."

"I don't think they're Carrara marble," said Lowell. "I scraped off some paint, and it looks like something else."

"Our house is virtually completed," said Mr. Warsaw. "The parlor floor is completely restored. *The New York Times* Sunday *Magazine* came and took pictures of it. Come by some time and take a look at it." He whipped a tweed cap from somewhere, suggesting that he was preparing to leave now that he'd finished talking about his house. "I have to go visit some people," he explained in a way that somehow managed to convey that neither he nor Lowell were people. He drew on a pair of kidskin gloves and looked at Lowell expectantly. "Well," he said sharply, "aren't you going to show me out?"

Lowell showed him out. Mr. Warsaw scuttled away down the street without a backward glance, like some kind of immense bipedal rodent. Lowell waited on the stoop for a moment, half-hoping to hear the sounds of a violent mugging, but no such good thing happened, and he went back indoors. He disliked Mr. Warsaw, and he had an imaginary conversation with him while he drank another beer and finished untangling his wires.

A few days later, however, he tried to pay the Warsaws a visit. He had decided to give them the benefit of the doubt. This was easy to do because Lowell had drunk a great many more beers that night and as a result he had no confidence in his memories when he reviewed them the following morning. He remembered that he hadn't liked Mr. Warsaw, but on the other hand, he'd been drunk. This was a powerful, and possibly conclusive, argument in Mr. Warsaw's favor. Lowell always retrospectively loathed himself when he'd been drunk in someone else's presence, even if they were drunk too. He was certain he'd disgusted them, although this was seldom the case; in actual fact, people almost never realized he was drunk even when he was bombed out of his mind, possibly because he never did anything conspicuous or odd (usually he just went to sleep), and they were always surprised and a little annoyed when he made his apologies afterward. Sober people had a great advantage when there were drunk people around: they were sober. It really gave them the upper hand. They knew what was going on.

Viewed in such a light, it seemed far less important to Lowell that he hadn't liked Mr. Warsaw than that Mr. Warsaw probably hadn't liked him. It would go far toward explaining his behavior: instead of being peculiar and compulsive, he could have been pissed-off and disgusted, in which case Lowell had blown another opportunity to make meaningful contact with his neighbors. It was like trying to contact the *maquis*. Lowell began to feel pretty paranoid and unhappy about the whole thing, and he set out on his visit in an unusually humble and disturbed state of mind.

The Warsaw house would have been easy to spot even if Lowell hadn't bothered to look up the number in the phone book beforehand. It stood out like a prince among beggars. With its mellow sand-blasted brick facade, its tastefully painted cornice and trim, its immaculate windows, polished oak door, and tubs of flowers, it gave the impression that it was the only inhabited building on the block, despite the fact that it betrayed no signs of life while all the other buildings were visibly teeming with humanity. Here and there along the street broken windows had been replaced with sheets of warped, unpainted plywood. Half the front doors appeared to be off their hinges, all the brownstone facings were flaking in a way that unpleasantly suggested rotting teeth, and naked light bulbs could be seen burning weakly in bare and garishly painted rooms beyond cheap and often ragged curtains hung from sagging bits of string. Despite the coolness of the weather, people hung from the upper windows of the houses like shapeless lumps of laundry, their elbows cushioned with pillows, and down on the street small groups of drunken men stood around on the sidewalk or sat on the stoops, wearing the remnants of ancient suits with trousers too wide for their legs and belted too high on their bodies, passing bottles back and forth in crumpled paper bags. The scene was so hyperbolically poverty-stricken that it didn't look real; it looked contrived, like a set for some kind of incredible squalid version of *Porgy and Bess.* As Lowell walked down the street—conspicuous, he was aware, not so much by his clothing and color as by his air of purposeful, energetic activity —a pack of children streamed past him from nowhere, yelling and screaming and running and waving their arms more frantically than seemed biologically possible. They raced to the end of the block, then turned and raced past him again to the other end of the block, where they fell upon one of their number, apparently chosen at random, and began beating him unmercifully.

"Hey, man," said one of the nearby drunks, lurching a step in Lowell's direction, "what the fuck you think you doing here?"

"Visiting friends," said Lowell with a neutral grimace that he hoped would discourage conversation while not inviting hostility.

"I said," repeated the drunk, "what the fuck you think you doing here?"

"Yeah," said another drunk. For some reason Lowell suddenly realized that all the men in sight were wearing hats. Not a man was without one. He wondered what it signified.

"Shee-it," said the first drunk, staring with slack-jawed malevolence as Lowell reached the Warsaw's steps and ascended them with what he trusted was studied nonchalance. There was no doorbell, a circumstance that Lowell found a trifle unnerving under present conditions, but a little diligent searching revealed an egg-shaped brass knob set into the doorframe to his right. Above it was a tiny brass sign that said PULL, which Lowell promptly did. A dull clunk resounded from somewhere within the house, as though a large lead object had fallen off a table. Lowell wondered if he'd done something wrong, despite the fact that he'd done the only thing available. A casual glance over his shoulder revealed that virtually everyone in sight had paused in their pursuits in order to give him their undivided attention. Feeling conspicuous but not popular, Lowell overcame his inhibitions and gave the knob another hefty yank and produced a really heart-stopping thud. This time his effort was rewarded with the sound of footsteps, and presently the door was opened by a tall woman who bore a vague resemblance to Ringo Starr. She glared at him silently as though hoping to scare him off with her face now that the doorbell had failed.

"Mrs. Warsaw?" said Lowell.

"That's right."

"How do you do? I'm Lowell Lake. I met your husband the other evening."

Mrs. Warsaw pursued her lips in a manner that suggested that her husband met a lot of queer fish in the course of his travels and that she had no truck with any of them.

"I'm renovating the Collingwood mansion on Washington Avenue," said Lowell with as much cheer as he could muster, hoping the information would either intimidate her or tell her something good about him. "Your husband said I should drop by."

"I'm sorry," said Mrs. Warsaw. "I never show the house when my husband is not at home. It's been nice meeting you." So saying, she closed the door in his face and left him to his own devices. Lowell was certain she was still standing behind it. He could almost feel her standing there, listening to him. He wondered what would happen if he threw himself against it, clawing with his fingernails, shrieking obscenities and innuendos, kicking over the flower tubs, yanking up the plants, rubbing the roots in his hair, masticating the leaves and spitting them out with an unearthly howl. It was a tempting but unconvincing picture; Lowell had never done anything remotely like that in his entire life, and he knew he would never do anything like it now. Just thinking about it was pretty damned unusual.

Lowell turned and went slowly back down the steps while the first drunk commented on his adventure with a joyless but outrageously energetic parody of uncontrollable mirth, evidently having decided that this would get Lowell's goat more effectively than his previous display of unbridled hostility. This insight was correct. Lowell scarcely knew what to do with himself, but feeling that it would not be smart to indicate it, he set off vigorously in the opposite direction. It was considerably longer that way, but although his presence was noted and his purposes speculated upon by an unnerving number of people, he managed to gain the corner without further incident. The children had decided to throw rocks at passing cars. They threw a rock at Lowell too, but it missed. In a minute he was able to turn another corner and make his way slowly back to his house along the street of vacant, blasted buildings whose condition gave the impression that their inhabitants had been exterminated, perhaps recently, with tanks and hand grenades.

His house told him nothing. He walked around in it for a while with a hammer in his hand, looking for something to hit, but no likely target presented itself. When he realized that he had been standing in front of a wall for some seconds, staring at it blankly, he decided it was time to go back to Manhattan. On the subway it occurred to him that, unless things improved and his wife changed her mind, he would probably be the only man in the world with a pied-à-terre on the West Side and a country seat in Brooklyn. He wondered what he would do then.

His wife was at her mother's when he got home. No doubt he was being reviled at that very moment. It was a pretty safe bet. His mother-in-law should have seen him today. How she would have laughed.

He made himself a martini and turned on a rerun of *The Avengers*. It was one of the ones with Linda Thorson instead of Diana Rigg and watching it with a drink gave him a measure of peace. He was the only person he knew who liked Linda Thorson better than Diana Rigg. He made a couple more martinis and liked her even more. When the show was over, he ate some lobster salad he found in the refrigerator. Then he had some more drinks and watched some more TV. He couldn't remember what time he went to bed or whether his wife had come home yet, but she was beside him when he woke up the next morning. He had a vague recollection that at some point in the evening he had stood up and yelled, "I AM NOT A NERD!" He wondered if anyone had heard him. He hoped not.

The living room showed no signs that anyone had been drunk in it, with the exception of the small writing desk in the corner. It was open and a sheet of letter paper was lying on it. Acutely conscious of the stubble on his face and the various imperfections and malfunctions of his body, Lowell padded over in his pajamas and picked it up. There was a brief scrawl in his most drunken handwriting. "Dear Mother and Dad," it said, "I want to come home."

Lowell looked at this message for a while and thought about it as best he could under the circumstances, but it didn't seem to him that he really wanted to do that, either. He didn't know what he wanted to do. He crumpled up the paper and threw it away before his wife could see it, and then he went out to the kitchen in his bare feet and drank a great quantity of nice cold, fresh milk.

8

By the first of April Lowell and his wife had gone about as far as they could go with their work of demolition and tidying up. They had reached the limits of their competence, and it was time to summon architects and contractors if the work was ever to go forward. A determined but ill-fated attempt to erect a new wall—the thing, when completed, looked exactly like one of the partitions he'd just finished pulling down, only cleaner—and a drunken, equally ill-fated, and physically painful attempt to install a new sink had convinced Lowell that he had about as much skill in these matters as a Puerto Rican, which had the curious effect of making him think less of himself, not more of Puerto Ricans. No matter how many books he read, he simply wasn't up to the mark. This was not a new thing with him. He'd never been up to the mark. His model airplanes had seldom flown, often fell apart, frequently were never finished, and never looked much like airplanes, despite an attention to the instructions that bordered on the fanatical. His dog had been run over before he finished building the doghouse, which had persistently refused to come out right. He couldn't even catch a ball. Even when they came right to him, they invariably fell at his feet. He studied and practiced, but it was always the same. Possibly his body was wrong for catching balls, like the body of someone who could never learn to swim. (He couldn't swim very well, either.)

He wondered if he could catch a ball now. Once he had asked it, the question so intrigued him that he went down to the corner grocery and bought one of the pink rubber balls like the black and Puerto Rican kids had. He took it out in the backyard, picked a good blank spot high on the wall between a pair of mullioned windows, and (after setting himself) threw the ball at it as hard as he could. The ball bounced off with a wet sound. It came nowhere near him. It went over his head and disappeared into the junk-strewn yard of one of the houses behind him, where it was promptly seized by a dog and carried away to a corner where the animal covered it with dog spit and then rolled it around on the ground. Lowell made no attempt to retrieve it. His reactions to the whole brief episode were distinctly mixed. On the one hand, he felt like a fool. On the other hand, he still couldn't catch a ball. He decided to think about contractors a little harder than he'd been doing.

Unfortunately, he didn't know any more about contractors than he did about putting up a wall—rather less, in fact. A few of them persistently sent him badly printed, semiliterate brochures offering to cover his house with either aluminum siding or artificial stone that resembled nougat candy or, if he were so inclined, to buy it from him, lock, stock, and barrel, for big cash. Once a contractor's representative had come to the house, unsolicited. He was a pleasant but exceedingly tense young man who reminded Lowell, for some reason, of a chipmunk. He had a little slide projector and he showed Lowell pictures of a number of kitchens done in bright pink plastic. There were also several slides of a cozy den paneled in unreal-looking artificial wood. Lowell told the young man that these things were not part of his plan and showed him to the door, politely but with a certain amount of difficulty. The young man left brochures.

They were just like the ones Lowell was always getting in the mail, and he threw them out.

He wanted his house to be like claret and Dutch chocolate. He was a little vague as to ideas, but that was the general plan, and he was determined to have it. He had only to find someone to accomplish it. He tried the telephone book, but it wasn't much help; there were any number of contractors in it, but nothing they had to say about themselves indicated a capability for claret and Dutch chocolate. On the contrary, their ads suggested a distinct proclivity for bright pink plastic and artificial stone, synthetic wood and aluminum siding. He supposed he could go and ask one of his fellow brownstoners for advice, but on the basis of the fellow brownstoners he had already met, he didn't think he wanted to do that. It was all very depressing. For some reason he seemed to lack the energy or the will or something to think about the matter creatively. He didn't even seem to be able to think about it intelligently. Frowning with formless, unproductive worry, he wandered from room to room in the huge house, upstairs and down, gazing at the outlines of old partitions on the walls and ceilings, the disemboweled wiring, the dismantled plumbing. In one of the rooms he came upon his wife, somewhat to his surprise, although of course she had to be somewhere. "How long has it been since you spoke to me before I spoke to you?" she asked as he entered.

Enveloped in gloom, Lowell stopped in his tracks and stared at her with dull eyes. He tried to speak, but it was difficult to climb out of his pit so quickly, and the only sound he produced was a faint, sad mooing.

"That's what I thought," said his wife. She bent down and began to brush furiously at a patch of floor with a hand broom. A tear or a drop of sweat fell at her feet, and she brushed it away. "There," she said, straightening again. "I guess that does it. You can take me to the subway now."

Lowell mutely did as he was told, feeling as though his body had turned into some kind of semiflexible stone. He escorted her to the station and waited with her for the train.

"Step away from the edge of the platform," snapped his wife. "You always stand too close."

In a few minutes the train came, and she got on it and went home.

She didn't come to the house after that, which was probably just as well, because there was nothing for her to do. There was nothing for Lowell to do either, but every evening after work he dutifully came over to Brooklyn and put on his work clothes and wandered around the rooms of his house drinking beer. A curious inertia afflicted him, but if he drank enough beer, he would presently begin to feel tired, as if he'd worn himself out in the performance of some useful task.

Spring came exhaustingly that year, almost as though something were leaving his life rather than entering it, and in the cold April sunsets the house took on the devastated look of the streets, as if it had been attacked, not recently but months ago, by a squad of compulsively tidy commando assassins, who had raced up and down the stairs, chucking grenades into every room, and then had cleaned up after themselves. Where partitions had been, there were jagged outlines on the walls. Nothing remained in the bathrooms but the heads of pipes. Holes were scattered here and there in the walls, in the ceilings, in the floors. Lowell couldn't remember why he'd made some of them. There must have been a good reason. Electric blue in one room, green in another, shattered and stripped, the house didn't look as though Darius Collingwood had ever conceived it, or that the poor people had ever occupied it, or that Lowell was ever going to live in it. It looked ready to be demolished. A weekend came, and Lowell wandered out in the back to look at his pile of linoleum again.

It was a fine, warm day that was completely lost on Lowell but much enjoyed by his neighbors. In the houses opposite, the occupants were tumbling their bedding out the windows to air, festooning the weathered brick with pink and turquoise sheets and faded Army blankets, piling up the windowsills with pillows from Fulton Street and Athens, Georgia, calling to each other from floor to floor as if they hadn't met in months. Lowell stood by his linoleum and watched them for a while through a film of either hangover or despair, he couldn't decide which. Whatever it was, it had turned his mind to sludge. He supposed he ought to stop drinking so much, but he didn't think he could face it. There would be all that empty time on his hands.

Lowell was so mantled in gloom that some time passed before he realized that someone was looking at him from one of the upper windows of the old ladies' rooming house. Then for the next few minutes he was so engrossed in horrified contemplation of the creature that he was completely unable to analyze the significance of his presence there in anything like rational terms.

It was Demon Rum himself. Many years ago Lowell had briefly attended a crackpot Methodist Sunday school, and he was therefore able to recognize him at once, although not with pleasure. Tiny and emaciated, dressed in decaying rags and smeared with nameless filth, its skin the color and in places evidently the texture of dried diarrhea, a toothless idiot's smile on its face and its eyes vacant of both intellect and soul, it stood framed in the window like a lurid illustration in a hard-core temperance magazine that only adults were allowed to buy. He looked so depraved that it was amazing that he was still alive, and Lowell found it difficult to believe that he wasn't some kind of hallucination sent by the god of hangovers. As he watched, the creature seemed to take a fancy to him. It bent forward. As it did so, Lowell became aware (although not as swiftly as he would have liked) that the pane had been broken out of the window, and while he was mulling that over, the creature's smile broadened. Lowell could see right into its mouth. It was horrible in there. The lips gave little spasmodic twitches, as though preparing to deliver utterance. Lowell wondered what he would do if this loathsome being were to address him. He supposed that would depend on what it said. In a moment the whole question became academic, as it became obvious that the creature had not been preparing to speak, after all. It had been preparing to vomit, and it proceeded to do so. Lowell turned away, thinking very hard with his eyes tightly closed, and when he looked back a few moments later, the creature was gone. A glance at the ground told him that it had, however, unquestionably been there, and it was only then, swallowing hard, that he began to consider the implications of that fact, beyond its obvious merits as an object lesson. A remarkably clear picture of rape and carnage flashed suddenly across his mind's eye, almost as though it were being beamed to him from some external source —the bodies of the old ladies strewn through the halls with their dresses horribly up, the doorjambs bespattered with gore, etc.—but although the spectacle held him momentarily rooted to the spot, on the whole he did not think it very probable. For one thing, although he knew it happened every day to people in all walks of life and was an unusually well-documented phenomenon, Lowell didn't really believe that people killed people. Lowell didn't really believe in death at all. He'd never seen a real dead person in his entire life. All he'd ever seen was pretend-dead persons on TV. He supposed his life could be considered either sheltered or fortunate. Anyway, there it was.

Secondly, granting intellectually if not emotionally that death and murder were possible, Lowell didn't believe that anybody could murder that many old ladies, at least not all at once. There were at least a dozen of them, at least half of whom expected to be raped and murdered any minute and were semipermanently barricaded in their rooms. It certainly could not have been done by the creature Lowell had seen. It couldn't even have been done by three or four of them. The old ladies would have cut them to ribbons.

Thirdly, Lowell noticed that the lace curtains were missing from every single window in the back of the house. That was an even stranger occurrence than the appearance of the interloper. Lowell made his way to the front of the house. All the curtains were gone from the windows there, too, and the door was standing wide open. Lowell cautiously climbed the steps and looked inside. It was as he suspected: the house was empty. The doors of all the little rooms were ajar, and every stick of furniture was gone. With the possible exception of a faded picture of Jesus taking off his shirt, glued to the wall by the stairs and therefore unremovable, the house was stripped as clean as a whistle. One had to admire the efficiency with which it had been done, and Lowell looked about himself with a certain dull amazement. He was so used to having the old ladies next door that their sudden and utterly complete disappearance was kind of alarming, like going to sleep in one place and waking up in another.

From somewhere overhead there came a bubbling cough, followed by muffled, animal-like sounds of an indeterminate nature. Someone started coming slowly down the stairs. Lowell went home and locked the door.

Later that day, he called the real-estate man from the drugstore. His house was barricaded as solidly as Fort Knox, and there was some doubt whether he would be able to get back into it without climbing to the second story.

"Blocks are like airliners," said the real-estate man. "Some go up, some go down. You just happened to get on one that went down. That's a tough break, and I sure wish I could help you."

"I don't know what you're talking about," said Lowell, somewhat more shrilly than he would have liked. "I only called to ask your advice about closing up the house next door. What do you mean, the block is going down? Which block? My block?"

"You heard me," snarled the real-estate man in a voice from which all trace of faggotry had vanished. "Listen, if I were you, I'd talk about it with Mr. Grossman. Mr. Grossman has recently bought a lot of property around there and will not doubt offer you the best deal you can get."

"I don't understand a word you're saying."

"Live and learn," said the real-estate man, hanging up.

Lowell remained in the phone booth for a while. If he closed his eyes, he could pretend he was in a little elevator car whose cable had snapped. If he opened his eyes, he could see where he really was. It was not a good place. His dreams were bathos, his hopes were ashes, his marriage was a wreck, and his mother-in-law was right. That was where he really was, and it had cost him only seven thousand dollars, which meant there was also a good chance that he was a chump. He was racking up quite a score.

Presently the druggist came over to the booth and asked if there was anything wrong. Lowell briefly pondered asking him for some kind of a drug, but he decided that a drug wasn't really what he wanted, at least not yet, and he apologized instead.

On his way home he observed that a group of men had broken into the old captain's house and were busily engaged in stealing all the plumbing. They were also breaking out all the windows, apparently for the hell of it. While it was possible that they were only an exceedingly clumsy crew of workmen, Lowell did not think so, and he quickly returned to the drugstore and called the police. The police never came, and after a short break for supper the men came back and stole the furnace and the cast-iron fence. Lowell assumed that the old man was either dead or not at home, and he was only mildly surprised to discover that he didn't really care. He looked around for the old man the following day, but he didn't find him, and he never saw him again.

On Saturday two thin, elderly Negroes in pale dungarees came to the former old ladies' rooming house and painstakingly replaced the old mahogany front door with a much smaller plywood door with a tiny triangular window. During the following week his new neighbors moved in and immediately gathered on the steps and set about getting as drunk as humanly possible, as though they were being paid to do it or were participating in a contest. One was an enormous woman with immense, bullet-shaped breasts and a huge stomach that stuck out beneath them like a shelf. She was fond of sitting with her legs spread like a sumo wrestler, and Lowell found it exceedingly difficult not to look at her, but possible. The rest of the drunks were scrawny middle-aged men, and he never even bothered to try to tell them apart. They sat on the steps from dawn until far past midnight, shouting and carrying on, their faces slowly swelling shut, drinking Rheingold and throwing the cans in the street. They never seemed to do anything else with their time, and Lowell never saw them eat anything, although he occasionally saw them throwing up. Meanwhile, the top floor of the captain's house caught fire one night, and the roof fell in. Down the block, another house became empty.

Lowell took none of this lying down. Lying down was what he'd been doing when things were going relatively well, but now that the struggle was absolutely hopeless he stood up and began to fight like hell. He could do nothing about Mr. Grossman and his schemes, any more than he could command the waves or treat with the devil, nor could he get his wife back or quiet down the drunks, but he could get back to work on his house, and that is exactly what he did. With the distracted, slightly crazed intensity of a man trying to remember the periodic table in the middle of a bombing raid, he cleaned up his backyard in nothing flat. Then he swept all the rooms and washed all the windows and shoveled all the dried sewage out of the basement and put it in plastic bags. Meanwhile, a dozen seemingly adultless children, looking and dressing exactly like old-fashioned Hollywood pickaninnies, moved into a newly va-cated house across the street and began playing frantically in the traffic and pulling the bark off trees. Lowell celebrated their arrival by opening the yellow pages and purposefully summoning contractors to hear his plans and give him estimates. Actually, it was principally the contractors' recording devices and answering services that he purposefully spoke his summonses to, but they were better than nothing. He was on the move at last.

Only two contractors showed up out of the dozen that he called. God only knew what happened to the others—maybe they never played back their phone tapes, or maybe they just cruised past the block and kept on going—but in Lowell's position an inch was as good as a mile, and two contractors were a great improvement over none. The first one was a morose little man with the eyes of a bloodhound and the shape of a half-empty bag of damp flour. Wordlessly he followed Lowell upstairs and down. When Lowell pointed at something, he looked at it, and when Lowell talked about something without pointing at it, he looked at Lowell. After Lowell had taken him through the house and outlined his plans, he left. He never came back.

The second contractor was a Trinidadian who was much taller than Lowell and who gave the impression of being far stronger and somewhat more gentle, although he never performed any feats of strength or special gentleness. He was a rich, deep color that Lowell greatly admired, and he had a soft, melodious laugh that he used at every possible opportunity. He laughed melodiously when Lowell showed him the rotten main beam, and he laughed melodiously when Lowell showed him where the plumbing had been taken out. Laughing melodiously, he told Lowell that things were in pretty bad shape, all right, but they could be fixed. Lowell hired him on the spot. His name was Cyril P. Busterboy. He was a very formal person who always called Lowell "Mr. Lake," compelling Lowell to call him "Mr. Busterboy." It was not easy to do.

Lowell's work was extensive, and Mr. Busterboy was not cheap, but they were able to come to an agreement. Mr. Busterboy laughed melodiously as he drew up the document, and he laughed melodiously as Lowell signed it. The next day, to the utter delight of the drunks next door, a truck came and delivered a big portable refuse bin that resembled an immense green lunchpail. The truck deposited it at the curb with a great clanking of chains and much shiny expansion of hydraulic pistons, and as soon as it was in place men from Mr. Busterboy's crew began to fill it with the bags and bundles of dreck and rubble that Lowell had accumulated over the winter, some of which burst like soft corpses as the men carried them, making a horrible mess all over the sidewalk. Lowell took a day off from the office and watched the workmen in a state of nervous excitement. He had to keep stopping himself from picking his cuticles. They were already picked down so far that he was afraid of infection. "Do you realize that this house used to belong to Darius Collingwood?" he asked Mr. Busterboy.

"No shit," said Mr. Busterboy, who had a half-pint of J & B in his back pocket and had been drinking from it at intervals. Mr. Busterboy was covered with plaster dust, as were most of his men, and Lowell decided not to pursue the matter. After a while he went down to the corner store and bought a six-pack of beer. He returned and opened one, but he felt guilty about drinking cold beer in front of the workmen, and he gave the rest of the cans to them. That meant there wasn't enough for him. The next time he went to the store he brought back a whole case. He put it down on the top step and invited everyone to take as many cans as they liked. The case was shortly gone, and he went out and bought another, and presently they were all as drunk as hoot owls. A strange, lethargic conviviality overtook them, Lowell and the crew and Mr. Busterboy, as though time had slowed down to where it ought to be and pleasure was a seamless object, like a small, smooth stone. Work came to a halt, and they all sat around quietly with their beers, except for Mr. Busterboy, who had found a second half-pint of J & B somewhere and was inclined to tell himself jokes. The drunks on the other stoop regarded them solemnly; the drunker Lowell got, the more human they looked and the more solemn they seemed to have become, as if they disapproved of the whole affair from some higher morality but were powerless to do anything about it. An old man wearing a straw boater and a pair of incredibly bright, orange trousers paused on the sidewalk, slowly examined the bin, and then slowly examined Lowell and the men. He looked at them for a long time with absolutely no expression on his face whatever, and then he shambled off up the street.

Mr. Busterboy and the workmen departed at five, leaving Lowell with his thoughts, which were merry but not very clear or sensible. He drank some more beer, and pretty soon night fell. Lowell decided he was too tired to go back to New York. He opened another beer and went upstairs to the master bedroom, where he spread out a clean dropcloth, took off all his clothes but his shoes, and immediately passed out.

When he awoke sometime later it was still dark and he was still drunk, which he decided was just as well, because he was going to have one shitload of a hangover, and the longer it could be put off, the better. He turned over and gazed up at the ceiling with the peculiar but selective clarity he'd sometimes experienced in similar situations. He could see the ceiling just as clearly as anything, with the moonlight coming in the windows and the big hole in the upper-right-hand corner where the lath was visible, but he hadn't the faintest idea where he was. The knowledge came to him after a while, but then he couldn't remember what he was supposed to be doing there, aside from lying on his back on a dropcloth. It didn't seem like a terribly important question, and Lowell decided to go back to sleep again. These things always panned out. Then he heard the noise downstairs and sprang instantly to his feet.

Actually, it was his body that heard the noise downstairs and which sprang instantly to its feet. Although his mind was remarkably clear, it evidently wasn't very smart, and for a moment, as he stood there nude in the moonlight with his shoes on, he couldn't imagine what on earth he was doing there like that, and he started to lie down again like a sensible fellow. Then a beer can was dropped somewhere. Lowell's body went taut, alert and listening. Someone was moving around in the parlor. Before Lowell could make up his mind about the nature of his visitor or decide on a course of action, he found himself in possession of a crowbar, stealthily creeping with it toward the head of the stairs. Volition and action completely severed, his brain more or less along for the ride as his body moved forward with silence and deadly purpose, he dimly felt himself creep along the hall on floors the consistency of marshmallows, between walls as soft as mattresses. There were moments, as he crept cat-like down the stairs with his crowbar, that he seemed to go to sleep or something very like it, drifting effortlessly in and out of his detached consciousness with a slow, gentle motion, like the soft uncoilings of an undersea plant in the waters of a warm lagoon. Meanwhile his body continued down the stairs in his shoes, and every time he woke up, he found himself on a lower step.

A wavering, smoky moonlight drifted through the parlor doors into the hall. Lowell paused, his mind drifting sleepily along with it, his muscles tense and alert. The front door was standing wide open, and beer cans were scattered carelessly about the floor. They were not his brand.

Minutes passed. Then, with a stumble and a wheeze, a shadow of a man appeared in the doorway. Lowell sprang, and although he had never been agile and was not particularly strong, the crowbar went through the intruder's head as if it had been a rotten pumpkin. The dead intruder had been holding a can of beer. He threw it into the air when Lowell smashed his skull, and his body hit the floor first. The body didn't make much noise, but the beer can made one hell of a racket. A part of Lowell's mind marveled at how easy it had all been. Another part of his mind fainted. The front of him was an absolute mess.

Still peculiarly detached and now also in a state of partial shock, Lowell perceived the events of the next hour in an odd way, sort of like a movie from which big hunks had been edited, totally at random. One minute he was in the front hall, and the next he was in the backyard, pouring water over himself from a bucket. He didn't even know he owned a bucket, and hoped he would remember where he put it when he was done with it, but the very next minute he was standing in the parlor, dripping wet but unencumbered, as though having been transported there by magic in the twinkling of an eye, except that he was also in the middle of a thought that he couldn't remember having started. He was deciding that he would wrap the remainder of the dead man's head in one of the plastic garbage bags. That was a good thought, and he was glad he'd had it, even if he couldn't remember starting it. The plastic bag would keep the head from dripping all over the sidewalk when he carried the body out and put it in the portable garbage bin, and he went straight into the kitchen and got one. There was no sign of the bucket.

His mind averted its eyes while he wrapped up the head, and the next thing he knew, he was standing out on the sidewalk, heaving the body over the side of the bin. He was still naked, and the moon was very bright. The drunks were perched attentively on the stoop next door, but if they found anything noteworthy in the spectacle of a naked white man dumping a dead body into a portable garbage bin at three in the morning, they didn't let on. Lowell swiftly forgot all about them. The next time he encountered himself, he was busily engaged in loading the bin all the way up to the top with the remaining junk from beside the house, working with the superhuman strength and subaqueous movements of someone who was stoned out of his mind. When he thought about it, he realized that he was still pretty drunk. It seemed like an irrelevant thing to be, and he did his best to ignore it. Once he caught himself wondering why he hadn't called the police instead of going to all this trouble, but evidently the answer was in the part of his brain that had fainted; the question just hung there in his mind until he forgot about it, and his body went right on working as though nobody had spoken to it. He guessed he really ought to go indoors and put on some clothes, but by the time he had finished thinking about it, he'd finished all his work and it was time to go back into the house anyway. Once there, it made no difference whether he had any clothes on or not.

There remained the little matter of the bloodstain on the floor. Lowell could always try telling Mr. Busterboy that he'd brought home a whore and she'd turned out to be a virgin, but he didn't think anyone would really believe it was possible to be *that* virgin: the bloodstain was a good three feet across, and there were splashes on the wall. He supposed it would be possible to rip up the floorboards and dispose of them, but on reflection he realized that he really didn't want to do that, at least not now. He really wanted to go upstairs to bed. The luminosity seemed to be draining from the moonlight, and the darkness had begun to close in again. It was as though the room were slowly filling with sand and deadly gas, and Lowell was barely able to make it back to his dropcloth before he passed out completely.

He was awake again in what seemed like mere seconds, horribly, totally awake, shooting bolt upright as if electrodes had been applied to the bottoms of his feet. Sunlight flooded the room, a very bad kind of terribly bright sunlight that seemed to be made of ground glass. From outside the house there came a noise of grinding and clanking. The part of Lowell's mind that had fainted was awake now, and the part that had been drunk was sober; it was telling the other part all about what had happened after it left. "Jesus Christ," Lowell said.

He was glad it had been dark. Boy, was he ever glad. He

hadn't the faintest doubt that his runaway body would have
butchered the man if the lights had been on, but at least Lowell
didn't have to remember the look on his victim's face. Thank
God for small favors. He didn't even have any idea what kind
of face it was. For that matter, he didn't know what color it
was either. He searched his memory as thoroughly as he could,
but nowhere in it was the remotest hint as to whether the man
had been black or white. It seemed like the kind of thing you
ought to know about the man you've just killed. Maybe Lowell
hadn't killed anybody at all. Maybe it had been a dream, a
drunken dream. How wonderful to have had nothing but a
horrible nightmare. Too bad he was never able to remember his
dreams when he was drunk. He was left with the conclusion that
a terrible thing had happened to him. It was one of the most terrible things that had ever happened to anybody since the world
began. It just wasn't possible.

Wrapping himself in the dropcloth, he climbed slowly to his
feet and staggered to the window. Another surprise awaited him
in the street. The garbage bin was gone. Not a stick or scrap remained to show that it had ever been there. Lowell stared at
the empty curbside for a long time. Then a car came and parked
in the space, and a man got out of it and walked briskly down
the street. Lowell's last hope was gone.

The truck had come and taken it away. The bin was going
wherever bins went. Soon the garbage workers would start unloading it. They were in for quite a shock. Lowell could well
imagine it. He didn't know how, exactly, he could have improved his situation, but as long as he'd been in possession of
the body he had been willing to study the problem. There was
little use in doing that now. His goose was cooked.

He supposed he'd better put on some clothes. It would not im-
prove his case to receive the police dressed only in a dropcloth
and construction boots unless he was going to plead insanity,
and he knew he would never get away with it. He was the san-

est person he'd ever met in his life, and hundreds of people could be called upon to testify to his blandness and total lack of peculiarity. He would only make an ass of himself if he tried to act peculiar now. The attempt would make him self-conscious and he would undoubtedly blush and queer the pitch before he'd gotten past the introductions.

Getting dressed was hard. His clothes, thrown down with drunken abandon the evening before, were wadded and dank and inside out, and his body was all thumbs with hangover and terror and had to be lashed forward with threats and exhortations. Buttoning his shirt in all the wrong holes with one hand and supporting himself on the banister with the other, he dragged himself downstairs to the scene of the crime.

There was a bum sleeping in the middle of the floor. Lowell had been prepared for many things, but he hadn't been prepared for this one, and it gave him quite a turn. He stood and stared into the room for the longest time, leaning exhaustedly against the doorjamb while his nerves strummed like piano wires and his heart did its best to keep him alive.

This wasn't the first bum. It was another bum entirely. A part of Lowell's mind wanted desperately to believe that it was the first bum, and another part of his mind was convinced of it, but Lowell really knew better than that. He wasn't even sure that the first bum had been a bum at all. Maybe he'd been a building inspector. Maybe he'd been a cop. (Lowell wished he hadn't thought of that.) Anyway, whoever he'd been, this wasn't him. It was someone else. Lowell knew it was someone else because of the bloodstain. The bloodstain was a hard argument to refute. Lowell would be willing to bet that even Norville Gepford, champion debater of his class at Boise Senior High, would have a hard time refuting it, and Norville Gepford could refute anything. Lowell hadn't thought about Norville Gepford in years, and he almost immediately forgot about him again, although not before experiencing a queer twinge.

Lowell was even able to figure out how the new bum had gotten in: through the front door. Lowell had forgotten to lock it again after his murder, and it was standing wide open. For a moment he thought that he was going to have to kill this new intruder too, so that nobody would find out about the first one, and it was only with some difficulty that he managed to shake the notion off. His mind felt like it was full of green Jell-O, and even garbled thoughts weren't moving through it very well. He was in pretty bad shape.

Meanwhile the bum woke up, regarded Lowell dully and without much interest, and slowly proceeded to get to his feet, where he farted loudly. He was in pretty bad shape too. His nose was large and incredibly lumpy, as though recently stung by dozens of obscene bees, and his body was shaped like that of an emaciated pregnant woman. It was a rack of bones with an immense, sagging belly. Presently, when he was finished with scratching his kidneys, he glanced over at Lowell again with an expression that was inquiring and mildly irritated, as though a point of etiquette had been violated. With a sudden flash of lucidity that was well-nigh incredible under the circumstances, Lowell realized that the bum thought he was another bum. He was waiting for Lowell to do whatever bums did when they met other bums. This realization enraged him, but his condition was too delicate for such a strong emotion, and instead of bellowing with proprietary rage and brandishing his fist, he nearly sat down on the floor.

"Get out," he croaked. His voice was weak and sounded curiously artificial, as though emanating from an antique radio speaker emplanted in his throat. "Scram."

The bum stared at him for a moment. Then he wiped his nose with his sleeve, went to the far corner of the room, and prepared to take a shit.

"Now, you just stop that," Lowell ordered weakly. His eye

was caught by the bloodstain in the middle of the floor. There was blood on the ceiling too, not to mention the walls, and now a bum was going to shit in the corner. Lowell was very bewildered. Bewilderment only seemed to confuse him further, if that was possible. "The police," he heard himself saying, as much to himself as to his uninvited guest. "The police are coming."

The bum perked up briefly, as though he'd heard a familiar sound in the far distance, but when it was not repeated, he went back to his business, and Lowell vowed to pay no more attention to him. He closed his eyes and rested his forehead against the edge of the doorframe. He'd become so many different people that he no longer knew who he was anymore. Nothing seemed to fit together. Locked within the same imperfect and hungover envelope of flesh were a managing editor and a guilty murderer, a man who hadn't gone home last night, a man whose marriage was on the rocks, a homeowner, taxpayer, dupe, nice guy, and nonentity. All of these people were badly hungover, but otherwise they seemed to have nothing in common; they were all sort of tumbled together like rubbish in a desk drawer, and he couldn't make heads or tails of any of them. He just stood there with his eyes closed and watched them float past, like disembodied spirits in one of the nicer parts of hell.

"Shit biscuit," said a voice in his ear, very loudly. "Jesus Christ Almighty, it looks like somebody slaughtered a hog in here!"

Lowell slowly opened his eyes and discovered one of Mr. Busterboy's workmen beside him in the doorway, gazing into the room with a speculative expression. "I'll be a motherfucking son-of-a-bitch," he said. "Whooee."

Lowell guessed that if you didn't expect to see blood, brains, and bum shit when you looked into the room, they must come as something of a surprise. A melodious chuckle sounded at his elbow, and presently Mr. Busterboy moved into the edge of

Lowell's field of vision. That was good, because Lowell was too tired to turn his head and wasn't sure he would be able to even if he tried.

"Now, this is really too bad," said Mr. Busterboy. "This is enough to make a man sick. I can tell you, we've got a job of work to do today. We've got our work just about cut out for us. Get the fuck out of here. I won't tell you twice."

The bum left by the window. He did not change his expression.

"The police . . ." began Lowell.

"Won't do you a damn bit of good, and might cause you one hell of a lot of trouble," said Mr. Busterboy's workman. He picked up the crowbar and examined it as a sportsman does a rifle. "You be a lot better off just to forget the whole thing, you want my advice. Them police can be bad news when they sets their mind to it. *Bad* news."

"Leroy," said Mr. Busterboy, "why don't you go and start unloading the truck?"

"Okay," said Leroy, taking the crowbar with him. "Jesus, what a mess."

"Won't take no time at all to get this cleaned up," said Mr. Busterboy. "No time at all. You look like you had some night, not that this here ain't enough to turn a man's stomach by itself. You want me to drive you home? I'm going that way anyhow."

Lowell stared at him. Mr. Busterboy chuckled melodiously. "Looks like you could use a little hair of the dog," he said, digging a half-pint of Dewar's out of his back pocket. "Take about as much as will cover a sixpence."

Lowell took a tiny swallow. The liquor did absolutely nothing to him, but its wetness made him aware that there wasn't any spit in his mouth. Evidently there hadn't been any for some time. He took a big swallow.

"That was supposed to be a sixpence lying flat," said Mr. Busterboy, retrieving the bottle before Lowell could do it any more harm. "Let's get going."

Somewhat amazed that he could do so, Lowell discovered that he could stand unaided by the doorway. He followed Mr. Busterboy out to the curb, feeling as though all his vital fluids had turned to sewage.

Mr. Busterboy's car was a little English model, brand new and very shiny. It was painted a handsome green, and Mr. Busterboy explained that the motor was sideways. Lowell was prepared to believe anything. No sooner had Mr. Busterboy seated himself than the vehicle seemed to spring away from the curb of its own volition. Mere inches from the pavement, they whipped around the corner and drove like the dickens down Greene Avenue.

"Front-wheel drive," said Mr. Busterboy.

Lowell nodded to show that he had understood. His lower jaw showed a deplorable tendency to remain stationary as he did so, causing him to gape like a fish.

"Don't worry about a thing," said Mr. Busterboy.

Lowell regarded him with as much keenness as he could muster under the circumstances, but Mr. Busterboy's open, cheerful face betrayed not the faintest hint of dark and secret knowledge. It reflected absolutely nothing but the good time he was having with his little car and its front-wheel drive. Maybe it was a commonplace occurrence for him to arrive at work and find his client hungover and stubbly, standing in a room bespattered with gore. Lowell's crime was so much with him, the evidence so clear, the punishment so imminent, that it seemed incredible that the world was not shaken by it, or at least moderately interested. It was like being at war while everybody else was at peace. It was downright immoral of them.

Suddenly the devil came and took him to the top of the mountain. He experienced an overpowering urge to tell Mr.

Busterboy all about it. Only the thinnest membrane of silence enclosed his secret, and the temptation to break it was delicious and terrible. It wouldn't be like he was telling a policeman or anything. He'd only be telling Mr. Busterboy. People like Mr. Busterboy knew all about that sort of thing. Fortunately, at the very moment that the temptation was at its strongest, Lowell was nearly knocked unconscious by a wave of nausea, and by the time he recovered, the fit had passed. He felt too weak to talk, much less confess, and as they went over the bridge he leaned his forehead against the cool glass of the window and watched the river.

They drove uptown in silence, and by the time they reached Lowell's building, he'd recovered his senses to the point where he was intelligently panic-stricken and sick with fear. Something awful was going to happen to him, and he didn't have it coming to him. Perhaps the police were already waiting for him upstairs. Perhaps he would be approached by a burly man in a pork-pie hat the moment he got out of the car, and his elbow taken firmly. He only hoped they wouldn't handcuff him in front of his neighbors. He'd never be able to live it down.

"Nice place," said Mr. Busterboy, gazing out the windshield at Lowell's building. "Must cost a lot to live here." He laughed melodiously.

Lowell mumbled something, he scarcely knew what, and clambered out of the tiny vehicle with a maximum amount of difficulty. He was not arrested on the sidewalk, and no one was waiting for him in the lobby. Povachik was nowhere to be seen (had they told him to take cover? were they questioning him in the boiler room?) and Lowell was able to reach his apartment alone and unobserved in a building filled with old ladies, house-wives, pre-school children, sick secretaries, and other defenseless folk. He could have been anybody, and under normal circum-stances he would have reported it to the tenants' committee. Now he didn't know what to do.

There were no police in the apartment, but at first glance the place gave the impression that it had been the scene of a struggle. Clothing was strewn everywhere in wild disarray, every piece of furniture was out of line, an ashtray had been overturned on the floor, and a glass lay on its side on the coffee table. There was a dirty plate on top of the piano. The Eames chair was stacked high with newspapers. Someone had left an orange peel on the windowsill, and the sofa cushions were squashed and askew. Lowell experienced a moment of numb alarm. Himself a murderer, he suddenly saw murder everywhere, as commonplace as doorknobs and coffeepots, and it would not have surprised him to discover his wife's nude and broken body in the bedroom, a washcloth in her mouth and a stocking knotted around her throat. Instead he discovered an unmade bed and a discarded pair of panty hose. It took him a moment to realize that he beheld a scene of disorder, not violence. The place was not a shambles, but it was certainly a mess. Lowell dumped the papers out of his chair and sat down to look at it. Every lampshade in the room was askew, and the rug was full of lint and bobby pins. Clearly this was not the work of a single night. It must have been building up for weeks like the rubbish and sediment on the bottom of a pond, while Lowell came home late and got up sleepy and failed to notice a thing. Huddled over his obsession like a miser over a coin, he had failed to look up until a minute ago, only to find everything changed and odd.

After he had looked at it for a while, Lowell noticed a peculiar thing about the mess. None of it belonged to him. Not a single one of his belongings was anywhere to be seen. His clothes were neatly put away, his dishes had been tidied up, and not a single one of the discards, nor the tiniest scrap of debris, bore the unique and recognizable stamp of his personality. It was his wife's mess, every bit of it. Even the cigarettes in the overflowing ashtrays were exclusively her brand, a denicotinized and heavily filtered variety that tasted like warm air and were about as much fun to smoke as sucking on an empty straw. Search the room as he would, Lowell could discover no visible indication whatever that his wife did not live here alone. He had been erased.

He waited all day for the police to come and take him away, but they never showed up. He tried to watch television, but nothing was on but a lot of soap operas where people stood around looking agonized and self-conscious, delivering stilted, unlifelike lines of script punctuated by long, embarrassed pauses, as though they could not quite believe that anybody had really expected them to say that. It was so much like real life that Lowell couldn't stand it, and after a while he turned the set off and stared at the blank screen. At five-thirty his wife came home. "You startled me," she said. She dumped her parcels on the sofa and went into the bedroom to take off her girdle.

"I spent the night at the house," said Lowell.

"So I gathered," said his wife. She emerged from the bedroom and went into the kitchen. Lowell followed her hesitantly, like a shy guest at loose ends. He sat down at the table, wishing she would ask him to do something for her, and watched as she made supper without looking at him once.

The police didn't call in the evening either. Lowell sat in the living room, and his wife lay down in the bedroom. She turned out her light at nine-thirty. Lowell continued to wait. He knew that police stations didn't close for the night, but he had an idea that homicide detectives went home at a certain hour, and he wanted to wait until they gave up for the day. He wished he knew more about their schedule. He looked in the paper to see if there were any police shows on television, but the only thing even vaguely municipal was an old Lloyd Nolan movie about firemen. He tried the ten-o'clock news, but it was too busy with the war in Vietnam, the insurrection in California, and a case of juridical malfeasance in the Bronx to worry about a piddling murder in Brooklyn. Evidently Lowell hadn't killed anybody important. He didn't know whether that was good or bad, but by the time the news was over he couldn't stay awake any longer. He went straight to bed, where he fell instantly asleep and dreamed that his teeth were crumbling.

All the next day Lowell waited for his secretary to come into his office with a strange expression on her face and the news that some men wanted to see him, but nothing of the sort happened. If anything, it was an even duller day than usual. Lowell began to worry in earnest, and it crossed his mind to go down to the police station and give himself up. Fortunately, he did nothing of the kind. People gave themselves up only in movies, books, and England. It was also possible that they gave themselves up in America if they were overcome by guilt. Lowell wasn't overwhelmed by guilt. He was being driven out of his mind by suspense and nearly starved to death by tension, but he didn't feel in the least bit guilty about anything. His body had gone walking one night, and his brain had gone with it, dimly witnessing about two-thirds of a murder and half a cleanup. He could hardly believe that it had happened. He'd had dreams that he remembered better. If it hadn't been for the dreadful consequences involved, he would have forgotten all about it in a couple of days. That was exactly what he wanted to do, forget about it. One could scarcely consider this the sort of foundation upon which a scaffold of guilt and remorse could be erected. You would have to be some kind of masochist or other nut.

On the fourth day Lowell stopped his furtive purchases of the *Daily News*. His crime had gone unheeded in its pages, and he was beginning to hope that it had gone undetected too. By the fifth day he was nearly convinced of it. On the night of the sixth day he had horrible nightmares, but the following morning he felt almost like his old self again. His appetite improved, and he found it easier to answer the phone. By the end of the second week the memory had receded to the back of his mind, and it was able to frighten him only in unguarded or clearheaded moments, like the intimation of death. If he ever called it consciously to mind, it was only to rehearse the lies he was prepared to tell.

Meanwhile, Mr. Busterboy and his workmen, laboring with the remorseless energy of army ants, were slowly dismantling the interior of Lowell's house. Whenever they found a rotten beam, they took it right out. They ripped up the entire floor of the kitchen and threw it away, and for a week or two you could stand at the edge of the dining room and look down at the furnace and the lake of shit. Then they took the furnace out, and you couldn't look at it anymore. They made enormous holes in the walls and ceiling, and you had to be extremely careful where you walked to avoid falling suddenly into the room directly below. Mr. Busterboy and his men also broke a number of windows and accidentally dismantled, smashed up, and threw out one of the irreplaceable parlor fireplaces. They were very sorry about their mistake, and Lowell decided not to press the issue. He felt a curious alliance with Mr. Busterboy. He felt obligated toward him, grateful, and he didn't want him to think too hard about certain recent events. He wanted to keep him happy and contented, and he let his workmen do whatever they wanted. Lowell got along with them wonderfully. Soon he had to take a loan.

The drunks next door never said a thing. Lowell had a bad moment the first time he had to pass them, but they just sat there and looked at him with a very total kind of indifference, as if he were a traffic accident or a fly. For a couple of days he was afraid that they were staring at him, but then he realized that they were only staring at him because he was staring at them, and when he stopped doing it, so did they. There was obviously no danger from that quarter. They never even tried to hit him for beer money.

July came, and everyone went on vacation. Lowell's wife

bought a bikini and a quantity of black underwear and went off mournfully to spend two weeks with her parents at a New Jersey resort whose name sounded made up and which Lowell failed to find on any map. He let her go with scarcely a word. Everything was all wrecked between them anyway, and although he could probably have stopped her if he'd wanted to, he couldn't think of what he'd do with her after that.

He returned to the house one night while she was away. He'd avoided the place at night since the murder, and there was absolutely no reason to visit it now, but when he returned to his apartment that evening and contemplated the hours that separated him from that moment and the imperfect oblivion of sleep, he nearly cried aloud. He no longer drank, and he'd discovered that television nearly drove him out of his mind when he was sober. He didn't want to read; the thought of sitting in one place long enough to make sense of printed words filled him with a kind of panic. He looked around the apartment almost wildly. It had been cleaned up, and everything in it seemed deliberately calculated to bore him silly. He considered going to a movie; then he considered the huge, half-empty palaces in which most movies were shown. Then he considered the probable clientele. Soon he found himself walking toward the subway to Brooklyn. It would take him a while to get there and a while to get back, and then he might be tired enough to sleep.

Not even his house belonged to him anymore. It was out of his control and no longer bore the mark of his hand. It bore the mark of Mr. Busterboy's hand instead, which was a much better hand than his. He walked through the darkened rooms, joylessly inhaling the odors of fresh plaster and newly sawed wood, feeling as though a giant trap was slowly being constructed around him. The place no longer meant anything; there were no dreams or excitements left in it. Yet he was going on, step by step, and God knew where his steps would lead him. Probably nowhere in particular. He knew now that the police were never coming. He was safe, and the one great act of his life would never be certified by the public realities of arrest and trial. He would never know the name of the man he'd killed or what kind of life he'd had or why he'd come to Lowell's house that night to drink beer in the parlor and meet his fate. Lowell would never even be able to prove that it had happened. Mr. Busterboy had been as good as his word, and all trace of the deed had vanished. Where the wall had been speckled with gore like raspberry jam, a huge patch of sterile new plaster glowed in the darkness; where the stain on the floor had been, there was a hole instead. A few miles away across the East River was the apartment he could never get used to, the job where he had nothing to do, the dozen or so people he knew slightly and cared about not at all: a fabric of existence as blank and seamless as the freshly plastered wall he faced. Soon his wife would return from New Jersey. Soon everyone would be back, and things would go on much as they had before. From the street outside came the sound of laughter and shouting, bottles breaking, voices droning in the warm air, and children playing far past their bedtime. It all meant nothing whatever to Lowell. Standing in the parlor of a house no longer his, listening to the voices of people whose lives where closed to him forever, contemplating a future much like his past, he realized that it was finally too late for him. Everything had gone wrong, and he had succeeded at nothing, and he was never going to have any kind of life at all.

TITLES IN SERIES